# EXPECTATIONS

## A SEQUEL INSPIRED BY PRIDE AND PREJUDICE

SAMANTHA ADKINS

CITY LIGHTS
PRESS
— LAS VEGAS —

**Expectations**
Samantha Adkins



Paperback Edition

City Lights Press
An Imprint of Wolfpack Publishing
6032 Wheat Penny Avenue
Las Vegas, NV 89122



ISBN: 978-1-64119-173-9

GET YOUR FREE EBOOK

"It is a truth universally acknowledged that a married man in possession of a good fortune must be in want of a son." So begins "Expectations" by Samantha Adkins, a sequel to the timeless romance of "Pride & Prejudice". Many have wondered if Darcy and Elizabeth would find a way to a happily ever after with a traditional family as well. The answer here comes in an unexpected way, along a circuitous route that leaves the reader guessing… and turning pages.
—Katie O'Connor Kenig, *The Newsy Neighbor,* Nov. 2009

"The first chapter does a very good job of imitating the writing style of Jane Austen… I found this story to be a very pleasant read."
—Linda Waldemar – Republic of Pemberley, Dec. 9' 09

*For Jen, the penultimate P&P fan. Happy 29th birthday!*

*Love, Sam*

*'But here, by my carrying with me one ceaseless source of regret. . . I may reasonably hope to have all my expectations of pleasure realized. A scheme of which every part promises delight, can never be successful; and general disappointment is only warded off by the defence of some little peculiar vexation.' Elizabeth Bennet, Pride and Prejudice Vol. II, Chap XIX*

# VOLUME ONE

# CHAPTER 1

## JUNE 1813

It is a truth universally acknowledged that a married man in possession of a good fortune must be in want of a son.

This truth is so well known, that all families related to the man consider his heir to be their rightful descendent and all of his neighbours await the new arrival.

"My dear Mr. Bennet," said his lady to him one day. "Have you not considered that it is six months since our two eldest were married?"

"Why should I consider this?" replied Mr. Bennet, though he daily remembered the wit and sense they brought to his otherwise foolish household.

"But it is so. I have thought of little else since their nuptials. How can you not have?"

"I leave such consideration up to you, my dear. Why should I squander my time on matters which occupy all of yours?"

"Well, my dear, you must reflect upon the fact we have had no word from either girl since her wedding day."

"Now there, I have caught you in an untruth, for I see a

pile of no less than five letters from each daughter upon your writing table."

"Mr. Bennet, pity my nerves with your tiresome responses."

"My dear, I could hardly pity the nerves you use to trump every conversation."

Mrs. Bennet carried on, ignoring Mr. Bennet.

"Mr. Bennet, you must know, both Mr. Darcy and Mr. Bingley are men of large fortunes. Why just the other day, Mrs. Long mentioned such large fortunes must be insured by the acquisition of an heir."

Here Mrs. Bennet's voice dropped, uncharacteristically.

"You know I never tell a falsehood, I was only trying to be delicate in the presence of our two unmarried daughters."

"What did you say Mrs. Bennet? I can hardly hear you at so moderate a decibel."

Mrs. Bennet made an utterance of exasperation and raised her voice to its regular volume.

"I said, Mr. Bennet, I was trying to be delicate in the presence of our two unmarried daughters. I should not wish to startle them with talk of producing an heir."

"Now, Mrs. Bennet, do you not think you should lower your voice when speaking of such subjects?" Mr. Bennet admonished with a barely repressed twinkle. "Especially when our unmarried daughters might overhear you."

At this, Kitty coughed and Mary flipped quickly though her latest book. Mrs. Bennet, so used to Mr. Bennet's daily exasperations, continued on her quest.

"If you were only to visit our neighbours more frequently and inquire upon the visitations of their young men, perhaps our younger daughters would be married by now rather than being present to overhear my indelicate remarks."

"Heaven help us, Mrs. Bennet, for then who would save me from such indelicate remarks?"

"What I propose, Mr. Bennet, is a letter from you to our eldest daughters encouraging them in the matter I earlier mentioned."

Mr. Bennet had been pushed beyond his ability to banter and flew into a strong, though entirely brief, rage.

"My dear, surely you jest! How do you suppose such a letter would look?" Mr. Bennet's face had taken on a hint of rouge at his lady's impropriety.

"Of course, you would not come right out and say what I mean, only hint at the importance of subservience and attention to their husbands."

Mr. Bennet returned once more to his sarcasm and humour.

"I fear, my dear, they would not know of which I wrote. From where did our girls ever observe such qualities in this home?" At this, Mr. Bennet turned from the room and was not to be seen for the remainder of the afternoon.

"Really Kitty, do control that cough. You are ruining my nerves."

Mrs. Bennet breathed quickly while Kitty tried to apologize and return her mother to equilibrium. Mary, knowing her own attentions would only be ignored, turned another page in her endless book.

# CHAPTER 2

PEMBERLEY WAS INDEED VERY FINE. MRS. ELIZABETH DARCY marveled at her good fortune and no more so than when she gazed upon her husband, whom she fondly referred to as Darcy. Georgiana proved as good a sister as any of Elizabeth's natural sisters, excepting Jane who was now become Mrs. Bingley. Of course, Georgiana was younger and still unmarried, and could not be expected to be as close to Elizabeth as the sister she had grown up with. She missed Jane keenly and wrote to her often.

Pemberley
$18^{th}$ June

Dearest Jane,

My sister, can it be only six months since we saw one another last? I miss you Jane, more than I ever thought. Darcy is the world to me now and Georgiana is lovely, but no one could take your place. Being married is such a transition, would you not agree? I cannot explain myself so well to Darcy as I can to you and many things are not appropriate for so fine a young lady as Georgiana.

Darcy still will not agree to have her out. He is quite paralyzed by her former misfortune over Wickham. Oh, I hope you would not show this to Lydia. Does she continue to visit you, sister? You must refuse her constant requests. Darcy remains firm on that matter. She may stay no more than a fortnight and never with her husband. She should learn to get on herself, now that she is a married woman and so sure of herself, as you say. Do not pity her, Jane, for I know she has no pity for anyone but herself.

I have had the strangest letter from father, whom you know never writes. Have you a similar note? No more than a paragraph extolling the virtues of the subservient wife. And then he ends it with 'Never mind, Lizzy. You know your mother.' What is he getting at, I wonder? I thought you might know as you are nearer by.

My husband calls and to please father I will end and go be the 'subservient wife' for at least a moment. My affection to you and yours,

Lizzy

"DARCY I AM SO PLEASED you called," said Elizabeth soon after.

"Really dear? I detect some irritation in your voice."

"Forgive me, darling, I was only trying to explain something to Jane in a letter."

"Please do not allow me to disturb you, then. I can wait."

"Now Darcy, is that any way to manage your wife?"

"Elizabeth, I would hardly dare try such a thing with you." A moment of quiet affection passed and a giggle or two escaped Elizabeth's sitting room.

"In that case, I beg you to join me in the parlour. We have visitors," said Darcy.

"I saw no carriage from my window," Elizabeth gazed outside as she spoke.

"Come, Lizzy, you will want to see this."

Elizabeth followed her husband, hoping to tempt the information from him, but his lifetime of reserve kept him from revelation. They were certainly a handsome couple and often sought by neighbours as good company at a ball or dinner. Only Mr. Darcy's aunt, Lady Catherine de Bourgh refused to call upon them. She had written a letter which greatly insulted her nephew's choice of spouse and called upon every means possible to entice him to uphold the marriage contract made by Lady Catherine and Darcy's mother for their children to wed. Darcy was completely indignant and demanded they should never see her again. Elizabeth hoped, for the sake of her friendship with Mrs. Collins, that the relationship might someday be repaired. Mrs. Collins was a friend from Elizabeths girlhood who had married the vicar employed by Lady Catherine. Her husband, Mr. Collins, was most attentive to Lady Catherine and would never dare incur the wrath of his patroness by any act of disobedience.

Pemberley boasted a most agreeable front parlour and the sun shone prettily through the windows as Elizabeth entered on the arm of her husband.

"Jane!" Elizabeth ran to the side of her eldest sister and embraced her for so long the men began to clear their throats.

"The surprise was well planned then," interrupted Darcy at last. Elizabeth tore herself from her dear sister and attempted to resume her good manners.

"Mr. Bingley, we meet again at long last. Now let us sit together and tell me everything that was done to make this surprise so well. Georgiana, come sit with us and hear the tale." Georgiana was always mindful of her place as younger sister and sat to the corner, endeavoring not to be a nuisance. As both Mrs. Bingley and Mr. Darcy were reticent in their public speech, Mr. Bingley took up the story.

"We have Darcy to thank for the surprise, sister. He wanted to celebrate the six month date of our wedding celebrations between us all. Jane thought it might be dishonest and worried about leaving the Wickhams' alone at Netherfield, but the Wickhams' departed in time and Darcy insisted and made such a game of it that we could not resist."

"If you only knew the troubles I took not to mention the event in my letters." Jane interjected.

"My sister, you are blushing. I have only known you to blush when you first began to love Mr. Bingley," Elizabeth noted.

"Truly, I do not." Jane touched her cheeks and blushed further. Mr. Bingley touched her cheeks with affection and laughed softly.

"I fear we cannot hide a thing from you, sister. Perhaps you and Jane would like a moment while Darcy and I inspect the grounds. It has been awhile since I last saw Pemberley."

The two men took their leave allowing the sisters a chance to embrace once more. Both Jane and Elizabeth thought their husbands very fine as they stood in their youth and strength to exit the room. Jane glanced quickly at Georgiana and Elizabeth noticed her hesitation.

"Georgiana, would you mind fetching the letter from my sitting room desk? Then come back so we can all get to know one another better."

Georgiana, ever dutiful, followed the wishes of her sister-in-law, though she wondered why a maid had not been sent for.

"Now sister, we have a moment to ourselves, what is your news?"

"I think, Lizzy, you have already guessed, but I shall humour you. Bingley and I are to have a child."

"Oh, sister! I had hoped, but dared not say it. Congratulations!" Again, the sisters embraced and their joy echoed in the room.

"The baby will be born around Christmas, I think. Oh, Lizzy, what will I do?"

"You shall be the finest mother in England, Jane. Your good temper and caring nature can only overflow to your children. Have you been very ill?"

"Only for a few weeks. I wondered if this trip was wise, but I have been well for a fortnight."

"I am glad, Jane. I only wish I had some news for you, but never mind, here comes Georgiana."

Georgiana presented the letter to Elizabeth and resumed her needlepoint in the corner. Lizzy and Jane found it difficult to change their conversation, but felt it imprudent to continue around an unmarried woman.

"Tell me, Georgiana, do you still find time for your pianoforte?" Jane inquired.

"I do. My brother and sister insist on my playing almost every evening."

"I am glad, for I have never heard you myself."

"Oh, Georgiana, do play us something now. Just for the two of us? It would be the perfect way to mark my sister's first visit." Georgiana, seeking to please, smiled at her dear sister-in-law's request. This gave the sisters a while longer to discuss the upcoming changes in their lives.

## CHAPTER 3

Due to the previous relations between Mr. George Wickham and Miss Georgiana Darcy, Mr. Darcy was most cautious of her company. She only went out with a chaperone, usually Mr. or Mrs. Darcy or a hired man. While she was very glad for the addition of Elizabeth to her life and the ability to walk or visit in her company, she could not help but wish for a sister nearer her age. Of course, this was impossible as her parents were gone, but Georgiana occasionally gave in to wistfulness. She was coming on eighteen and began to worry about her future connections. Elizabeth guessed these unspoken wishes and worked to provide Georgiana with the company she deserved. The arrival of her sister and brother-in-law produced another reason for entertainment.

"Darcy, let us host a ball," began Elizabeth at breakfast the morning after the Bingley's arrival.

"My dear, is your sister not company enough?"

"Of course, but it is a good reason for me to meet the neighbourhood and I think your sister might enjoy the entertainment. She cannot be completely satisfied with only us old married women around all day."

"She has the Miss Lawsons," said Mr. Darcy who still favoured a small gathering to a large one.

"Yes, but young women need more than two friends. Come Darcy, it would be such fun."

"Will I ever be able to say no to you, my wife?"

"Let us hope not." Elizabeth began plans immediately and was glad to try her hand at running the house.

Jane, Elizabeth and Georgiana spent the rest of the day in planning. First was the party list, for which Georgiana's advice was most helpful. In six months, Elizabeth had begun to know her new society, but was far from meeting all the people who must be invited.

"What about Lady Catherine de Bourgh and the Collins"?" asked Jane.

"I will speak with Darcy. He has sworn never to have Lady Catherine on my account, but perhaps I can make him see the good in it. The Collins" would never deign to come without her consent, so I will not invite the one without the other."

Jane and Elizabeth had never hosted a ball. Their own parents had not the means and could only hope for invitations to the balls of their acquaintances. Georgiana revealed she had never hosted a ball either as her brother was of a solitary nature. Their mother had been gone since she was a girl and she had been far too young to learn all that must be done.

"We will require some assistance," Elizabeth decided and she sat down to write a letter to her nearest neighbor.

# CHAPTER 4

MRS. PATRICIA HIGHMORE WAS WELL-LOVED IN DERBYSHIRE. She had been born, raised and married in Derbyshire and her people had known the Darcys for generations. Mrs. Highmore was pleasant both in appearance and nature. She wore the latest fashions and her knowledge in the matter was frequently sought by her neighbours. She had sewn a little as a girl and received magazines from London and Paris to keep her updated. She and Mr. Highmore had two children, whom she loved very dearly. Her husband was often away in England as a member of the court, and while many women would accompany their husbands, Mrs. Highmore disliked parting with her children and so stayed home much of the time. This left her with ample time to visit friends. Though she had every right to prejudice by birth, appearance, abilities and marriage, she chose instead friendliness and helpfulness. She found both attributes served her well and she was a very popular visitor. No one left her off an invitation list and, being so frequently without Mr. Highmore, she was glad of this.

Mrs. Highmore had invited Elizabeth and Darcy to dine

within a month of their marriage. Her good humour and lively conversation endeared her to Elizabeth immediately. It was a lonely business to leave one's family and Mrs. Highmore and Elizabeth were becoming close friends. Mrs. Highmore arrived within an hour of receiving Elizabeth's letter.

"Elizabeth, I am so glad for the opportunity to meet your sister. You have often sung her praises and I see she is as lovely as you described. Welcome Mrs. Bingley to Derbyshire. I knew your sister-in-law Mrs. Hurst as a girl. How does she get on?"

"Quite well, last I knew," smiled Jane.

"Now as for the matter of your ball, Elizabeth, I have been waiting for such an occasion. It will be so good to see Pemberley put to proper use once more. There has not been a ball here since the Darcy parents were alive, may they rest in peace."

Mrs. Highmore turned to Georgiana at this point and offered her sympathies.

"It must be a great sadness to be without a mother at your age, Georgiana. You must be glad to have a sister-in-law to keep you company."

"Indeed, Ma'am."

"I suspect this ball is partly given to your benefit as well, Miss Darcy. Why, I do not believe you have been out in public since you were fifteen, am I mistaken?"

"You are correct."

"Surely, it is time again. I always wondered at your disappearance. You were once quite a popular dance partner, if I recall."

Elizabeth, sensing Georgiana's embarrassment at these references to her uncomfortable past, turned the conversation in another direction.

"We hoped you might enlighten us on the customs and

expectations of the area, being either too young or too far removed from them as we three are."

"You are very wise to seek my advice, why only last year there was a ball given, and I will not mention any names, but guests were forgotten and wine ran out to all but ruin the host's reputation. Now what have you decided so far?"

Mrs. Highmore reviewed their guest lists and, complimenting them on their good start, she added invaluable insight on others who ought to be added. She recommended a wine house and musicians for the event.

"However, I would insist you have Miss Darcy play at least one waltz for the dances. I have always admired her talents and I believe they would only improve her reputation in Derbyshire."

"Oh, I could not." Georgiana insisted.

"It is becoming more popular, Miss Darcy, I assure you. It is lovely to have a change from the quartet once in a while. I am certain you are working on something even now that would be appropriate. Perhaps you could play us something?"

Although Elizabeth tried to protect Georgiana from everything causing discomfort, she believed Georgiana could use a bolster to her confidence. She often worried that Wickham's most damaging effect on Georgiana had been the breaking of her spirit.

"Play something, dear, if only for our enjoyment. You need not decide right now if you will play at the ball."

Georgiana acquiesced as was her nature and played for the three ladies as they completed their planning.

# CHAPTER 5

The Wickhams were currently living at North Yorkshire on a recommendation from the Darcys. They had only just returned from an extended visit to the Bingleys at Netherfield. Their present lodgings had seemed cheap accommodation at first, but the monthly fees were quickly becoming unreasonable in comparison to the Wickhams spending. Mrs. Lydia Wickham had not learned the care of a household from her mother, either because she had married at such a young age or because she had always been her mother's favourite. Her face still beamed with youth, but the shade of innocence had been much erased in the ten months of marriage to her handsome Wickham. To his great irritation, she had begun in the fashion of her mother to question him, and make suggestions as to his business.

"Do you think, dear, that we ought to host a dinner party?"

Wickham turned a deaf ear to his wife. Only in public did he pay her much heed as he saw the benefit of the attentive husband in good company. The ladies found it quite endearing and it made him appear trustworthy to other men.

"Lydia, we have not the means at present," said Wickham while attending to other matters.

"We need to make our statement to the neighbourhood. We need to become part of society."

An unrecognizable mutter was all Wickham could muster.

"I fancy a new dress, Wickham; I fear I am becoming a bit fat around the middle. It surprises me, when we have not eaten nearly as well as I had thought. Why at Netherfield, they had several courses with every meal. Even at home, we would regularly have meat."

Wickham continued as before.

"Wickham, do pay attention. Do you not care about the appearance of your wife and her nutritional needs? How would you explain this plumpness around the middle? I will need to speak to cook about all of the potatoes; it could be she is fattening me up like the hogs."

Lydia left to speak to her servant and Wickham drew in a deep breath of quietness. If only he could find a way to find some peace. He returned to his papers and the cleaning of his guns, nearly dropping one a moment later at the squeals echoing through their modest dwelling.

"Wickham, Wickham! You will never believe this. You are going to be the happiest man this side of . . . well I do not know where, but you will be surprised."

"Oh lord," muttered he. Lydia returned to the parlour flouncing and jumping, but then becoming strangely still.

"What is it, my dear?" said Wickham without looking at her.

"Mother never told me how it all worked. I learned what I could from my friends and the farm hands and anyone else I might overhear, but I would never have guessed."

"Yes, yes. What is it you are getting at, Lydia?"

"I will be a mother, Wickham." Wickham looked greatly

confused. "You will be a father; just imagine, like in the nursery when I played dolls with Kitty. A baby, Wickham, do you see dearest! I am to have a baby and you will become a father and I shall be the first of my sisters to accomplish this as well! I will bear the first grandchild, but I must take care of myself." At this, Lydia flung herself like an invalid to the chaise and began demanding water bottles, tinctures, hot clothes and the doctor.

"Well, well, Lydia." Wickham managed to pat her hand. "It certainly is a surprise. I will leave you in peace and go fetch the doctor."

After the first shock of news, Wickham returned to his talents of scheme and forethought. Was he not considered a son by the Old Mr. Darcy? Surely then, his offspring had a right to inheritance and if the offspring were to be male, this may be a sizeable amount. Wickham smiled for the first time at the news of his child and Lydia mistook it for what she wanted it to be.

"Oh, dear, you must be very proud – and to think I shall be the first of my sisters to have a child. Oh, they will all be so jealous – I should write immediately to tell them our good fortune."

"I have another idea, dear wife. Why not a visit to Pemberley? Would it not be better to tell them in person and see their faces for yourself?"

"Wickham, do you so quickly forget? You have been banished from the place forever, poor soul. How cruel that your only relation in the world should so abuse you!"

"Aha, but I should not accompany you. You have not been banished, and your own sister would never turn you away. I will go on to London and see about some business. You should be well looked after for a fortnight, I am certain, and your sister Elizabeth should thoroughly spoil you when you tell them the news."

"How will you stand to be apart from me, though, my dear? We are still newlywed and we have not spent a night apart since our wedding." Lydia held out a hand to him. Wickham patted it quickly and gave it back to her.

"I will bear it, dear, for your own good. I should not want you to be estranged from your sisters on my behalf. I will not withhold from you the right to visit, as Darcy has done to me."

"Oh you are the world to me, Wickham. Thank you, thank you for your generosity." Here the lady broke into the most unbecoming fit of tears and Wickham solaced himself with the thought that soon he would have his time and mind back to himself, if only for a fortnight.

# CHAPTER 6

NEWS OF THE WICKHAMS HAD YET TO REACH THE INHABITANTS of Pemberley. Despite Mr. Darcy's protests, they were ensconced in a hearty game of Whist. Even Mr. Darcy was playing at the encouragement of his wife. She had the power to make even the dullest of activities captivating enough for him. Georgiana again decorated the occasion with the melodies of Beethoven. Four was all that was needed for a hand of Whist, but they promised Elizabeth would trade places at the next round. The Bingleys and Darcys enjoyed one another's company immensely and easily returned to the banter they all enjoyed before marriage.

"Tell me, Mr. Bingley, what is the most singular memory you have of Darcy before Jane and I had the pleasure of his acquaintance?" began Elizabeth, dropping yet another trump card onto the pile.

"Elizabeth, I must protest this line of questioning. It is not becoming to remember past mistakes," said Darcy.

"You will have your turn, do not worry husband. I will ask the same question to you of Mr. Bingley when he is through. He will remember that you get your chance when he considers his story. He will not dare influence your bad feelings."

From the piano-forte, Georgiana wondered at the teazing nature of her sister-in-law, but especially at the patience and good humour with which her brother received it.

"I will tell you, Mrs. Darcy, of the first time I met your husband."

"Is this absolutely necessary, Charles? Consider your own wife."

"You will have your turn, Darcy. No more interruptions," scolded Elizabeth.

"I was in London at the tender age of twelve. Darcy was brought to our home as a playmate for me, but being five years my senior; he felt it quite beneath him to entertain me. Instead, he situated himself in front of the fireplace to read a book. All of my entreaties to play trains, a puzzle or to draw went ignored. I gave up and played quietly at his feet, trying not to induce his looks of cool disdain."

"Will you not end there," said Mr. Darcy. "I was so enjoying this card game."

"I could, but will not for the sake of your kind wife. I dare not refuse her when she has always been such a good sister to me. You, Darcy, are to blame for keeping me from my Jane almost a year when we could have been married much earlier."

"Go on then, Mr. Bingley. I shall endeavor to restrain my husband's interruptions."

"You will remember I have two sisters my junior. Georgiana was still a baby and not yet fit to play with Louisa and Caroline, so they decided to join our twosome. However, knowing their company might be considered an intrusion, they decided to take us by surprise. They crawled into the room out of our sight and brought with them instruments of detention. Both of my sisters went directly for Darcy who was their primary attraction. They knocked him from his chair and tied his arms behind him. He fought valiantly and might have escaped with my help, but I was tired of playing alone and decided instead to join the antics of my sisters.

"Even then, he had much of the pride he now possesses and refused to call for help. We tied him to the chair and my sisters forced him to listen to the parlour conversation they had picked up from mother. They fed him cakes and tea and I banged around on a drum. It is amazing I did not lose his good opinion forever. I have always thought perhaps he was glad of the diversion from his own high expectations."

At this final sentence, even Georgiana could contain her laughter no longer; she giggled so violently that her piano piece was ruined and could not be recovered.

"Please, may I join you for the telling of Mr. Bingley's tale? I have had quite enough piano playing for tonight."

"Certainly sister," said Elizabeth and pulled up another chair for Georgiana. "I fear our card game is much forgotten. Now Darcy, how will you defend yourself?"

"Surely you would not encourage revenge, sweet Elizabeth," admonished Darcy, but to please her he chose quite a different story.

"I beg your pardon, Mrs. Bingley, for what you must now hear. I hope it will not cause you to lose much respect for your husband. He was fifteen when he first came to visit Pemberley."

"Ah, Darcy, I should have known you would give up my secret."

"I can only think you meant it be told when you began your own story, Charles. You must have known this was coming."

"I tell you I did not. I had nearly forgotten the whole affair."

"I assure you, he could not. Now if you will allow me to

continue – at fifteen, Charles was quite the addition to our neighbourhood. I heard many of my female acquaintances marvel at his arrival. He was as tall as you see him now, though rather thin. He was agreeable and smiled even more than he does today. I had accepted his friendship since our first meeting and looked forward to setting out on horseback for some shooting during his visit.

"At this time, I believe, our Charles was quite enamored with the writings of the Gothics. He had brought several along and would read them long into the night by candle-light; I knew for we shared a room while he visited. I picked one up in idle curiousity one evening, but could hardly finish the ridiculous thing.

"He must have fallen asleep in the middle of one of his books that evening – I had long retired and left him to his foolery. I woke around midnight to see a most peculiar sight – Charles was standing on the bed post, his colouring so white I briefly wondered if he was dead.

"What is it, Charles?" I asked him, but he could not speak for fear. I jumped from my bed and looked around the room for any sign of his fright. I saw the window was open and a light shone from the lamps outside. I followed the light to find a shadow on the wall.

"Is it the shadow?" I asked and Charles nodded his head. Upon closer inspection, I saw that with a tilt of the head, it looked to be the outline of Charles" late governess.

"She is back to skin me for reading her books!" Charles managed.

"I laughed so heartily I woke the Bingley sisters. They came running from their room down the hall and banged on the door, demanding to know what was so funny." Laughter rang through the parlour at this end, until Mr. Bingley finished the story.

"Darcy, my good friend, never betrayed my fright, until

now. I yelled through the doors that it was none of their business and to get back to bed before a ghost got them. In my own defence, I will say I had the most dreadful governess."

Jane and Elizabeth had tears streaming from their happy faces and Elizabeth gasped; "Enough! This cannot be good for Jane. We must return to less jovial amusements. I will take my place at the piano and play a somber march."

The rest of the evening was spent in secret smiles between sisters, friends and newlyweds.

# CHAPTER 7

GEORGIANA HAD GROWN UP IN A QUIET HOUSE WHERE HER opinion was rarely sought. At eleven years her brother's junior, she had always been the baby and was treated well, though often left to solitary amusements. After her parents' death, life became even more solitary, for an older brother does not consider the social needs of his little sister. She had been at school and liked it, but her brother found it preferable for her to be established first in London and then Ramsgate. It was there she had been most bitterly disappointed and indeed, humbled. George Wickham had always been a favorite of her father's. He had been almost a brother to her as a child, and wonderful for playing games and reading stories. She had assumed him a good man and allowed herself to fall in love with him. His proposal of a secret elopement had seemed wonderfully romantic and as her mother and father no longer lived, she thought it could hurt no one. She had been only fifteen, but when her brother visited them, unannounced, two days before the elopement was to take place, Georgiana realized the pain this secret marriage would cause him and confessed everything to him.

His reaction was quite a surprise and her innocent attachment soon showed its sinister nature. If Mr. Wickham could not be trusted, who then could be? She had become quite removed from society then and promised she would never again be fooled. Only the introduction of Elizabeth to her life now brought her back from seclusion. She was grateful for her company and the vivacity she brought to Pemberley. If it was her station in life to be sister-in-law to Elizabeth and then Aunt to their children, she would be satisfied. The knowledge that Elizabeth's sister, Lydia, was now married to the man who once ruled her heart would serve as a reminder to Georgiana that she was not meant to marry. With this decided, Georgiana strived to embrace the life she now lived and aimed to be a helpful member in her household, while allowing her brother and his wife as much privacy as they desired.

In the effort to maintain her welcome and cherished position in her household, Georgiana made frequent visits to her female acquaintances. Julia and Penelope Lawson were special favorites and the following morning, Georgiana called at their home, Sunnings.

"Georgiana, how good of you to come. We hear you have visitors, tell use all you can!" said Julia. Julia was blond and spirited. She was Georgiana's age and their birthdays were only a month apart. Georgiana had never been in her company without laughter. Julia found everything interesting and made even the dullest situations an occasion. They had attended school together when they were younger and, although Julia's friendship was often sought by other girls, she remained loyal to Georgiana. Penelope was younger and plainer than her sister. What her natural appearance lacked, Penelope made up for in compliments. She complimented everyone in anyway possible. This sealed her popularity in society.

"It is Elizabeth's older sister, Jane and her husband, Mr. Bingley. They have come as a surprise to Elizabeth on the occasion of their six month anniversaries."

"How romantic," sighed Penelope. "Your brother has always been so good to you and now he is the most doting of husbands. I cannot wait until I meet such a man."

"You speak of little else, sister. I fear you may miss the joys of life while you pine away for some man to make it for you. Have you learned nothing from your older sister and our good friend, Georgiana? To be single with means is freedom!"

"Of course, I admire your good examples, but can you say you are not a little excited for engagement and marriage?"

Georgiana was certain such excitement was not part of her future. Instead, she dreaded the marriages of her friends. A married woman soon sought the company of other married women in her neighbourhood and Georgiana was quite resigned to the life of a spinster. She kept these thoughts from her friends, though, and tried to be excited for their prospective attachments.

"I rarely think of such things," said Julia with a flip of her head. "Come; let us find some other mode of conversation."

"Perhaps I have something that will please both of your sentiments; I have more news from Pemberley. We will be having a ball – the first since the passing of our mother and father – You are both invited."

"Great heavens, why did you not start with that news?" said Penelope. "Tell us, when is the momentous event to occur?"

"The seventh of July will be the date. Elizabeth and Jane spend much of their days trying to make it just right for our society. I fear the previous opinions of my brother and the current disdain of my Aunt have made them anxious to make the perfect plans.

"Their sweetness can only make the whole neighbourhood fall for them. What can we do to help?" spoke Julia.

"Only say you will come and never mention a fault."

"I will endeavor to compliment them at every opportunity," said Penelope. Georgiana was grateful for the kindly natures of her friends.

"The day is beckoning ladies," said Julia when talk of the ball had run out. "I think I know how we might amuse ourselves."

Penelope and Georgiana turned to Julia with dancing eyes. Julia's ideas were always remarkable and they were in the mood for entertainment, as young ladies so often are.

"I think we should make a course for the horses. There are three available for us and I think the fields are well dried for riding. I propose we set up jumps and put on a show for ourselves. Do not fret, dear Georgiana, we will not damage your pretty dress. We have plenty of riding clothes to spare."

Georgiana always feared the day her friends would outgrow their fun-loving ways – she and Julia were both seventeen and Penelope sixteen. Georgiana swore she would not be the first to call attention to their advancing age and so she eagerly embraced Julia's idea and they quickly made for the fields.

Half an hour later, bedecked in riding costumes, the girls waved goodbye to Mrs. Lawson and promised to return for dinner. They took another half hour to set a course through the adjoining woods and then collected their horses from the stables. Georgiana nearly forgot all thoughts of Mr. Wickham and her own shame, which so often plagued her, and very much enjoyed their exercise in the woods.

"Does my sister not ride beautifully?" enthused Penelope.

"I have never seen her do anything poorly."

"I only hope mother will not discover our activities. She has been encouraging us to settle down of late. If Julia does not consider a husband, our mother worries enough for the both of us."

"You are both well established in society and still very young. Why would your mother worry that you be settled?" Georgiana had no experience of a mother at this stage of life.

"There are certain expectations, you know," Penelope shrugged. "Come, it is your turn, Georgiana."

Georgiana was not as experienced on horseback and so her friends had allowed her a shorter course to run with only one jump near the end. She concentrated and enjoyed the heat of an early summer day to warm her through. On the final jump, she held tightly and laughed when it was through. When she returned to her friends, she noticed they had been joined by their older brother and blushed deeply.

"Good day, Miss Darcy," said Mr. Lawson. "I see my sisters have you up to their unladylike pastimes once again."

All of Georgiana's hidden shame returned in the presence of handsome Phillip Lawson. She could speak not a word in reply and only tried to return her tangled hair to a state of obedience.

"I am sorry, Miss Darcy. I only speak in jest. You look well upon our horses."

"Leave us, Phillip," said Julia. "We never sought your company. I am certain you have other things you can do."

"Very well, sister. I only came at Mother's instructions to ensure your safety and to remind you of dinner in an hour. She wishes Miss Darcy to stay." Then Mr. Lawson kissed his two sisters, nodded at Georgiana and strode back to Sunnings.

"You should not speak to him so unkindly, Julia. Perhaps he wanted the pleasure of conversing with our friend," said Penelope.

"He can speak to her inside where we can appear like proper ladies. Come on, we have time for one last ride!"

# CHAPTER 8

WHILE THE LAWSON GIRLS – MAINLY JULIA – TRIED TO FIGHT against the expectations of their sex and station, their mother was amongst the chief upholders of its continuance. Mrs. Lawson had been married at sixteen and had served her husband very well in her lifetime. She bore him first three sons and finally two daughters. She insisted upon proper education for her boys and proper training for her girls. At sixteen, she insisted the girls stop all formal education that they might not become too intelligent for their future husbands. Mrs. Lawson insisted upon proper attire, good friends from the right families, and decorum on all occasions. She made it her business to arrange many situations where her daughters would meet the right men and kept them from any society of the wrong sort. Her daughters had three thousand a year upon their marriages and she insisted they marry men of no less than twice that amount. The girls knew nothing of their mother's background as she kept no company with her former relations. Her daughters would be very surprised to learn that their mother insisted on good society in the hopes of saving her children from the life she knew before Mr. Lawson proposed.

Although Mrs. Lawson was stern and forceful, she retained a tender heart. Upon the death of Georgiana's mother, she endeavored to make up for all that would be missing from the girl's life. Mrs. Lawson had always loved children and it was only pure joy for her to welcome another daughter under her protective wing. She hoped one of her sons would marry Miss Darcy so that they might become true family. For this reason, Georgiana was placed between two of her sons at dinner. The eldest, Phillip on her right was full of teazing and made it his aim to bring a smile to Georgiana's face. Barrington was the second son who was most serious and sat to her left. Though the Lawson children might argue and teaze one another, they were resolved to protect one another from the watchful eye of their mother. They kept one another's secrets that they would each have a chance at a bit of fun now and then – this had been their way since they lived in the nursery and when Georgiana became an unofficial part of their family, they included her into their schemes.

"I do love *horse*radish," announced Phillip once their roast beef was served. "I know my sisters are fond of the stuff, but I did not realize that you, Miss Darcy, had a taste for the wild."

Georgiana blushed at the obvious reference to her afternoon activities.

"I believe all good English people have a taste for horseradish," she attempted to close the topic.

"I assure you, Miss Darcy, that I have never had a taste for the stuff, but at your recommendation, I will make another attempt," said Barrington, helping himself to a large spoonful of the condiment only to make the most hideous face while tasting of it. Phillip laughed heartily at his expense.

"Stop *horsing* around, brother. You know you detest the stuff."

During the next course, Phillip again sought to bring a blush to Miss Darcy's face.

"I propose we play a game after our meal. I hear that Miss Darcy has a bit of a *horse*shoe in her purse when it comes to playing at cards."

Again, Georgiana's cheeks burned at the word. "I am no luckier than anyone else," she managed.

"Phillip, I insist you stop mentioning the word horse. It continually brings a blush to Miss Darcy's cheeks and I can see she wants nothing to do with your conversation," admonished the senior Mr. Lawson.

Phillip quit his public attack on Georgiana and resorted instead to whispering his provocations.

"I hope, Miss Darcy, that you do not take offense at my comments."

"I assure you I do not."

"It is only that I took pleasure in watching women of your age enjoying the games of children."

Although Georgiana had always been a complacent and obedient type of girl, Phillip was drawing from her a side of self-preservation which she did not know she possessed. Perhaps the influence of her new sister, Elizabeth, had also taught her to respond to a man's provocations.

"We only enjoyed the activities that you yourself regularly partake in."

"I assure you it has been many years since I made a course to play at with my friends," said Phillip, smiling.

"I do not see how your hunting parties are any different, except that you carry a gun and shoot at innocent creatures." Georgiana surprised herself with her presence of mind and blushed once again. Phillip controlled his obvious delight at her comment.

"Now I see I have sparked your ire. It pleases me that I still hold such powers," Phillip smiled.

Mr. Barrington Lawson aimed to break up the whisperings by interrupting quite loudly.

"Miss Darcy, I hear we are to have the pleasure of a ball at Pemberley."

"Yes, to mark the marriage of my brother and the arrival of her sister and husband, Mr. and Mrs. Bingley." Georgiana was relieved to escape her former conversation.

"Do the Bingleys find Pemberley to their liking?" spoke Mrs. Lawson.

"They only speak well of everything they see and everyone they meet, but I believe this is also their temperament – They are a very agreeable couple. Of course, you are all invited to the ball. I was sent to ask your company."

"We would be delighted to attend, it will be wonderful to see Pemberley in celebration once more – when is the grand event?" said Mrs. Lawson.

Georgiana told them the details and thanked them for accepting the invitation. As soon as the family returned to their suppers, Phillip continued his whisperings.

"I request the permission of the first dance, Miss Darcy – and if it please you, the second and third."

Georgiana blushed again, but before she could reply, the younger Mr. Lawson made his request loudly.

"Miss Darcy, please give me the honour of first dance at your family ball."

"I am sorry, Mr. Lawson, to withhold the honour from you, but my first three dances have already been secured."

"Well then, I would be pleased to request the pleasure of the fourth," Barrington said, maintaining his dignity.

"Yes, thank you Mr. Lawson. It would be my pleasure." She nodded also toward Phillip in agreement to his petition, but she worried at his attentions. Three dances with the same man in succession would certainly start her neighbours talking and might inspire the expectations of Mrs. Lawson. She would not like to crush their hopes, but if they ever learned of her past indiscretion, they would certainly dismiss her from their society. She saw no way to refuse him, however, and only hoped people would view their closeness as that of a brother and sister.

Mr. Lawson later questioned his wife on the odd behaviour of his eldest son at dinner.

"Why all the mention of horses?" he said. His wife was most delighted to share her opinion on the matter.

"I think our hopes may be coming into actuality, Mr. Lawson," smiled his wife. "You remember, my dear, that our son's name means "lover of horses", he must be teazing her about her own feelings toward him."

Mr. Lawson was quite surprised by her statement, but it pleased him well and he smiled at his wife's clever mind.

# CHAPTER 9

DINNER AT PEMBERLEY WAS A MORE SUBDUED AFFAIR. Elizabeth had received word from her sister, Lydia, that afternoon announcing her arrival the following morning. Mr. Darcy had forbidden Lydia's husband, Mr. Wickham, ever return to Pemberley due to his indecent behaviour towards Georgiana two years prior, but could hardly refuse the sister of his wife. They only worried at the feelings of Georgiana. While Mrs. Bingley was aware of this situation, she had never revealed the secret to her husband and so they could not speak freely on the subject over dinner and Mr. Bingley, though vaguely aware of a sense of unease, was blissfully unacquainted with its source.

"Is it not a coincidence your sister should visit while we are at Pemberley," he wondered aloud with a smile.

"Indeed," replied Darcy.

"I only wonder why she should come all this way alone. Surely her husband could delay his business in London a day or two to bring Lydia to Pemberley."

"It really is not our business to question," said Jane

quietly, but Mr. Bingley did not notice the warning in her voice.

"I hope there is not a lover's quarrel between the pair," he joked. "She would not make for a pleasing house guest if that were the case. I propose you invite Mr. Wickham as a personal guest to your home on the event of the ball. He could surprise Mrs. Wickham and we could all enjoy the spectacle of their reunion." Mr. Bingley was quite pleased with his scheme, but it was met with no enthusiasm.

"It is a lovely proposal, Mr. Bingley," said Elizabeth. "However, I am quite certain their union is a happy one and do not wish to cause Mr. Wickham any guilt on being unable to accompany my sister during her visit. Tell us, Mr. Bingley, what news do you have of your two sisters?"

Mrs. Darcy's clever distraction brought relief to her husband and sister and they listened to Mr. Bingley"s news of his sisters for the remainder of the meal. Mr. and Mrs. Hurst had produced a most acceptable heir whom they had named for Mr. Bingley.

"Little Charles is the very essence of my sister, Louisa. He is a most becoming fellow and always content in every situation – he was born to them only this spring."

After dinner, they retired to the parlour where Jane and Elizabeth continued with plans for the ball and Darcy and Bingley played at backgammon.

"How do our sisters Mary and Kitty get on at Longbourn without us?" Elizabeth asked when she tired of the planning.

"Father has stuck to his promise to keep a closer watch on Kitty in the hopes she will not turn out like Lydia. She often complains about the restrictions and pines for her previous freedoms, but I can see improvements in her actions every time I see her. Kitty has begun to show some interest in books, which father takes as a sign of some sense."

"I had nearly forgotten Jane how well you speak of everyone. I fear I will not get the whole answer from you," teazed Elizabeth. "And what of Mary?"

"She is not much changed. I hope she and Kitty will draw closer now that it is only them in the household, but they are of quite different temperaments. I fear they are lonely without their sisters in the house. The younger Miss Lucas visits often enough to keep the girls from tiring of their situation."

"I wonder if they should be married before long. Does Father really keep them from *coming out*?"

"Indeed – Father is much changed by our marriages. I think he misses you greatly Lizzy; whenever you send a letter, he reads it aloud to anyone who will listen."

"I will have to make sure I carefully consider every word I write!" Elizabeth grew slightly teary at the stories of home. She had never been away so long and realized a married woman must change her idea of home.

Mr. Darcy interrupted at this point in the conversation. He and Mr. Bingley had finished their game with the former as champion. An idea came to him which he felt he should share in the company of their close friends.

"Elizabeth, I have realized that I have been remiss on a rather important piece of business since our marriage."

Elizabeth could hardly think of anything her husband had forgotten, and especially anything he would want to share in company.

"What is it dear? Are there some papers we have not yet signed?"

"It is something much more important than paper and longer lasting. It will need to be completed before the ball and I fear it might take some of your time away from preparations."

"Do tell us, Darcy, we are all very curious." Mr. Bingley was never one for patience.

"It is the marking of your entrance into our family -- A sure sign you have joined the Darcys and it will remain in our history forever."

Elizabeth guessed now what he meant but dared not say so for fear she was mistaken. She merely smiled and hoped for his answer.

"Your beauty will be a welcome addition to our walls, my dear. Your portrait must adorn them to show our guests your proper place in our family. What do you say, Eliza?"

Elizabeth was quite delighted and her sister equally if not more so.

"You will need to begin immediately, I fear - Does tomorrow morning suit?"

"Certainly," Elizabeth was honoured at his thoughtful contribution to their preparations.

Eventually Georgiana returned home, looking rosy from her evening out. Mr. and Mrs. Darcy dreaded the news they must tell her and in an effort to provide some privacy, Jane pressed her husband to turn in early on the excuse that she was tired.

"Did you have an enjoyable evening?" Mr. Darcy asked his sister once the Bingley's left.

"I always enjoy the company of the Lawsons. They have been so good to me over the years. They have all agreed to attend our party."

"I will mark them down," said Elizabeth and looked at Darcy to see if he would tell Georgiana the news; he took her hint.

"I fear we have received some news which might cause you some discomfort," began Darcy.

"Is someone ill?" Georgiana said.

"No, it is rather a visitor to Pemberley who may remind you of what you would rather forget."

Elizabeth could not stand the look of worry on Georgiana's face and interrupted to end the suspense.

"It is my sister, Lydia. She has written to say she will visit us for a fortnight while her husband attends to some business in London."

Georgiana's rosy cheeks turned ashen at the news. They gave her a moment to consider its meaning.

"Will your sister's husband be accompanying her during the visit?"

"No, she will arrive alone by carriage with only her maid. I have asked that man never to show himself at our home and I mean that he never shall." Mr. Darcy replied.

"That is a comfort." Georgiana composed herself and forced a smile. "I can only be glad for the company of any sister of yours, Elizabeth. You need not worry about my response; I will be cordial and willing to make her stay as pleasant as possible."

Elizabeth felt a surge of pride at her Georgiana's bravery. "Thank you, Georgiana. I hope you will not be troubled in any way. Your composure is to be praised."

After a few more inquiries into Georgiana's time at Sunnings, they retired to contemplate the day ahead.

# CHAPTER 10

MRS. WICKHAM SPENT A MISERABLE NIGHT AT A ROADSIDE INN on her way to Pemberley. She had insisted upon stopping before their designated lodgings due to her pestering hunger, against the better judgment of her driver. The Inn had a reputation for rowdy visitors and bad food. Lydia ate up her supper quickly and demanded more only to spend much of the night in agonies over poorly cooked ham. There had been banging at her door in the attempts of quieting her groaning and various obscenities were yelled through the walls when she would not cease. Mrs. Wickham complained loudly upon her departure and refused to pay her bill – mainly due to the fact that she could not afford it. Her driver finally stopped the argument by escorting her to the carriage and returning to give her brother-in-law's address at Pemberley for the forwarding of the bill. Mr. Darcy was known even in these parts as an honest man of means.

Mrs. Wickham's complaints continued as they journeyed on to Pemberley. They now had two hours to make up due to their early stop the night before, and the driver took it upon himself to drive faster in order to end his appointment with the grousing lady. This increased the effect of any and all obstructions in the road making Mrs. Wickham's journey all the more lamentable. Her only consolation through the journey was the thought of her sisters' faces at her news. She arrived at Pemberley quite irritated, hungry and sore, and refused to tip her driver for his troubles. He looked to Mr. Darcy's footman to make up for her lapse in judgment.

"Tell my sister and brother that Mrs. Wickham has arrived. Be quick now, I have had the most dreadful two days of travel – I am certain I shall feel the effect on my nerves for my entire visit," she announced.

When both Elizabeth and Jane arrived to welcome her, Lydia's spirits and nerves were miraculously restored.

"Sisters, I am so relieved to find you both here to receive me. I have the gravest of news."

Lydia's vocabulary had always been impressive in verbiage, though rather lacking in understanding; for this reason, her sisters were not alarmed.

"Welcome to Pemberley," said Elizabeth. "I trust your travels were agreeable."

"Hardly! What manner of Inns you have in this country. It is only my strong constitution which brought me here intact. I was made ill by the fare and forced to listen to the most horrific of language whilst I attempted to rest my aching body. My nerves are barely intangible. Quickly, sisters, fetch me refreshment and a comfortable seat that I might share my news with you."

Jane and Elizabeth exchanged glances but accepted Lydia's orders. Though Lydia was their much younger sister, her marriage provided her relief from their former reproofs. When Lydia had devoured a plateful of sandwiches meant for all three and multiple cups of tea, she finally allowed herself to share her information.

"Well sisters, it is well you have treated me tolerably for

you are both to become aunties!" Lydia's face was all pride and delight. Jane and Elizabeth were true in their congratulations.

"Will not mother and father be pleased to finally have grandchildren!" she continued. "I dare say they have waited long enough; we all feared you two would never marry and here I am the first to provide an heir."

"It is wonderful news, Lydia," Jane did not wish to upstage her sister with her own news.

"To think I will be a mother before I turn eighteen! Mother was already nineteen when you were born Jane. Oh! She will be so pleased with me. I only wish she were here with us all. Now, I must rest and wash before dinner. You have prepared something special for my arrival, I trust. Three courses would be sufficient. Lord, but I am tired."

Elizabeth herself showed Lydia to her room and promised to provide all her favorite foods for supper. Elizabeth took a long breath of relief when the door closed behind her younger sister.

The Darcys held dinner as long as they could for Lydia who had fallen into a deep sleep. They finally sent the maid to wake her for a very late dinner. She was famished and fell to eating almost without comment to her hosts. Jane and Elizabeth covered their smiles at her behaviour and discussed Elizabeth's first sitting for her portrait.

"Was it very difficult to sit still so long, Lizzy?" Jane asked.

"I fear it was. You would do so much better than me, I am certain. You know I have never been accomplished at stillness and calm."

"Did you get a chance to look at the image?" Mr. Bingley asked.

"The artist does not feel comfortable having anyone seeing his work before he has finished. He told me several stories of young women destroying his work because he had done them injustice in the initial sketches. He insists we must pay full price in the event of such an occurrence. If we are dissatisfied with the final work, he will not charge us to rework the painting."

This finally drew Lydia from the devotion she paid her food.

"Why are you being painted?" she said.

"We will be hosting a ball during your stay," said Mr. Darcy.

"Lord! Why did you not tell me? I have not a single thing to wear and I am big as a manor."

"We did not get the chance before you arrived, sister. Do not worry about your clothes, Jane, Georgiana and I will be having something made in the coming week. You can be included in our party," said Elizabeth.

Mrs. Wickham, of course, had no money and endeavored to obtain her costume without charge.

"I was not prepared for such extravagance," she replied. "I do not have the permission of my good husband for such expenses."

Mr. Darcy looked heavenward momentarily, but smiled at his wife and ventured to please her by her family. He also aimed to make up for what lacked in Mr. Wickham who, at one time, had been almost a brother to him.

"Please accept your dress as a gift, Lydia. Feel welcome to order the loveliest you can imagine," he said.

"I am happy to see your fortune equals what you expected in life," said Lydia meaningfully, her husband had prepared her for this visit. "Of course, you would not want your nephew or niece to want for anything and while providing for his mother is a kind gesture, a child needs more than a pretty mother to get ahead in life. If only my husband had what was coming to him."

Lydia, unfortunately, was nearly without manners and

referred to a promise made by Mr. Darcy's father to provide for Mr. Wickham a position in the clergy. What only a few sitting at the table knew was that Mr. Wickham demanded and received from Mr. Darcy money in lieu of his livelihood. Fortunately, Lydia was of short attention to any one topic that did not directly concern her and moved on to another delectable dish.

Georgiana tried to watch the wife of her former betrothed without judgment. She aimed to see her solely as the sister of Elizabeth and a guest to their home, but could not help but wonder how two sisters could be so entirely opposite. Georgiana wondered how a woman could be so self-involved. She spent much of the dinner considering her previous involvement with Mr. Wickham. Thankfully, she was seated as far from Mrs. Wickham as was possible in their small party. She could consider her thoughts nearly without interruption. She pondered, though, how she could politely avoid Mrs. Wickham for the duration on her stay.

When Mrs. Wickham finally sated her voracious appetite, she began to speak at length about her dutiful and popular husband. She spoke of his great accomplishments, the company they kept, and their hopes for the future. She again referred to her belief that it was solely Mr. Darcy's fault they did not enjoy all of the wealth they deserved.

"Of course, we do not have the comfort and respect we are due, should life have turned out as my husband expected," she glanced meaningfully at Mr. Darcy. "It is not easy to make a living on my husband's salary. We are as frugal as possible, given our circumstances. Do you know, Lizzy, of any inexpensive lodgings in your vicinity?"

Elizabeth attempted to distract any hopes Lydia might have of moving closer to them with politeness.

After supper, Georgiana wrote a letter to the Lawson's announcing her plans to visit the following morning.

# CHAPTER 11

ALTHOUGH THE DARCY'S WERE ESTRANGED FROM LADY Catherine de Bourgh, which in turn caused them to lose favour in the eyes of her patron, Mr. Collins; Mrs. Charlotte Collins, nee Lucas, and Mrs. Darcy still exchanged letters regularly. Mrs. Collins letter arrived the following day filled with raptures over her newborn son. While Mrs. Collins spoke only fleetingly of her husband, the letter brimmed with her son's little sounds, looks and many talents. He was three months old and named William after Mr. Collins and Charlotte's father.

"Lizzy, I cannot tell you how fulfilling life is when a child enters it. I can hardly stand to part with him when the nursemaid comes. I wonder why we have made it so strange to raise our own children. The poor spend every waking moment with theirs – working, caring for their other children and teaching them all at once. I wonder how they do it, but am also quite glad for a moment or two to myself. Baby William does have the most shocking scream when he is hungry or dirty. It is a blessing then to pass him to the nurse,

I will confess. Of course, I must not admit such astonishing thoughts to Lady Catherine or my husband. Lady Catherine often stops by to favour us with her many opinions on what Baby William should wear, how he should be fed, what schooling we should consider etc. It was her kind suggestion which provided us with a nursemaid. Mr. Collins is very grateful for her views on these matters. They would think me most peculiar, as you likely do as well. I wish you could come and meet him, Lizzy, but I do not see how that might be accomplished. I will content myself with the coming visit of mother and Maria within a month. They have already been twice and I think Maria may have found favour in the eyes of Mr. Collins" cousin.

"Yours affectionately,
"Charlotte."

ELIZABETH PLOTTED with Jane on how best to approach Darcy on the subject of Lady Catherine and the Collins". Lydia was napping after a large breakfast and Georgiana had left for Sunnings, so the two older sisters had some time to themselves.

"It seems Lady Catherine is quite fond of giving advice," Jane suggested.

"You always have a way of putting even the most undeserving people in the best light possible," complained Elizabeth. "However, I would welcome any suggestion you might have."

"Perhaps you could write to her for advice on the planning of your first ball?"

"Now, that is an idea, Jane. When did you become so cunning?" Elizabeth looked proudly at her sister.

"I do not think myself cunning, only helpful in repairing an argument between two families."

"Call it what you will, Jane, I think the idea has some merit, but how do I convince Darcy?"

"There, sister, I think you have the authority. You know your husband much better than I."

"I hate to abuse his goodness to me. Do you see what he accepts from Lydia on my behalf? I am sure it puts both my husband and his sister to great pains even to have her in the house, but he never complains and is continually obliging. Is it fair to impose further on his goodness to me?"

"Possibly not, Lizzy, but perhaps he mourns the separation between himself and his aunt."

"Indeed Jane, you have a way of putting things in the most agreeable perspective; however since she has also slighted me, I think I must put forward my great desire to see Mrs. Collins again."

"Shall we visit Mr. Darcy and Mr. Bingley then?" said Jane with mirth in her eyes.

"Indeed. I think we should invite them to tea!" The women smiled as they remembered their courtships and sent word to their husbands for tea.

"Excellent," spoke Mr. Bingley a half hour later when he and Mr. Darcy joined their wives in the morning sitting room. "I was beginning to tire of Darcy's company. I do not know how you stand him day in and day out, Mrs. Darcy!"

"You can see my friend still endeavors to put himself ahead of me in the company of women," said Darcy.

"He is wise to seek our good opinion," said Elizabeth.

"One never wishes to find the wrong side of a woman's favour."

"I see I should work diligently at it," bowed Mr. Darcy.

They discussed briefly the passing of the morning and plans for the afternoon when Elizabeth thought it was acceptable to bring up her petition.

"I received a letter from Mrs. Collins this morning," she began while refilling her husband's teacup.

"She is nothing if not devoted," said Darcy. "She writes at least once a month."

"Quite as often as Jane and I. She has had a son and writes of all the wonders of motherhood." Elizabeth placed another teacake on Darcy's plate and he took it without noticing.

"That should be a help to you, my dear," said Mr. Bingley to his wife.

"Indeed," said Jane, taking up some knitting.

"She wishes I could see baby William," Elizabeth dared.

"Is that of interest to you, Lizzy?" Darcy spoke.

"I would not wish to disappoint her."

"When would you like to go, then?" Darcy rose to look out the window.

Elizabeth was encouraged by his agreeable speech and apparent eagerness to move.

"I thought, perhaps, we could invite them to the ball."

"Impossible," spoke Darcy who turned back to his wife. "I am certain they will not wish to travel so far with a newborn."

"Of course, I had not thought," said Elizabeth. "However, I do not see how I could visit Hunsford when Lady Catherine is so near."

"Ah, do you wish for me to write my aunt for forgiveness, then?" Darcy's voice was no longer quite as genteel.

"I would never dare tell you what to do, especially when your pride was at risk," said Elizabeth. "I only spoke my desire to see an old friend. I do not know how it is to become a reality."

Darcy turned taciturn at this point and Mr. and Mrs. Bingley were left to revive the conversation. They did so valiantly until Mrs. Darcy excused herself for the sitting of her portrait.

# CHAPTER 12

THAT MORNING, GEORGIANA SET OUT EARLY FOR SUNNINGS. She wished to avoid all contact with Mrs. Wickham and so took a picnic for her breakfast. She walked, singing, along the path connecting the two houses and was pleased to enjoy the early sunlight through the pretty trees. She felt herself relax as she always did when alone in nature and looked forward to conversing with her friends. She heard the approach of a horse and stopped her singing – she hoped the rider would carry on without noticing her or with nothing more than a nod, but Phillip Lawson was only too pleased to meet her.

"You are out early, Miss Darcy," said he, "But where is your horse? We could have enjoyed the morning together and you might have taught me to jump more proficiently."

Georgiana was angry with the blush this produced.

"I would not consider myself equal to the task. I wonder that you have any friends at all when you insist on reminding them of their shortcomings," she could hardly believe her fiery remarks.

"Ho, ho! I did not expect you so quick this early in the morning. I only wished to invite you to enjoy it together."

"I am quite happy on my own, I assure you Mr. Lawson, and I spend no time of the day in "slowness". Good day." Georgiana attempted to walk on, but Mr. Lawson dismounted his horse and followed after her on foot, letting his horse follow behind.

"My apologies, Miss Darcy. I fear I have pushed you beyond your limit."

"I am not so faint of heart as that. I am most capable of defending myself from any man."

"Again, I have misspoken. Forgive me Miss Darcy and grant me permission to walk you to your destination."

"I need no companion; I was quite enjoying the solitude."

Mr. Lawson acknowledged his defeat, bowed, said "Good day, Miss Darcy," and returned to his saddle. Georgiana expected relief at his departure, but could only repeat their conversation a hundred times in her mind for the remainder of her walk. She felt she might have faced less vexation if she had remained at Pemberley.

Georgiana arrived finally at Sunnings and was welcomed by Mrs. Lawson and her daughters. Georgiana realized she had forgotten to eat her breakfast and tried to hide it from their view. She tucked it into her light cloak before the maid hung it away in the closet.

Mrs. Lawson had invited Mrs. Highmore to provide her daughters and Georgiana with the best advice on ball gowns. Until Mrs. Highmore's arrival, the girls decided to visit the pond which provided them privacy to speak freely.

"I don't know how I shall stand a morning of fashion," said Julia. "Why can I not trust my own feelings on the subject?"

"Do not be ungrateful, Julia," said her sister. "You are becoming more and more independent by the day."

"It is the weather. I feel the need to travel and to get away from Mother's watchful eyes. Georgiana, could you not persuade your brother to allow you and me to spend the summer traveling?" said Julia hopefully.

"I fear it would be futile without his accompaniment or that of your parents."

"If only we enjoyed the freedoms of men! Do you think any of my brothers or Mr. Darcy ever spent so long at home when they were our age? It is unbearable."

Penelope tried to turn the subject.

"I noticed my brother paid special attention to you at dinner two evenings prior."

"Oh, leave her be!" said Julia. "I am certain she does not want us prying into her private affairs."

Usually, Georgiana would be grateful for Julia's statement, but on this particular day she found the need to share her distress.

"I do not wish to speak ill of any of your family, but I fear your eldest brother is using me most unkindly."

"I think he means only to tease. I do not think he meant to be unkind, but he is badly trained to converse with a lady. He has had only us as his experience with young women." Julia said, trying to soothe her friend.

"I saw him this morning as I walked to Sunnings and he was most insulting."

"If only I could speak to him as a brother and demand he treats you well." Julia crushed her bonnet in her hands.

"Please, do not speak to him, Julia. I should not be sharing this burden with you, only I have no one else I can speak to."

"Let us teach him, then, in a less direct way!" Julia became animated and crammed her misshapen hat back onto her windblown hair.

"Sister, we are not children any longer." Penelope admonished, but Julia ignored her.

"We will be married away and respectable ladies soon enough, in the meantime, let us enjoy our youth."

Though Georgiana was, by nature, very compliant and Penelope a great believer in proper behaviour, Julia's exuberance was contagious and the three were soon plotting a proper revenge on Phillip.

"We must not cause any physical harm," said Penelope.

"Nor do I wish to cause any public embarrassment," added Georgiana.

"Do not fear, my friends. We will only play with his expectations and none but us will know the outcome. Oh, but we must hurry before Mrs. Highmore arrives."

By tea time, a letter was placed in Phillip's pile, mixed in among the rest. He never read his before noon, which gave them some time to complete their ruse while Mrs. Highmore visited.

"How well your daughters look," exclaimed Mrs. Highmore when they met for tea. "Miss Darcy as well. I am certain you will all be claimed for every dance at the ball. Be sure to rest well beforehand to save your stamina."

Mrs. Highmore, like any person of great encouragement, was a welcome addition to Sunnings. She brought several fashion magazines with her and a few swatches of material for them to consider. The girls carefully studied the dresses in pairs while the other of the group sat to write a letter. Julia eventually excused herself with complaint of a stomachache to finish off their plan.

"I hope you will be well soon," said Mrs. Highmore. "Stomachaches are such a bother. I suffered many at Julia's age, I think now that it was merely nerves."

Georgiana's stomach actually was beginning to feel unwell at this point, but two stomachaches would cause suspicion, so she tried not to think of the plan at hand or the effects it would have on Phillip Lawson. Too soon, the women were called to lunch.

"Good day, Georgiana," Mr. Lawson senior greeted her upon entering. "It is always a pleasure to have you at Sunnings."

"Thank you sir, I hope I do not wear out my welcome."

"Impossible, my dear," said Mrs. Lawson. "I only wish you were here oftener." At this, she glanced at Phillip to gauge his reaction to Georgiana's visit. Again, Phillip took his seat to her right, but did not pester her with any mention of horses. Georgiana began to regret their prank, but it was securely in place at this time and already, Phillip reached for his letters. He remained at this until their soup arrived and she saw he had not yet read the letter in question. He finally spoke to Georgiana.

"I trust you enjoyed your *solitary* walk this morning." Phillip did not smile or jest as usual.

"I did thank you – and you your riding?" Georgiana began to regret her treatment toward Phillip, but certainly she must become accustomed to such ways if she was to remain single all her life.

"Naturally, it was a very fine morning."

Barrington cut in at this moment to tell a long and involved story of his achievements at school. Georgiana nodded in agreement between mouthfuls of soup and then noticed Phillip had finished his and was reading the false letter. Georgiana looked away quickly. At the end of the letter, Phillip glanced her way briefly but made no comment. Mrs. Lawson smiled at the careful inattention she noticed between the two.

The rest of the meal was spent in suspense of whether or not Phillip would be taken in by the plan. Julia, Penelope and Georgiana watched each other carefully and repeatedly stopped themselves from smiling. At the end of the meal, they excused themselves and ran outside to compare what they had seen. Then they split up to watch their posts.

At each post was another letter to entice Phillip onward. The letters were written in all capital letters and the first was received by him at lunch;

"Mr. Lawson;

I request the enjoyment of your company as I have something of interest to share with you. Please meet me at the gate to the meadow.

"Signed,

"A Lady."

At the meadow gate was a second note which read;

"Mr. Lawson;

I could not stay in the meadow as I feared it too open for a meeting such as ours. I ask you to humour me once more and join me instead at the large tree by the pond."

At the large tree was a third epistle.

"Mr. Lawson;

I fear the insects are too troublesome and ask instead that you would find me in the covered hut by the garden."

Georgiana waited behind the covered hut in anticipation of Phillip's arrival and his response to their charade. Julia and Penelope met Georgiana there with news that Phillip had found each of their letters. They waited breathlessly for him to open the hut.

Georgiana felt uneasy at the prospect of his discovery, but her friends kept her in good spirits. They heard his footfalls presently, but were unable to see him without revealing their hiding spot. Suddenly they heard the creaking of hinges and jumped up to see Phillip's reaction. They were alarmed to see it was Barrington who opened the door to let out a large hog dressed in a bonnet and old doll's dress. The hog snorted and rolled at Barrington's feet and behind him stood Phillip, laughing.

"It appears I was correct in requesting your assistance in the matter," said Phillip. "I would not like to meet a lady such as this on my own. I trust you will know how to handle her."

"Does it thrill you, brother, to bother me with such juvenile pranks? I should think you had better things to be doing with your time." Barrington stormed back to the house, swatting at the mud on his trousers. "And put that pig back in its sty."

"Thank you Barrington," called his brother. "I will certainly consider my sisters in my next prank." He walked then behind the hut and found the cowering girls.

"Well, I see you girls are up to your childish games once more." He held out his hand to Georgiana to help her to her feet. The hog barreled over then, sniffing at her pockets. She remembered her hidden breakfast and gave it to the pig in a fluster. "Truly, Miss Darcy, I would not have supposed you were behind this. Get on with it then, sisters, I believe you have a pig to return." With that, Phillip tipped his hat and followed his brother back to the house. The girls were left with the mess they had created.

"We should have remembered the quick thinking of our brother," lamented Penelope.

"I hope we have not made things worse," said Julia.

Georgiana felt herself duly reprimanded and promised herself she would return to her regular practices of study and obedience. However, not wishing to dishearten her companions, she put on a brave smile and told them not to worry. It had been good fun and no one was the worse for their tricks. They undressed the hog with some difficulty and returned it to its pen where Georgiana bid her friends goodbye on the excuse that she must return home to wash.

# CHAPTER 13

THE DAYS BEFORE THE BALL TOOK ON A PATTERN OF SORTS. Elizabeth sat for her portrait in the mornings. Jane occasionally joined her, endeavoring to keep her as still as possible for the artist. Lydia wrote daily letters to her mother explaining every detail of her gown for the ball and all of the preparations she was doing for it. She also wrote to her husband, but these letters went unanswered. She put on a brave face and explained to all around her he was very busy and important and was probably preparing things as well as possible for his new family, but Jane and Elizabeth secretly worried over his gaming habits. To cheer Lydia, Jane frequently reminded her that their own father was very reticent to pick up pen and paper. Darcy and Bingley hunted when the former was not occupied with matters of business and tenants. Georgiana did not go as often to visit the Lawsons, hoping to avoid Phillip. She worked at her playing and singing and took long walks and rides. In secret, she attempted to improve her horse riding.

The time passed quickly as it does in the company of good friends. Elizabeth found herself occasionally dreading the ball rather than facing it with the excitement of her youth. She considered that as she was now a married woman, such things no longer held the same appeal as when single men were an object of interest. She wanted to avoid her mother's habit of arranging for the marriages of others; however she found that the one secret joy she had in hosting the ball was in hoping Georgiana might find a worthy husband. While such thoughts had previously been vulgar to her, she found marriage had softened her acceptance of speaking of the marriages and expected children of others. Instead she must look forward to the enjoyment of all her guests and the new friends she might make. She fervently hoped she would not disappoint anyone with her ability to run a house.

Elizabeth continued to persuade her husband to reconsider his attitude toward his aunt. He agreed to allow Elizabeth to write a letter requesting Lady Catherine's advice regarding the ball. Two days before the event, a reply was sent. Elizabeth brought the letter with her as she and Jane took a walk toward the bridge. The sun was sparkling and summer birds delighted them with song. They sat to rest in a copse of trees where Elizabeth handed the epistle to her sister to be read aloud.

"For our amusement, Jane, let us have it. How has Lady Catherine permitted herself to patronize me?"

"It is a long letter, sister. Are you certain you wish that I should know all of the details of your family business?"

Elizabeth laughed at Jane's impeccable manners. "Who in the world can I trust more than you, sister? You have kept even Bingley from knowing the indelicate relationship between Wickham and Georgiana. Read on!"

Jane obliged her younger sister as she so often did.

"Rosings

"3 July

"Mrs. Darcy,

"You must know how much exertion it requires for me to answer your letter. I had no intention of communicating with you again after the way I was received when I visited Longbourn. Then to learn that you had, indeed, usurped the longstanding engagement between my daughter and nephew! Certainly, you have caused me much grief and trouble. However, in the hopes of preserving my late sister's good name and her exquisite taste and breeding, I will permit myself to provide the information you have requested.

"A ball, my dear, is not something one plans lightly. I see by the time you receive this, you will hardly have time to follow much of my advice. You have already made several errors, primarily in that you have allowed yourself so little time for preparation. I always give myself at least three months for such grand occasions. Hopefully, your guests will be forgiving to you, a foreigner to Pemberley and one of altogether other upbringings."

"How well she justifies her insults!" Elizabeth laughed and Jane read on.

"You will have already sent the invitations, I assume, which are of the utmost importance. These present the very air and expectation of the ball. They must be sent on gilded paper with the inclusion of all of your family names. I recommend you make additional reminder invitations which may undo some of the harm which the error of your initial invitations may have caused. It is critical that you sign each one personally with the best of calligraphy. I do not suppose, however, that you are acquainted with the art. In that case, you may hire someone to sign for you, which has become an acceptable practice nowadays.

"I must regretfully refuse our invitation, which I assume

you mean to send. My daughter Miss de Bourgh is not well at the moment and I cannot leave her to travel. The nurse requires the utmost attention and care or I declare she would kill Anne with her country-learned ministrations."

The letter continued for six full pages covering every aspect of party-giving which could be considered, including linens, necessary cleaning preparations, recipes for White soup and negus and proper techniques for introducing guests.

"Well sister, she is very generous with her advice," Jane said, breathlessly at the end. "This might be a letter worth preserving for future parties."

"How well you put her, but there are some helpful hints and I must send my thank you promptly. I will let you rest awhile before we walk back. I should not have made you read the entire letter, but I so enjoyed your good reading of the whole."

"It is good, Lizzy, that you endeavor to repair the rift between your families. Lady Catherine would be a good ally."

"I only hope she will never make it to one of my balls. Imagine everything I must do to make it acceptable for her ladyship!"

"It is a pity Miss de Bourgh is not well. What a worry that must be to her mother."

"I think she will rise to the occasion as she does everything else, but I do not wish her ill. I will remember to send my wishes for her health."

After a quarter of an hour resting in the copse after the letter was read, the sisters returned at a leisurely pace to Pemberley.

# CHAPTER 14

THE DAY OF THE BALL ARRIVED IN RAIN. THE LADIES OF THE house regretted that gowns and shoes would be ruined by mud, and made arrangements for wet overcoats, overshoes and umbrellas by the front entrance. Darcy and Bingley cancelled their plans to go fishing, which would have allowed them to avoid much of the commotion surrounding preparations. The portrait was finished and hung in the grand room covered by a sheet. None but the artist had looked upon it yet and Elizabeth hoped his reputation was to be trusted. She had invited him and his wife to the ball for the unveiling.

At breakfast, Lydia complained that her dress was too tight and declared she would need the skills of the best seamstress for the morning. Elizabeth eyed her sister's heaping plate with amusement and promised the best seamstress in the house would come to her rooms with expediency. Despite the mocking tone Elizabeth initially gave Lady Catherine's letter, she consulted it several times throughout the day. Elizabeth felt she must make her husband proud and show that, although her upbringing was lacking in many areas, she could learn to be mistress of a grand house like

Pemberley. She was grateful for the experience and efficiency of their housekeeper, Mrs. Reynolds, whom she had liked from the moment they met on her fateful first visit to Pemberley. Elizabeth often credited Mrs. Reynolds for turning her opinion for good toward Mr. Darcy.

Jane felt poorly after so much strain from the previous days and rested in her rooms for the remainder of the morning. Elizabeth missed Jane's calming influence, but told her it was only a party and the baby was much more important. Jane must rest until she felt fully recovered.

Darcy and Bingley took to billiards for the morning in lieu of fishing. Darcy hoped this activity might excuse them from much of the excitement in the house, but Bingley would rather have been in the thick of it all. They were well into their first game when Bingley noticed they were completely alone without even a servant to overhear them. He took this opportunity to confront Darcy.

"Have you had the chance yet, my friend, to approach your wife with the secret you previously kept from her?"

Darcy looked nervously about the room and did not answer until he was certain they were alone.

"No, man, and pray do not mention anything to her or your wife."

"I have kept your secret, even from my sweet Jane, though I know her to be trustworthy enough to keep something even from her closest sister. In fact, I feel she has kept matters from me which she felt were not at her liberty to share."

"I thank you for that."

Bingley took a shot and missed badly. "I do not think you should have any fear of confiding in Elizabeth. She seems to have a kind and forgiving soul."

"I have yet to see how the information directly concerns her."

"Really? What if she were to bare you a child?"

"It has not happened yet. In that case, I might reconsider."

"Why wait, Darcy? What if she were to find out from elsewhere? Surely there are people in the house who know? Or in Lambton?"

"Those people have been well paid to hold their tongues. I think also of Georgiana in the matter. I do not wish to worry her."

"I will not mention it again on this visit, but I strongly urge you to bring this matter before your wife."

"I will thank you for keeping all thoughts on the matter to yourself."

Darcy's agitation did not affect his ability at billiards and he won the game neatly at the next opportunity.

BY LUNCHTIME, Lydia was in tears over her dress and Elizabeth alone was left to bring her to sense.

"Lydia, I am certain it cannot be as bad as you claim. I will come to your rooms directly after lunch and inspect it myself."

"It will not do for the wife of a previous resident to look anything but her best!" Lydia shouted. "I cannot put my husband to shame in the presence of so many of his prior acquaintances."

Elizabeth gave a knowing glance to her husband. Lydia could hardly worsen her husband's reputation in Lambton. His previous debts had all been cancelled by Mr. Darcy himself as no attempt at repayment had ever been made by Mr. Wickham.

"You will look lovely, Lydia. You hardly need any adornment at all in your glowing condition." Elizabeth cajoled.

Lydia consoled herself with a healthy portion of ham and

Elizabeth was thankful that the eating of it caused some quietness on her behalf.

"Georgiana, have you decided to play for the ball?" Elizabeth turned to her much quieter sister-in-law.

"I will, only because you have requested it," she said. "I do not believe people wish to hear me half as much as you have said."

"You are too modest," said Bingley. "I am certain I have never heard better, but do not tell my wife!"

"Your wife would only echo your sentiments," said Darcy. "She is by far the most complimentary of ladies I have ever met."

"I am surrounded by such talents," said Elizabeth. "I am pleased you will play for us, Georgiana, but I should never wish for your discomfort."

"You need not worry, sister. I have played for crowds before and though I do not relish being in public, there is some joy in it for me, I confess."

"Now Mrs. Darcy, what will you have us do this afternoon?" said Mr. Bingley, who was very much looking forward to the evening's activities.

Elizabeth consulted her lists and was pleased her brother-in-law volunteered to share some of the burden and offering her husband's assistance as well.

With Darcy in charge of checking the victuals and wine, and Bingley to arrange the musician's transportation, Elizabeth was free to attend to both of her sisters. She checked on Jane first and found her in much better spirits.

"Only a bit of morning sickness, I expect. I have, perhaps, been exerting myself too much."

"You must rest for the remainder of the day. I will have the maid bring you some refreshment for the afternoon."

"You are very kind, sister. I only wish I were not a burden and could assist you in this grand fete."

"Nonsense, I have put both of our husbands to work and any omissions I have made by now are too late to repair. We can only hope the wine will erase any of my mistakes!"

Elizabeth left Jane then to attend to Lydia, whom she feared would be quite a bit more demanding on her time and resources.

Lydia's room was in disaster. She had three maids busy sewing, ironing and cleaning all at once. The dress was in pieces and she stood in a petticoat before the mirror.

"Lizzy, what am I to do? You will have to cancel the party."

"There, there." Elizabeth resorted to the tactics she learned to bear her mother through her various bouts of nerves. Although she would rather have rebuked her younger sister for being so ridiculous, she used patience and forbearance.

"You have the best of my maids and if you will only sit down and let me have a look, I am certain you will be stunning by the time of the ball."

Lydia allowed herself to be led to a chair and covered with a blanket. Elizabeth sent for tea in the hopes of its soothing effects.

"You must take care not to overexert yourself. You are carrying the load of two people now."

"Oh, I had nearly forgotten. What would my dear Wickham think if I damaged his child?"

"There is a good girl." Elizabeth turned to the dress and gave a few instructions on where it might be taken out a bit and helped to pin it back into place. She had the maid take the dress to another room so that Lydia might not see what work was to be done until it was time for her toilette.

"It will be ready in time for the ball. You must rest now, Lydia, so that you can enjoy yourself tonight."

"If only Kitty could see me now! I do miss her company, I must confess."

"I wrote to Father asking that she and Mary might attend, but he is resolute they will not be let out for several more years."

"Oh Father, he is so mean. How does Mother bear him?"

"I see your tea has come. Have a cup and then spend your afternoon in bed. I see it is now made and cleared of all encumbrances. I will leave you to your rest and send up the maid in time for the toilette."

"If only Wickham were here, I should be much more at ease. Do talk to Mr. Darcy on his behalf. It is so spiteful to keep him away."

Elizabeth made no such promises and left her sister without use of any maid. She felt she would likely say something uncouth to her sister if she stayed a moment longer.

# CHAPTER 15

THE RAIN STOPPED BY MIDAFTERNOON AND BY SEVEN O'CLOCK, only a few puddles remained. The Darcys, along with the Bingleys as guests of honour and Lydia as supposed guest of honour, greeted their friends and neighbours with smiles and friendly remarks. Mr. Darcy was placed in charge of the coats due to his more reserved nature. Georgiana was prevailed upon to smile, though her comments were few and so quiet they could hardly be heard. Only when her friends the Lawsons arrived was she audible enough to understand. Elizabeth insisted Georgiana accompany Julia and Penelope to the ball room.

There were many new faces and names for Mrs. Darcy to learn and remember. She relied on her husband for a whispered reminder. She was overwhelmed at his society and momentarily despaired Lady Catherine had been right in warning Elizabeth she should never fit in. However, her spirits were easily turned by the arrival of Mrs. Highmore.

"Mrs. Darcy, Mr. Darcy, Pemberley looks grand! Your mother and father would be so pleased to see it in its glory once more. What a clever pattern of candles you have placed at the entryway. My husband sends his official greetings, and regrets his absence tonight. I have brought my nephew in his place. This is Mr. John Spencer."

"Good evening, Mr. and Mrs. Darcy. I hope I will not intrude on your evening, I only arrived at my aunt's this afternoon."

"Not at all," said Elizabeth. "We hope you will enjoy our little party."

"I am continually in the habit of enjoying what life has to offer. I feel it is my duty as a gentleman."

John Spencer had a pleasing smile and looked to be about five and twenty. He had stylish dark hair and a handsome coat. He was shorter than Elizabeth cared for, but was possessed of a most charming smile. Elizabeth strived not to imagine any pairing for her sister-in-law before the fact was known, but could not keep from picturing the two together.

Once the guests were arrived, Elizabeth took to the matter of the White Soup. She made certain there was plenty to go around and served it for a while in her role as hostess. While so employed, her husband saw that all were well refreshed with spirits and negus. Elizabeth was therefore alone when she was approached by Mr. Wolfe, whose name she had forgotten since their introduction at the door. He was tall and fair with friendly eyes.

"How pleasing to see a lady serve her guests," he said. "It has become the custom of late that only the servants do such tasks."

"I trust you will enjoy the soup nonetheless." Elizabeth reddened at his suggestion that she was behaving in the manner of a servant. Lady Catherine's letter had said nothing on this matter.

"When served by such a lovely hand, I could not enjoy it more. Tell me, how does the wife of Mr. Darcy spend her idle days, for I know he is not one for conversation?"

"I find little time for idleness, sir, and my husband provides me with the most enjoyable conversation I could wish for."

"It is rare to find a woman so fond of her husband. In fact, I would say it is almost unheard of in modern marriages. I hope you will not take my questions as insults. I merely hoped you had discovered Mr. Darcy's excellence. Some of less discernment than you might only see his pride."

Elizabeth decided to forgive the man, for at one point, Darcy's pride had indeed prejudiced her against him.

"I have indeed."

"Might I have the great honour of your company in dance, Mrs. Darcy?"

Elizabeth agreed to the third dance after her duties were fulfilled. The first and second must go to her husband.

Lydia had attached herself to Georgiana as she found in Georgiana a patient listener and a valuable asset in impressing herself upon high society.

"La! What a lot of people to meet and beaus for dancing. Of course, I have no need of beau with my faithful and handsome Wickham, but a lady still has need of a dance partner. Who do you suppose I should dance with, Georgiana?" Before Georgiana had any time to answer, if indeed she wished to provide any answer at all, Lydia filled in the conversation for at least the two of them. "I think I know who fancies you! You are so fortunate to have me here, a married woman, who will look out for your best interests. I will arrange for you to have every dance filled by only the most infamous of men! Why here comes one now, do not worry yourself, dear, let me see to all of the arrangements."

Georgiana briefly wondered what Lydia thought infamous meant.

John Spencer approached then, with his eye firmly set on Georgiana. Lydia's help was obviously not necessary.

"Good evening ladies," he introduced himself and his relationship to Mrs. Highmore.

"Oh, how well you young men look these days!" said Lydia. "Why, my husband always had the good fortune of being part of the militia with all of their fine costumes, but you have made the most of country foppery."

Mr. Spencer's brow furrowed at Lydia's comment, but he decided to ignore her unintended insult. "I have not had the pleasure of knowing your name, Madam," he addressed Lydia, though his eye frequently moved to Georgiana.

"You must be a visitor to these parts, for I am sister to the Darcys, Mrs. Lydia Wickham."

"Wickham? That name is familiar. Does your husband come from this country?"

"La! Certainly. He was raised in this very house alongside Mr. Darcy. They were practically brothers until Mr. Darcy decided he would rather not be so close to someone not directly his kin – To think he went against the wishes of his late father to put my Wickham out of his rightful inheritance."

"Ah," Mr. Spencer had heard a different set of circumstances from his Aunt, but dared not refute a sister of the Darcys. "Could you do me the honour of introducing your friend?"

"Well you are new to these parts if you are not acquainted with Georgiana Darcy!"

John Spencer was quite acquainted with her through his aunt, but had undertaken not to reveal this prior knowledge. He bowed to Georgiana and took her hand. Georgiana instantly blushed and wished she could be rid of her talkative relation.

"Tell me, Miss Darcy, do you have a dance free tonight?"

"I am taken for the first four, but then have a place."

"May I have the pleasure of that spot?"

Georgiana acquiesced, but could not help but glance at Mrs. Wickham who looked expectant of her own invitation. John Spencer noticed her gaze and offered an invitation to her as well.

"Well, I am a married woman, but I feel there is no ungodly reason why I cannot. You are most fortunate that my first dance is free."

Mr. Spencer smiled and bowed to each of the women before removing himself to speak to others in attendance.

Georgiana was most pleased to see the Lawson sisters approaching after this introduction. They had been in conversation with others of their friends, but returned faithfully to her side, for they knew of her propensity to shyness. Lydia insisted upon their introduction and continued to chatter on about all of the costumes in the room, the young men in attendance and referred often to her "dear Wickham" and her ability to find them all good husbands by the end of the night.

"For you girls are all older than I was at my hapless marriage. Youth does not last, I am told, and I know no woman who envies the life of a spinster."

Penelope looked diligently for amiable qualities in Georgiana's sister-in-law, while Julia tried not to laugh at Lydia's ironic attempts at high language accompanied by incessant chatter and bad manners. Julia forced herself to hold her tongue for Georgiana's sake, but sought to remove them all from Lydia's company at the earliest convenience.

Fortunately, Mr. Darcy called for the attention of his guests at this point and made his announcement to the group.

"It is my great pleasure to have all of you at Pemberley tonight. I want to take this opportunity to present a new addition to the walls of our home. I will ask the artist, Mr. Trent, to do the honours of unveiling his work."

Mr. Trent took a moment to build an air of suspense in the room. Then, with a flare, he pulled the rug from the painting and his lovely work was displayed for all to see.

"It is my great privilege to present to you, Mrs. Darcy."

The hall gasped and then applauded his work.

"What do you think, my dear?" Mr. Darcy whispered to his wife.

"I am very pleased," she whispered back and her feelings at that moment were of the utmost love and gratitude toward her mate.

Mr. Darcy called for the music then and insisted the Bingleys lead off the dancing. Shortly after, Darcy and Elizabeth joined them.

PHILLIP ARRIVED PROMPTLY at Georgiana's arm and without waiting for an introduction to Mrs. Wickham, led his partner to the dance floor.

"I am well aware how fortunate I am to have your first dance, Miss Darcy," Phillip began. "I have behaved most abominably toward you in the past fortnight."

Georgiana was surprised at his confession and only nodded in acceptance of it.

"My sisters, you see, have always inspired my worst conduct and I fear you have been caught in their midst."

"I thought, perhaps, you considered me as one of them."

"Hardly!" he responded quickly, but then forced himself into composure. "I only felt you had been so melancholy in recent months that it was my business as a family friend to remind you to smile."

Georgiana blushed at the thought of Phillip knowing something of her past.

"I see I have said the wrong thing again. Please accept my apologies."

"No, no. It is most gentlemanly of you."

"I admit I was also inspired to find your temper at last. Ever since you were a child, you have been the most obedient girl I ever met."

"I fear I may have said more than I ought." Georgiana said.

"Do not apologize to me, Miss Darcy. It has only given me pleasure to hear your true thoughts on my conduct."

The music changed then and Georgiana felt glad of her promise to have three dances with Phillip Lawson.

"So, can we be friends then?" he said once they had the chance to speak again.

Georgiana offered her friendship immediately, but felt strangely disappointed. She could not know why, especially when it was her aim to remain single for the rest of her life. Phillip showed her the utmost respect for the rest of the dance, but before it ended, he made one more attempt on her behalf.

"I feel I asked too much of you in requiring three dances. I do not wish to send the wrong impression to any of the gossipmongers in this company. I will give you the opportunity now to remove yourself gracefully from your commitment to myself, if only to spare your reputation."

Though Georgiana had worried over the prospect of three dances in succession with the same man, she realized now she would rather inspire idle talk than leave Phillip, however, fearing he may in fact be wishing to escape her company, she accepted his proposal and was immediately approached by another in his place.

MR. WOLFE TOOK his place then with Mrs. Darcy. Mr. Darcy greeted him warmly and mentioned to his wife that Mr. Wolfe had always been a great dancer.

"I trust you will find my wife among the best dancers in attendance," Darcy boasted proudly.

"I have no doubt," said Mr. Wolfe and the dance began. "I must confess I have been most interested in meeting the woman who has captured our Darcy. I often wondered if he would ever be settled into matrimony."

"Have you been so settled, sir?" Elizabeth inquired.

"Unfortunately not, for although I have the means, I fear I have yet to meet a woman who could abide me long enough."

"I see you possess a degree of modesty which is not disagreeable in a man. I am certain you would not still be single if it were not truly your wish."

"You are very quick-minded, I can see. I would suspect nothing less in the wife of my good friend. Yes, there is a story there, for once I was married, but I fear my wife did not make it to our first anniversary."

Elizabeth felt herself very ill for bringing such a memory to mind so early into their acquaintance and took great pity on him.

"Please forgive me, sir. I was not aware."

"There is nothing to forgive when one has no prior knowledge and I am tired of people avoiding her remembrance in my present. Mrs. Annabelle Wolfe was a lovely woman. We married when she was only eighteen and greatly enjoyed our time together. For us, the honeymoon will truly never end."

"I am sorry never to have known her." They danced in silence for a moment before Elizabeth spoke again.

"Tell me, how do you know my husband?"

"From our schooldays, I would say. He was a year or two ahead of me, but would often defend me in the schoolyard. Many older boys were fond of tormenting the younger, but he would not stand for it and I have had the highest regard for him since."

The music ended then and as they bowed to one another, Mr. Wolfe remarked, "Mr. Darcy did not boast when he called you a great dancer. You are very skilled."

Elizabeth accepted the praise as well as she could and left Mr. Wolfe thinking him a worthy gentleman.

Lydia took Elizabeth's side shortly after and began to ask for introductions to all her best society. Lydia remarked on the styles of the evening and listed all the men who had asked her to dance. She said several times how well her husband would do at such an occasion if only he were invited. Elizabeth was most relieved when a gentleman approached her sister to dance. Her relief soon diminished; however, as she heard her sister's laughter ring through the hall and felt shame at the great impropriety of a married, pregnant woman flirting with all of the single men. She could only find solace in the fact that Lady Catherine was not present.

As promised, Georgiana joined Barrington Lawson for the fourth dance. He was staid and rather awkward in his movements, but he was most attentive to Georgiana. He asked after each of her family members individually and then told her of the health of each of his family members. She was glad for his prolonged soliloquy as it allowed her to ponder the words that had passed between her and Phillip. Her previous dance partner had been much too lively to allow such reflection. She was all too surprised when at the end of the dance Barrington requested a private meeting with her the following morning. Georgiana could only nod her assent and dread what was to come. Before she could consider that for long; however, she noticed Elizabeth beckoning her to the piano. She had nearly forgotten her promise to perform in the confusion which developed during her dances with Phillip. Her insides flipped now to consider he would be amongst her audience.

Georgiana, though, was never one to run from responsibility and followed her sister to the pianoforte. She steadied her nerves with a deep breath and then forgot her fears and all other matters of the heart as she began the piece she had prepared. It was simpler than she was capable, but rich in tone and beauty. She felt the thrill of playing while people danced to her music. She had only played for dancers in small rooms before, and the effect of her music in a much larger area was deeply gratifying. Her fingers were long and confident and her face a portrait of joy. Several onlookers remarked on her transformation at the keyboard when they had always imagined her either very proud or very shy. Only Lydia could find fault in Georgiana's performance when she remarked to Julia Lawson, who unfortunately stood near, that she found the piece very out of style and hardly worthy of so grand a ball. Julia, who had never truly mastered the control of her tongue, responded that Lydia's own behaviour as a woman so near confinement was much less worthy of the situation. Lydia was momentarily silenced by the comment, but when she realized only she had heard the offensive remark, she sought to rectify Julia's ill breeding.

"Of course, you are not a married woman," Lydia said with great pity. "I cannot expect you to know all of the responsibilities it requires."

PHILLIP LAWSON WAS QUITE TAKEN by Georgiana's transformation at the piano. He was without a partner for the waltz and simply watched her play for its duration. He applauded loudly at the end and remarked to several nearby on her great ability and composure in an audience so large. He strode toward her at the song's finale with the aim of congratulating her on her accomplishments. He was unable to carry out his goal, however, by the arrival of John Spencer who then accompanied Georgiana to the dance floor, leaving Phillip to find someone else to converse with.

Mr. and Mrs. Darcy took to the floor once more and he smiled warmly at her.

"What is it, my dear?" asked she.

"I am so pleased that you agreed to be my wife, Eliza, for who else could have given my sister such confidence?"

"You allow me too much credit, for consider only what my younger sister is. If I had such great powers, would not her behaviour be more what it ought?"

"A teacher can only teach to the abilities of her student, my dear. You cannot blame yourself for Lydia's conduct. That is up to her husband now."

"So then, may I pass off my deficiencies on you, Mr. Darcy?"

"What deficiencies, Mrs. Darcy? I have seen only your abilities."

"Then you are well deceived, Darcy. You have only as far as your aunt to look for what I lack."

The couple laughed and Darcy thought how much more he enjoyed dancing with Elizabeth than any other woman in the world.

Mr. and Mrs. Bingley had danced the first two dances together, but then Jane requested she be allowed to sit the rest of the evening. She insisted her husband not suffer for her condition, but he would not hear of leaving the side of his beloved.

"There are plenty of young men for the ladies here, my dear. I could ask for no better entertainment tonight than the pleasure of your company."

He was very attentive to her for the duration of the

evening and they excused themselves from the festivities as early as was polite.

"It is such a lovely party, Lizzy," said Jane. "I am certain you have made all of Derbyshire fall in love with you."

"You are very kind, sister. Now take care of my nephew, will you?"

Jane blushed at the reference to her condition and removed to their chamber for the remainder of the evening.

Elizabeth was quite pleased with the ball and had wine and refreshment to spare. When the party broke at midnight, she was pleased to hear the compliments she received, but was mostly relieved to be finished her duties for the evening. She considered that a small and agreeable company was much more to her taste than a large and fashionable one.

The Lawsons were the last to leave and they congratulated the Darcys on their success. Phillip looked for a moment to speak to Georgiana and found one just before they departed.

"I hope you will allow me a short interview on the morrow, Miss Darcy," he whispered as the others spoke.

Georgiana panicked at the thought of two brothers arriving at once the next day. She could not see how she could either agree to or deny the interview. She could only nod and pray the two would come at different times.

"I bid you goodnight, Miss Darcy, and look forward to the morning."

Georgiana excused herself as soon as the Lawson's left to return to her chambers for a sleepless night.

# CHAPTER 16

THE EIGHTH OF JULY ARRIVED FAR TOO EARLY FOR THE inhabitants of Pemberley, who were all tired from the evening prior, but none so much as Georgiana. She had considered so many scenarios of her day to come and none of them gave her any comfort. She forced herself to prepare for the day; despite the humiliation it was likely to bring her. If only she had her former companion Mrs. Annesley to advise her. Mrs. Annesley had been both a comfort and an aid in developing Georgiana's social education. She had returned to London in January after Elizabeth joined the family. Georgiana wished she could share her worries with Elizabeth, but with her family visiting, she did not have the time she usually had to spend in conversation with Georgiana. Once she had dressed and had her hair arranged she ventured downstairs for a cup of tea. Food was not at all tempting, but the tea provided a measure of strength.

To Georgiana's great dismay, Mr. Barrington Lawson arrived at Pemberley before all of its inhabitants were even awake. Mr. Darcy welcomed him and asked him into the breakfast room.

"Good day, sir," spoke Barrington smartly.

"Good day, Barrington. To what do we owe the pleasure?"

Barrington was surprised to find his intentions had not been shared with the household. However, after a moment's hesitation, he regained his confidence.

"I have requested a private conference with your sister, Georgiana. I was expecting she would have shared this piece of information with you herself, but perhaps I am come too hastily."

Mr. Darcy was visibly alarmed, but after some moments in consideration, he considered Barrington was a man of good reputation and family. Although he wished to protect Georgiana from all harm, he felt none could come at the hands of so dull a man. He only wished Elizabeth was present to steady him and bring about that lightness of mood which she always created in a room. Elizabeth, however, was in bed with a headache after the stress and worry of the previous day.

"I think you will find the parlour unoccupied. I will show you the way."

In one of Georgiana's imagined scenarios, her brother had thrown Barrington from the house with a firm warning never to return. How she wished now that he had reacted in such a way. Instead, Georgiana was ushered into the parlour and before Darcy left he only whispered;

"If you need me at all, please ring the bell. I will remain outside the door. You have no need to settle for anything you do not wish for, sister."

She felt some comfort in his words, but found she needed to sit the moment he left the room. She could look only at the small blemish on Barrington's shoe as he summoned the courage to speak.

"Georgiana," he began in earnest. "You must be well aware of the high regard I have always held you in. You and I come from very similar families and I have no doubt you would make me a very respectable companion. I can offer you much in the way of material possessions and agreeability. I have always sought to be peaceful and compassionate toward my fellow man. I will promise to hear your preference in any decision which might directly affect you. I feel that at our ages, it is no longer preferable to live at home with our families. A short distance from them is now appropriate to the development of our adulthood. My parents have always been kind to you and I have observed you are especially close to my sisters. For these reasons, I trust you will accept my proposal of marriage."

His speech was so reasonable and yet so devoid of emotion that Georgiana found it much simpler than she imagined refusing him in a similar tone.

"Mr. Lawson, I am most indebted to your proposal. I have always been fond of your family and have greatly appreciated the attentions of your mother and sisters. I hope then, I will not disappoint either you or your family when I do not accept your proposal. Although you have made excellent arguments in favour of our union, I must confess I have no feelings of love for you, besides that between our two families. Please accept my deepest regrets."

Barrington's face registered shock and disappointment, but neither emotion touched Georgiana. Instead, she felt a rather giddy relief that this portion of her day was now completed.

"I suppose you have many other options to consider," he said after some deliberation. "I only hope you will not come to regret this decision, for I am not a man to repeat my offers."

Georgiana shook her head to assure him of her decision, at which point he took leave of the room and nearly knocked over Mr. Darcy, who had been joined by Mrs. Darcy.

"Good day," he said, in all politeness and left the house speedily.

When Georgiana was certain Mr. Lawson could no longer hear, she motioned for her brother and Elizabeth to join her and did not keep them long in suspense.

"Mr. Lawson has proposed and I have refused him. I hope this will not cause you any disappointment."

"Hardly, dear Georgiana," said Elizabeth. "You are only a source of pride and delight to your brother and me."

Mr. Darcy nodded in agreement and Georgiana felt a sudden pang of hunger along with a sparkle of anticipation at the arrival of the older Lawson brother. She felt she must then inform her brother and Elizabeth of his intention to visit.

"My, my," said Elizabeth. "I had no idea our ball was such a great success. I confess I was not aware of your visitors. I only wonder if you have the heart to disappoint two young men on the same day!" she winked at Georgiana and placed her hand on top of her husband's in the hopes of steadying his obvious agitation.

Darcy and Bingley left the house shortly after to see to the tenants. Darcy felt he had neglected them long enough during the ball preparations, but with the expectation of Phillip Lawson's arrival, he wavered on his decision to go out. Elizabeth assured him he would be sent for the moment he was required and that she would make sure Georgiana was well looked after, if not by her, then by Jane. After the men left, Elizabeth suggested a game of charades for the women to pass the time. She hoped it might keep Georgiana from stewing over her expected guest. Lydia, unfortunately, chose this time to rouse herself from sleep and joined the women, causing all of them some degree of irritation.

"La, but I am tired from the ball. I do not think any of the men guessed at my condition. I had nearly every dance filled, which I consider rather an accomplishment for a married woman without her husband. I noticed you, Jane, did not make it through the evening. I suppose it is because you are so much older than I," Elizabeth required all of her patience not to scold her sister. She passed around sweets instead.

"Lydia, we were just about to play charades. I remember you were always quite good at the game, you could begin."

Lydia acted very poorly, but Georgiana was able to make out that she was a lampshade.

"I forgot to mention, Georgiana, that you have a most unladylike friend."

Georgiana could not guess to whom she referred.

"Miss Lawson, the older one, had the impertinence to suggest I was ill bred in attending a dance in my condition. She mentioned in public that I was soon to be in confinement and I am only consoled in the knowledge the room was applauding Georgiana's passable performance at the piano and so could not have heard her comment. I have never been so insulted."

All three women could only admire Julia Lawson's ability to speak what they all felt, but before anyone could respond, Mrs. Reynolds arrived in the room to announce the arrival of the very lady under discussion.

Georgiana and Elizabeth glanced at one another, each wondering if the other knew of Julia's visit. She was soon shown into the room and greeted each woman warmly, speaking of the weather and the success of the previous evening. However, it was clear she wished only to speak to Georgiana, so after a few rounds of charades, Elizabeth suggested they take the air.

"Georgiana, I could hardly maintain myself in there. How do you manage yourself around Mrs. Wickham? She is insufferable."

If only Julia knew just how insufferable!

"I am so pleased for your visit, Julia, but I must confess it is a surprise."

"I will not keep you in suspense a moment longer, for you must be expecting this." Julia handed over a letter with the Lawson seal. "From my eldest brother. Do you wish for me to leave you alone to read it? I will pick berries by the water until you have finished."

Georgiana was grateful for her friend's sensitivity. She glanced about for any other audience and, satisfied she had perfect privacy, she opened her letter.

"Dear Miss Darcy,

"I regret I will not be able to keep my appointment this morning. I have been called away on important business to Ireland. I do not know the date of my return. I trust I have not greatly disappointed you and hope you will accept my humblest apologies. I understand my brother was rather disappointed by you this morning. The hearing of it gave me much pleasure.

"Phillip Lawson"

GEORGIANA WAS SURPRISED by the depth of her disappointment. She hardly knew when her expectations had begun, but recognized they were stronger than she could admit. She wondered if he had heard anything of her ties to Mr. Wickham and chastised herself once more for her previous folly.

# VOLUME TWO

# CHAPTER 1

AUGUST 1813

ALTHOUGH THE DARCY'S REGRETTED THE LOSS OF THE Bingley's company in the middle of July, the departure of Mrs. Lydia Wickham brought much relief. Mrs. Wickham, on the other hand, would sorely miss the meals at Pemberley. She complained endlessly of the lesser fare served by her cook, Mrs. Croft, who soon after quit her position leaving Lydia in great distress as she could not even peel a potato. To alleviate the stress this caused on their unborn child, Mr. and Mrs. Wickham left immediately for an extended visit to Netherfield. Mr. and Mrs. Bingley began to discuss their need to quit their present residence.

Georgiana was relieved she would no longer have need to find ways to avoid her home. She had more time to spend in conversation with her sister in law, and though Georgiana showed the letter from Phillip to Elizabeth, they did not speak of him after Elizabeth ensured Georgiana was not overly disappointed. Georgiana merely said she wished him well on his travels. She told herself her relationship with Phillip had merely consisted of a few upsetting conversations and a couple of dances. Georgiana felt she had no right to speak of any feelings she might have toward him and sought to extinguish any thought of him that came unwillingly to mind.

Miss Penelope Lawson found greater luck at the Darcy's ball in her engagement to Mr. John Spencer. At the end of the evening, he discovered that Penelope was everything he had ever wanted in a wife and after a few visits to Sunnings, their future was secured. As oldest son, he was entitled to seven thousand a year and those concerned on both sides were very pleased with the match and nuptials were hastily prepared.

Elizabeth began to feel she had a greater understanding of her position as mistress of Pemberley. The ball had acquainted her with most of her neighbourhood and she contended to call on and receive these acquaintances as often as possible. The end of July became rather unbearably hot, however, and she suggested to Mr. Darcy they take a holiday to the Lakes, which she had planned on taking the year before with the Gardiners, but had been prevented due to Mr. Gardiner's work. Mr. Darcy thought it a fine suggestion and asked if her Aunt and Uncle Gardiner might like to join them.

"That is a fine idea. They have wished to visit us at Pemberley and I promised my Aunt a ride about the grounds in our finest phaeton. May I invite them here first that we might travel altogether?"

"Of course, my dear," Darcy laughed. "You have no need to seek my permission; you must consider Pemberley your true home now."

"I only thought Lady Catherine might disprove of my relations coming so often to Pemberley."

"Hang my aunt. I have no need to seek her approval," Darcy's temper rose.

"I had a letter from her today, dear. I do not think I boast when I say I may be gaining her favour."

"You are too good to seek her favour. She should be begging for yours."

"My Darcy, you are the finest husband a girl of my *family obstacles* could hope for." Elizabeth was fond of teasing him on this, his initial complaint of her.

"Elizabeth, I feel sometimes I allow you too much liberty, but your aunt and uncle are among the finest people I ever had the pleasure of knowing."

"Then I shall write to them today."

Arrangements were made for the first week of August. The Gardiners planned to leave their youngest two with the Bennets and hoped that Kitty and Mary would find the patience to endure them. They would bring their eldest two to Pemberley and then on to the Lakes where Georgiana promised to play with them. She had no younger siblings of her own and felt she would enjoy having children around. Elizabeth suggested Georgiana invite one of her friends for company and to help with the children. Georgiana was very delighted to ask Julia who had begun to tire of her sister's upcoming nuptials.

"May I go to the Lawson's directly?" Georgiana asked when Elizabeth voiced her idea.

"Of course! I only hope you will not be proposed to before you return."

Georgiana coloured at this reference to her encounters with the Lawson men and Elizabeth chastised herself for being so thoughtless.

"Do forgive me, sister. My teasing is most improper."

"Of course not, sister." Georgiana pressed Elizabeth's hand. "I am only glad you feel so at ease around me."

Georgiana left then to make her invitation in person. She had no worries of running into Barrington, who had left

Derbyshire for a tour of Europe over the summer. Julia resented the ease with which he traveled about and Georgiana hoped to bring provide her friend with much joy in her invitation. Phillip had not been heard from since he had left. Georgiana doubted very much that she would run into him today.

Georgiana took the phaeton at Elizabeth's suggestion.

"You must," she insisted. "I promised my aunt a ride about the grounds in the phaeton quite a long time ago. It has not been out in weeks and you will know if it needs repair."

This convinced Georgiana, who was secretly pleased to avoid too much exposure in the heat of the day. Julia met Georgiana at the door upon her arrival.

"Thank God! I am about out of my head with talk of weddings and trousseaus. How very wise of you to bring the phaeton. Where shall we ride?"

Julia hopped into the carriage before Georgiana could send her greetings to the Lawson family. She promised herself she would make up for her bad manners upon their return.

"I think the forest path will offer some shade, miss," spoke the driver and the two young women agreed to his suggestion.

"La! It's hot today. Do you not long to be at a cool stretch of sea on a day like today?" Julia waved her summer hat to cool her reddened face.

"I think I may have a better plan."

"You a plan? You usually leave such scheming to me, Miss Darcy. Tell me quickly!"

"Well, in truth, we have my sister in law to thank. She has suggested we go to the Lakes and has invited me to ask you along."

"The Lakes! It is perfect! Thank you Georgiana, but do you really mean to ask grumpy old me?"

"Of course, Julia. You are never grumpy."

"But I am. Everyone says I am jealous of Penelope for being married first and I fear it might be so."

"If you wanted to be married, Julia, you would be in a moment. Did you not see all the men lining up to dance with you at the ball?"

"Ha! This is exactly why you have always been my best friend. You know precisely what to say at every moment. I would be delighted to join your family to the Lakes."

"I am so pleased, but before you accept too hastily, I must add we will have some responsibilities on the holiday."

"Really? Who would want me to take on responsibility? Does your sister not know I am one of the least responsible young ladies in Derbyshire?"

"Your mother must be at you, I can hear her voice in your speech. The responsibilities are to assist in the care of Elizabeth's cousins."

"Delightful! Why they would likely follow all of my hair-brained ideas without hesitation. How many will there be?"

"Only two. The other two will stay with their aunt."

"If only they could all come. Yes, Georgiana, I think this will be the perfect tonic for all that ails me. When do we leave?"

Georgiana gave the details and the two young women discussed the many sights they wished to see. Julia had been twice to the Lakes and Georgiana had been only once before her parents died. The driver was right in selecting the coolest path through the forest and Julia felt her youthfulness return. When they came upon a pond, she suggested they stop to bathe.

"I haven't any bathing clothes!" said Georgiana.

"Nor I. We are so far off, who would see us?"

"What about the driver?"

"We shall send him on to Sunnings. We are close enough

to walk back, which would also allow our clothes to dry in time."

Georgiana looked around the pond in every direction to ensure they were completely alone. They had whispered so the driver could not know their plans. She had always hated saying no to Julia, who was so lovely in her enthusiasm. After some moment's pause, she agreed to the plan.

"Drive on, Mr. Winters," Georgiana instructed the driver. "Refresh yourself at Sunnings. We will walk from here."

The pond was too small and open to be called picturesque, but the water was so cool and the air around it so fresh that Julia and Georgiana felt it the most perfect pond in England.

"Can you believe my sister will marry John Spencer?" Julia said when they had splashed about and completely soaked themselves.

"Do you not like him?"

"He is very handsome and well enough settled in life."

"Then why would Penelope not marry him?"

"He is short and has a most peculiar haircut."

"Is that your only complaint? I am sure you could overlook that." Georgiana laughed.

"But he is dull and speaks only good things."

Georgiana laughed even more and took a moment to regain her composure before saying;

"Perhaps you are jealous then, if these are his only faults. Your sister also speaks only goodness and is not such a giant as to require a taller husband."

"But she shall be gone to me forever, Georgiana. If I had other sisters, I might not mind so much, but we have been together so long now, I fear I will be very lonely."

"There is a good reason then to dread their marriage. I should hate to lose Elizabeth now that she has come to stay, and I have only known her less than a year. Will they live far away?"

"Not so far, but further than we have ever been from one another. She is such a good sister." Julia sniffled and Georgiana did her best to console.

"Marriage is full of hardship for women," railed Julia after some minutes. "She must leave her home forever and all the people who love her, and then there are the children. Did you know I have had two cousins pass away under that affliction?"

"I did not know," said Georgiana softly. "But Penelope is young and strong. You must not worry yourself. I know it is not much, but I may offer you some consolation in the promise that I shall never marry."

"Georgiana Darcy! How can you make such promises? Why you were nearly married to both of my brothers only a month ago."

Georgiana confessed then her relationship to George Wickham. After keeping the secret so long, she was relieved to share her burden with such a close friend. Julia was most alarmed to learn of his deception and Georgiana's secret agony.

"No wonder you wish never to marry, my dear dear friend. How awful this is the very man to marry Elizabeth's sister. Was it terrible to have her visit?"

Georgiana smiled in the relief of having a friend to share her sorrow. "It was not so terrible. Both my brother and Elizabeth are aware of my past and did their best to shield me from every discomfort."

"I am so relieved you have trusted your secret to me and in return, I will share mine. But I see you are shivering and mother will be expecting us for tea. Let us leave this fairy pond and warm ourselves with exercise."

After they had returned to their outer garments, the pair

made haste for Sunnings. It was nearly time for tea and they did not wish to incur Mrs. Lawson's displeasure. Julia was right in suggesting the heat would dry them quickly. As they walked and dried, she confessed to Georgiana.

"My secret is not as compelling as yours, I fear. It is only that I have entered a book of poetry to be published."

"Poetry! I had no idea," said Georgiana.

"Mother would say it was completely unladylike, but it is something I love. It makes me feel vibrant and lets me share the thoughts I cannot due to rank and responsibility. Do you think it is unbecoming?"

"No! Never, Julia. It is very becoming indeed and I cannot wait to read your verses."

"I will not show them to anyone until they are published. Even Penelope has not read them, which has been quite a feat. I have written at the oddest hours and in the strangest places."

"Then how have you had them submitted?"

"Ah, that is another secret and I cannot share two in one day," Julia's eyes sparkled. "I may tell you someday or you may learn of it many years from now. But I am most pleased to be accompanying you to the Lakes. I have heard there are many poets and artists who use them for inspiration. Perhaps I may meet one of them in our travels."

"You are very surprising, Julia. Thank you for sharing your secret with me. I am certain your writing will be met with praise."

They arrived at the house then, nearly dry, but rather unkempt for tea at the Lawsons. They hurried to Julia's room to hide all signs of pond-dipping and thanks to the fortuitous arrival of Mr. John Spencer; they were able to avoid all suspicion.

## CHAPTER 2

Penelope's wedding to Mr. Spencer was a model of grace and respectability. Mr. Highmore made a rare appearance at the ceremony to the great pleasure of his wife. Julia was the Maid of Honour and Barrington the Best Man as Mr. Spencer had no brothers of his own. As the eldest in his family and only male, John Spencer would be able to provide Penelope with the kind of living with which she was accustomed. They would take a house within five miles of Sunnings and Penelope had already begun ordering decorations for their modest residence. She hoped to spend their honeymoon shopping for treasures to make their house a home of style. Julia maintained her tongue and did not utter one word of criticism during the days prior. She looked forward to the promise of the Lakes as her reward. She was also grateful for the wedding preparations as they distracted her mother and sister, allowing Julia more time for poetry. She and Georgiana spent many enjoyable hours together and after the wedding, the Gardiners came.

The family arrived in time for dinner and Elizabeth and Darcy were very pleased to have them all at last. Elizabeth had done her best to organize a delicious supper featuring all her aunt and uncle's favourites. She had their rooms papered in airy country wallpaper and bought books for the children to read while they visited. Samantha was the eldest of the Gardiner children at nine. She was at an awkward stage between childhood and adulthood with protruding knees and elbows and was possessed of a shy manner. Jennifer was seven and quite tall for her age. She had lovely long blonde hair and a more outgoing nature. All of the Darcy's approved of their good behaviour at supper.

Julia was also present at dinner to meet the Gardiners and was invited to stay the night. She brought a gift for both the children.

"I hope you will not object to presents which have already been enjoyed," she said when she handed them each a parcel wrapped with green ribbon. The children opened them and discovered a ball and cup game each.

"Samantha's belonged to my older brother Barrington and Jennifer's was my younger sister, Penelope's. I fear the rest of us lost or broke our games. Barrington and Penelope are the most responsible of the Lawson children."

"Thank you, miss," the children said with curtsies.

"Oh dear, we must get rid of those good manners immediately!" cried Julia. The children looked to their parents for some hint of their indiscretion, but Julia soon alleviated their fears. "Please call me Julia, I insist."

Julia and Georgiana sat with the children while Mr. and Mrs. Gardiner caught up with the Darcy's.

"It was a pity we could not visit at Christmas as planned. I fear I was dreadfully ill," said Mrs. Gardiner.

"We feared for her life, I dare say," agreed Mr. Gardiner. Mrs. Gardiner quickly changed the subject.

"Do you remember our visit here, only last year?" Mrs. Gardiner asked.

"Of course, we remember it often," said Elizabeth, smiling at her husband.

"I had no inkling you might someday be mistress of Pemberley when we came. What a lot of good luck our trip to the Lakes was then cancelled," said Mr. Gardiner.

"I like to think it was Providence which brought you here," said Mr. Darcy.

"What news do you bring from Longbourn?" asked Elizabeth after a pause of happy reflection.

"They are all well and I am happy to say your mother's nerves were in good form," said Mr. Gardiner.

"Your sister and Mr. Bingley dined while we were there and Jane looks very well," said Mrs. Gardiner. "The children were disappointed she would not be able to watch them during our holidays this year, but I assured Samantha and Jennifer they would greatly enjoy Miss Darcy and Miss Lawson. I hope our two boys will find friends in Kitty and Mary. Kitty seemed to find my Emmett rather entertaining."

"Do the Wickhams still visit Netherfield?" said Elizabeth.

"Mr. Wickham was called away quite suddenly soon after we arrived. Lydia accompanied him, but they left no word as to their intended destination," said Mrs. Gardiner.

"How mysterious," said Elizabeth to be polite, but she worried the Wickhams would be a continual source of strain for all her family.

After supper, the men retired to discuss maps and draw up an itinerary for their trip to the lakes. They would stay one more day at Pemberley before setting off on their journey. Georgiana, Julia and the Gardiner children sat in the parlour practicing the ball and cup game. Samantha was the most skilled and was soon showing the others how to improve their abilities.

Elizabeth and her aunt were left to speak freely to one another at the opposite side of the parlour. They had always been close and Mrs. Gardiner had many questions to confirm Elizabeth's happiness in marriage.

"You look very well, my dear," said Mrs. Gardiner to her niece.

"Thank you, aunt. I have never been more content."

"Ah, then your husband is all that I thought him to be. But how do you like being mistress of such a large house?"

"I still have much to learn, but Mrs. Reynolds has been most gracious and even Lady Catherine has written me with some advice."

"Well that is an accomplishment, I should say. Does she visit you yet?"

"Not yet, but for Darcy's sake, I am doing my best to mend broken bridges."

"You are very wise, Elizabeth and I am most pleased to see you so well settled. I only wish I could say the same for your sister Lydia." Mrs. Gardiner confirmed Elizabeth's fears when she whispered that some rather large debts had been left in Meryton which the Bingley's took care of immediately.

"I fear they will be a chronic source of debt to my sister and her husband. I shall send something to help them with their burden," decided Elizabeth.

"We hope they may be somewhat relieved of their many intrusions when they move from Netherfield."

"Will they leave?" Elizabeth had not heard as much from Jane.

"Jane asked me to tell you, for they only recently decided. They plan to take a house within thirty miles of Pemberley."

"What wonderful news you bring me, Aunt, for I continually regret the absence of Jane's presence. Will they leave before Michaelmas?"

"Indeed, for they hope to be well settled before Jane's confinement."

All of the inhabitants of Pemberley greatly enjoyed their evening and were delighted by a short concert by Georgiana, Julia, Samantha and Jennifer later on. Before all retired for the evening, Elizabeth promised the Gardiners a ride around the grounds in the phaeton the next morning.

# CHAPTER 3

All of the Gardiners enjoyed their day at Pemberley. Jennifer quickly grew fond of Georgiana who taught Jennifer several new songs on the pianoforte and was delighted to listen to Jennifer's early skill for music. Even shy Samantha found a friend in Julia who shared her love for poetry. Mr. Gardiner and Mr. Darcy went fishing and caught enough fine fish to provide their supper. Mrs. Gardiner was charmed to have her wish come true of a ride in "a low phaeton, with a nice little pair of ponies . . . all round the park" provided by her thoughtful niece.

"Thank you my dear," she said when they were through. "You have made me very happy in remembering my little dream, but I must say what gives me most pleasure is to see you so well settled here with your gentleman husband."

Julia returned to Sunnings after breakfast to prepare her trunks for their trip to the Lakes. She would rather have stayed at Pemberley, but felt she should give the Gardiners some time alone with their relations.

The day went quickly for all and was over too soon. All

knew they would have a wonderful time at the Lakes, if only for the company.

The morning of their departure saw rain. It was the first rain in weeks and the company wondered if they may have waited too long for their escape from the heat, but by midday, the skies cleared and they were well on their way. They would stop at an Inn in Leeds for the night. Mr. Gardiner and Mr. Darcy agreed they should not travel too long in a day so as to keep the women and children as comfortable as possible. They took two carriages for the journey. For much of the way, Mr. and Mrs. Gardiner rode with Mr. and Mrs. Darcy and Mrs. Gardiner noted with approval that Mr. and Mrs. Darcy often held hands. Elizabeth had never been so far north and was continually delighted by the scenery and new towns she met along the way.

"If only we had time to stop in every one and meet all of its inhabitants," she remarked.

"If this is truly your wish, my dear, we should make that our summer holiday for next year." Mr. Darcy replied.

Georgiana and Julia were also pleased to ride with the Gardiner children. The children never complained of the long hours in the carriage and entertained each other and their elder companions with stories they made up along the way. Samantha and Jennifer had never been to the Lakes and felt very mature to be thought old enough to accompany their parents on the journey. However, they did not talk so much as to annoy their companions.

After a night in Leeds, the traveling party set out for Kirkstall Abbey, a short drive off on the way to the Lakes. Mr. Gardiner had read it was a very attractive site and as none of the party had ever been, they might enjoy the new experience together. The children found the early morning mist a delicious addition to their tour of an Abbey, but the elder travelers worried for the horses and coachmen and insisted they not drive too quickly.

The Abbey rose suddenly in the mist and Samantha and Jennifer were rapturous in their approval.

"It is just as it should be," spoke Jennifer in hushed awe.

"The dead monk will already be about his prayers," proclaimed Samantha.

"Why should dead monks remain at this Abbey?" laughed Julia, but her laughter sounded eerie in the thick fog, bouncing from the stonework of the monument.

Jennifer whispered with authority, "There is always one angry monk left behind to guard an abbey."

The elder Gardiner's came to check on their children and to lead them through the Abbey.

"Do you think it is safe Mr. Gardiner?" said Mrs. Gardiner. "Perhaps we should wait with the carriages for the mist to clear."

Samantha and Jennifer insisted they were old enough and careful enough to take the tour, but Mrs. Gardiner would only allow it if the girls stayed by her side. Julia and Georgiana were left to walk the grounds on their own. They enjoyed a chance to speak of their own interests.

"Have you composed any poetry yet?" Georgiana whispered to Julia.

"Only in my head. I am so glad I had the chance to share my secret with you. It should allow me more time for writing."

The Abbey was quite large and had suffered the loss of its tower in a storm several years prior. The women could not help but be affected by the ghostly aura the Gardiner children and the mist gave the place. Still, it was breathtaking. Julia spoke of her brother Phillip then, wondering if he had returned in their absence. As Georgiana considered her own thoughts of Phillip Lawson, she glanced through an old window to be met with the grinning face of Mr. Wickham. She screamed and in her unsettled state, fainted amidst the rocks and vegetation.

Julia ran to her side and called for help. It took several minutes for the party to find them and when they had, Georgiana awoke from her faint looking ill and confused.

"What was it, Georgiana?" cried Elizabeth in distress. Georgiana, naturally, could not speak of what she saw in so large an audience.

"Just my imagination, I suspect," she laughed, thinly. "I thought I saw the ghost monk."

This gave the Gardiner children quite a thrill and they wished to seek him out immediately. Their mother forbade it and this time they took her advice to return to the carriages until the fog lifted. Mr. Darcy heard the sound of hooves retreating as they returned to their horses, but made no mention of it to the already excitable party.

In a quarter of an hour, the fog dissipated as the sun grew stronger above. The Abbey turned from mysterious and foreboding to innocent and peaceful, surrounded and overrun by wild plants.

"It is a lovely spot," said Elizabeth. "But I fear it is quite ruined by the fear it caused our Georgiana. If it is alright with everyone else, I suggest we return to our travels."

The Gardiner children were the only ones who lamented the idea and they were soon on the road again.

The party returned to their attitudes of relaxation and mirth as they viewed valleys, bridges and mountains along the way. They arrived at Lancaster by afternoon and had time to settle into the Inn before suppertime.

Julia then had the opportunity to question Georgiana in detail of what she saw at the Abbey.

"Wickham!" she cried after the telling. "How gruesome.

You must be still in quite a state over him to see him in a place you have never met him before."

"I was not even thinking of him at that time." Georgiana would never speak of whom she had been thinking. "He looked so very real and older than when I had last seen him."

"Is it possible he follows our path to the Lakes?"

"He may have heard the Gardiners speak of our travels when he visited Longbourn, but why should he wish to follow us?"

"Perhaps he loves you still." Julia said with eyes wide.

"Please do not speak of such things to me. He is married and to the most disagreeable girl I have ever met. Forgive me! I should not refer to my sister's family with such dishonour."

"You have been very upset today and have no reason to apologize for anything you might speak of either Wickham. I should not consider them in anyway related to Mrs. Darcy. You must rest now."

Georgiana took her friend's advice, allowing Julia nearly an hour to write her poetry on writing paper in tiny print.

THE FOLLOWING MORNING, they would travel from Lancaster to Kendal and then on to Ambleside, where they would stay a fortnight. The men decided it would be best to station there awhile and take small trips by foot to various nearby sites. The Gardiner children regained their seats with Georgiana and Julia and had their chance to question Georgiana of the ghost she had seen. To take away all pressure from her friend, Julia took over answering and created a tale of such horror that even Georgiana was made to laugh over the event. This inspired Samantha and Julia to imagine stories for every building they passed and they were entertained for the remainder of their tour, along with the many sites along the way. Lake Windermere was magnificent in the heat of the day and they promised to take the ferry on their return trip.

They secured lodgings in Ambleside and were able to stretch their legs after their many days of travel. The women set out for the shops before they would close for the evening while the men made enquiries at the pub for the news and recommendations for excursions in the area. The children accompanied the women on their errands.

"I should like to find a notebook for the stories Jennifer and I have been creating about our trip," said Samantha, much to the secret pleasure of Julia who wished to do the same for her poetry. Jennifer wanted to find some new music, for she had seen a pianoforte tucked into a corner at the Inn and wished to impress her friends with a new tune upon their return.

Georgiana and Julia accompanied the children on their errands while Mrs. Gardiner and Mrs. Darcy looked for hats and trimmings at a nearby shop.

"Miss Lawson is a lovely friend for Miss Darcy," remarked Mrs. Gardiner. "I wonder if they might visit us in London. Do you think it might be appropriate for me to ask them?"

"Both we and the Lawson's have a house in London, of course, but if they should wish to visit without their families, you are a most respectable family. Georgiana would be very happy in your home, I am sure, and Julia seems quite taken with your girls."

"I will ask them, then, if you are certain it will not offend your husband."

"He is not the man he was when first we met, Aunt. I only worry what his aunt might say!"

While Georgiana looked with Jennifer for pleasing music, she recognized a young man from her school days. He was fair and handsome in a summer sport coat. She saw that he noticed her and, realizing it was her duty to begin or refuse conversation, she felt her old habits of reserve return. Georgiana had learned much from Elizabeth in the arts of conversation, but without her or Julia around to offer their delightful discourse, Georgiana worried she might run out of things to speak of. Jennifer, however, had no such qualms and, noticing the young man holding a copy of a dear tune; she clapped her hands and introduced herself.

"I see you are holding my favorite piece! I am Miss Gardiner of London and this is my new cousin, Miss Darcy of Pemberley. You will find it is not difficult to learn, though it seems so at first. Oh sir, you must have this tarantella!"

The gentleman smiled at Jennifer's enthusiasm, which faltered now as she realized his strangeness. Georgiana took pity on her blush and continued the conversation.

"Good day, Mr. Black. I believe we are acquainted with one another from my school days."

"Yes, Miss Darcy," said Mr. Black with a pleasing nod. "I recognized you as soon as you entered, though you have changed since I knew you. I believe you have grown taller."

"As have you," laughed Georgiana for they had been mere children when last they met. "Do you live now at Ambleside?"

"I have come for the summer to work on my poetry, for it is a great place for poets."

"So I have heard. My good friend. . ." but Georgiana realized she must not reveal Julia's interest on the subject as it was a great secret. Mr. Black would certainly remember Julia if he remembered Georgiana. "My good friend Miss Lawson has joined us for our tour of the Lakes. You may remember her from school?"

"Ah yes," said Mr. Black who began to look nervously about him.

"She will join us momentarily if you wish to remake her acquaintance as well."

"You are very kind," said Mr. Black, looking to his pocket watch. "I must beg your pardon as I am expected. It was very good to meet you Miss Gardiner and to see you again Miss Darcy. Happy travels."

Georgiana worried her halting speech had chased Mr. Black away. She knew if her friends were here, he would not have found excuse to leave so soon. To Jennifer's approval, he purchased the tarantella she recommended and quit the shop.

BY DINNER TIME, the shops began to close and the little group returned to the Inn for the toilette. Just as they arrived, Elizabeth realized she had left her purse at one of the stores and excused herself to return for it.

"You could ask your maid, now," said Mrs. Gardiner.

"It will only take a minute, I promise. Tell Mr. Darcy I will return soon."

She left and returned to the last place she visited. After tapping at the window, she retrieved her purse and left a coin in thanks for its safe keeping. When she exited the store she walked directly towards the smiling face of Mr. Wickham.

"Wickham!" she cried in a mixture of surprise and alarm. "Whatever are you doing here?"

"I might ask you the same thing, sister."

"We are on holiday. I thought you would know from your visit to Netherfield."

"Ah, that is correct; I remember hearing something of the sort from Mrs. Bennet."

"But where is Lydia?" Elizabeth looked around for her sister.

"I fear my dear wife is not up for travel in her condition.

She is now into her period of confinement. I had some business to attend to and, regrettably, was forced to leave her for a fortnight."

"She must be anxious for your return." Elizabeth stumbled then in her conversation for she knew she was expected soon at the Inn, but was in no position to invite Wickham to join them. At the same time, she felt very ill to dismiss herself so soon from his company. Fortunately, or perhaps not so fortunately, Wickham carried on the discourse.

"I will not keep you Elizabeth from your family holidays. I would not wish to meet either your husband or sister-in-law, if only . . . no, I shall say no more."

"What is it, Wickham? You may speak freely to me, if not my family."

"It is only that I feel ill-equipped to provide for my dear Lydia and our coming child due to my abysmal circumstances in life. When I left, she could speak of nothing but his requirements upon his birth. She begged me to bring back something for our expected child and, though I have great hopes for my business here, I fear returning to her without the desires of her heart."

Elizabeth was resentful and suspicious of Wickham's supplication, but being clearly in possession of her purse and wishing to return as quickly as possible to her party, she collected enough to provide for a baby's essentials. Wickham feigned the position of gentlemen at first and refused her money, but Elizabeth insisted and argued it was her niece or nephew in question.

"Tell Lydia that Mrs. Bingley and I can be counted on to send her anything the little soul needs upon his birth," she said truthfully.

"You are very kind Mrs. Darcy. I feared your husband might forbid you from such gestures, but I see now you are a true and loyal sister. I must bid you good day, for I am presently expected."

The pair departed in opposite directions and Elizabeth hurried to the Inn. On the way, she considered it was more than coincidence which saw Mr. Wickham at her side the very moment she was alone. She remembered Georgiana's face at Kirkstall Abbey and wondered what burdens the Bennet relations were and would continue to be upon the Darcy family. She must tell her husband, even if it caused him disquietude on this lovely holiday.

# CHAPTER 4

Both Elizabeth and Georgiana were concerned over the reaction they received when sharing their news. Mr. Darcy was most upset with the knowledge that Wickham may have followed them to the Lakes in search of money. He forbade Elizabeth from giving any more money directly to Mr. Wickham. They agreed any further requests should be denied him and that a small sum would be sent instead to Mrs. Wickham. Elizabeth cried in shame which caused Mr. Darcy to feel he may have been too harsh. He apologized for his anger and promised it was really directed at Mr. Wickham and not Elizabeth.

"You are not to blame, my dear, for a good and trusting heart. I only hope to keep you from being ill used in the future."

They forgave one another and promised no Wickham would come between them in future.

Julia was not at all excited to hear of Georgiana's meeting Mr. Black. Georgiana had thought them friends or at least acquaintances in school days and believed Julia would be happy to see him on holiday.

"I have no wish to see that gentleman, Georgiana. I hope if you do see him coming, you will alert me immediately."

Georgiana made some attempt at finding out the nature of Julia's ill-feelings, but was of such a kind and empathetic nature, she could not press anyone to reveal a confidence they were not ready to give.

Neither man in question was seen for the next three days as Mr. Gardiner and Mr. Darcy kept their party busy with walks and rides to the various Lakes, waterfalls and bridges in proximity. All of the party marveled at the beauty of their surroundings and found great enjoyment in their company. Upon the fourth day, however, Mrs. Gardiner begged a day of rest out of respect for her advanced age and her children wished to stay with her. Mr. Gardiner accepted her proposal and felt a day with the family would be enjoyable for them all. The Darcy's and Julia decided it would be a good day for a more challenging walk to Blea Tarn.

They began early in the morning when the mists remained to filter the sunlight. Georgiana shivered slightly at the memory of her meeting with Wickham's ghost, but refused to let the thought ruin her outing. They went by Clappersgate, crossed the Brathay and continued with the river to the hamlet of Skelwith-fold. Elizabeth stopped at a particularly sunny cottage, charmed by her surroundings.

"Darcy, is this not the loveliest cottage you have ever seen? It is so peacefully set and in perfect harmony with its surroundings."

Darcy agreed with his wife and the party gazed about them in acknowledgement of her sentiments. At last, Elizabeth begged them to continue, so as to make their goal of the tarn by teatime. They soon passed the houses of Skelwith-fold and turned to climb a hill. This led to a stunning view of Brathay River and Langdale Pikes.

"You have blessed me with the gift of this trip, Mr. Darcy," said Elizabeth. "You must promise we will return as often as we can."

"We will settle here, if that is your desire, my lady."

"You spoil me, Darcy, but I love you for it."

They continued to Colwith-force and up Little Langdale and finally to Blea Tarn. Julia and Georgiana arrived first; leaving the Darcy's to enjoy the sights at leisure. Georgiana instantly recognized the form of Mr. Black fishing at the lake, but before she could warn her friend, he turned to see them.

"Julia, it is Mr. Black. Do you wish us to turn back?" Georgiana whispered speedily.

Julia looked quite alarmed and dismayed at this news, but could not ask her companions to turn back on her account.

"He must not ruin all of our days. I will simply hang back from his conversation."

Georgiana had never known Julia to avoid another person and found it quite mysterious. She decided to notice the flowers at her feet and await their company before continuing on to make introductions.

The Darcy's arrived presently and Elizabeth continued in her praise of the scenery. Mr. Darcy noticed Mr. Black and walked toward him to discuss his tackle. The women arranged their modest picnic upon the blanket carried by their man. After some time spent in appreciation of the view, Mr. Darcy joined them accompanied by Mr. Black.

"I believe I have found an acquaintance of yours, Georgiana, and yours Miss Lawson. This is my wife, Mrs. Darcy and here is Mr. Black, whom I have asked to join us for refreshment."

Georgiana relayed their meeting from a few days earlier

and Elizabeth made small enquiries into his family. Julia only nodded and scarcely looked upon him. Georgiana noticed Mr. Black glanced frequently at Julia, but never directed his conversation toward her.

They had a very enjoyable lunch of breads, cheeses and tea and Mr. Black roasted three fish upon a small fire for them. He recommended several other walks and told Mr. Darcy what types of fish to expect at which lakes. At the earliest opportunity, Julia excused herself to inspect the flowers and before Georgiana could join her friend, Mr. Black entered into conversation with her.

"Are you fond of poetry, Miss Darcy?"

"I am indeed," she said.

"And who are your favourites?

Georgiana mentioned her fondness for Pope, Coleridge and Cowper.

"You are certainly well-read, but have you made an attempt at the craft yourself?"

"I fear I have no talent for writing. I restrict my skills to the pianoforte."

"Yes, I remember now a small recital at school and you were very good. But I fear I forget what accomplishment your friend Miss Lawson is most skilled in."

"She has many talents, Mr. Black. I would hate to limit her to only one." Georgiana must not mention Julia's love for poetry, though it seemed most fitting to the conversation. "Perhaps you could speak to her on the subject yourself."

Mr. Black smiled at this remark. "I would make you a little wager, Miss Darcy, but I feel you are far too well-bred for such bad habits. In any case, I think if you were to closely observe Miss Lawson in my presence, you would find she will never speak to me."

"I am certain you are mistaken."

"Am I? Watch closely when she returns and if she will

speak to me, you are correct, but if she will not, you must make a prediction as to why she will not speak to me. I will join your party on the way out, if I have your permission, that you may present your conjecture to me."

Georgiana was baffled by such a strange arrangement. "Do you know, Mr. Black, the answer to your own question?"

Mr. Black would not answer this last question, but instead removed a book from his bag and presented it to Miss Darcy.

"If it pleases you, I should like you to have this book. I think you might find it of some interest, as you share my fondness for poetry."

Georgiana was quite surprised by the sudden gift and could only say thank you. She saw that Elizabeth noticed the exchange and was glad for someone to share the information with. Georgiana must ask later what it might mean. She did not wish to speak of it to Julia and hid the slim volume in her own bag.

Mr. Darcy and Mr. Black soon returned to their fishing poles. Julia returned and she, along with the Darcy women, worked on her flower guide. It was a glorious afternoon full of bird song and sunlight. Julia resumed her enjoyable ways when out of Mr. Black's presence and Georgiana dared not ruin the mood with mention of his conversation. Out of politeness, Elizabeth did not mention his name either, but planned to question Georgiana later in privacy.

All too soon, the afternoon was spent and the party reconnected to return to Ambleside. Mr. Darcy invited Mr. Black to join them and then took the lead with Elizabeth. Mr. Black joined Georgiana and Julia, much to their dismay.

"Did you enjoy your time here, Miss Lawson?" He began, winking at Georgiana. Julia gave a slight nod, but did not speak.

"Miss Darcy was telling me of the poets she admires. Pray

tell us, whom do you prefer?" Julia looked angered and only gave a shrug in answer.

"I understand Wordsworth is becoming well-known in London. Have you had a chance to read him?" Again, Julia made no answer, and in sheer discomfort, Georgiana answered for her and she and Mr. Black carried the conversation for the rest of the walk to Skelwith-fold, at which point, he joined Mr. Darcy and Elizabeth stepped back with the women. Georgiana and Julia were both relieved and spoke merrily to Elizabeth as though she had been long lost to them. They continued in this manner just until Ambleside when Mr. Black stopped them all to take in a view. He positioned himself to take the rest of the walk alone with Georgiana and then was able to quiz her.

"So, you see I am correct. Now you owe me a guess at her behaviour. Does she act so in front of all men?"

"Hardly. She is usually a wonderful companion and very kind to everyone. I can only suppose that at some point you have wronged her."

"Ah, the very conjecture I hoped to avoid, for your good opinion of me cannot be had if you think such things. You have my word I have done no such thing to Miss Lawson. I only hope you shall soon discover the truth. Until then, Miss Darcy, I bid you good day. I hope we shall see one another again soon."

Soon after, he made his departure with good wishes to the entire group, but before he could get away, Mr. Darcy invited Mr. Black to dine with them.

# CHAPTER 5

In preparing for dinner, Julia mentioned how much she wished for Mr. Black's departure and Georgiana took the opportunity to discover more.

"Forgive me for asking, Julia, for I cannot remember you disliking Mr. Black while we were at school."

"I do not dislike Mr. Black," said Julia abruptly.

Georgiana did not wish to upset her friend, but felt she must discover if Mr. Black told her the truth.

"He seems an amiable young man, but a word from you would be more than enough to convince me he is not welcome in our party and I should speak to my brother on your behalf."

Julia sighed. "I have no such word against Mr. Black. Please do not mention my complaint of him to anyone, least of all your brother."

Georgiana could gain no other information from her friend and felt their previously enjoyed closeness diminish with Julia's secrecy. Still, Georgiana was happy to learn Mr. Black had not deceived her with his good nature.

At dinner, Mr. Black took his place between Georgiana

and Julia and did not seem the least dejected when Julia proceeded to give all her attention to the Gardiner children, continuing her refusal to speak with him. Mr. Black spoke animatedly to Georgiana and, though she was somewhat uncomfortable in such a tête-à-tête, she was entertained by Mr. Black's interesting questions of her time at school, in town and at Pemberley, as well as telling his own tales of a summer spent with artists in Ambleside.

After dinner, Georgiana and Jennifer played and sang at the piano and even Mrs. Darcy was prevailed upon by her husband and Aunt to play some dancing songs for their company. Mr. Black asked Georgiana to dance then and the Gardiners also danced while Mr. Darcy danced with the Gardiner children and Julia. After two dances spent with Georgiana, Mr. Black bowed and made his way to Julia. Her face reddened at his approach and showed such violent emotion that Georgiana was certain she would not agree, however the pair took to the floor and Georgiana replaced Elizabeth at the pianoforte. She watched the pair closely and was quite certain that, though Mr. Black spoke to Julia while dancing, she never replied with a word.

Georgiana had not mentioned to Julia the book Mr. Black gave her at Blea Tarn; however, when Georgiana took it out to read before bed that evening, she noticed it was published by a Mr. H. Black. She could not help but comment;

"Could this be our Mr. Black?"

She showed it then to Julia who became rather agitated, but she would only say:

"I could not know," and returned with diligence to her own writing. The book was devoted to writings on the Lakes. How Georgiana wished she could know what the book meant to Julia, but she could not distress her friend further.

The following morning, the Darcy-Gardiner party took

leave of their lodgings at Ambleside to continue their tour of the Lakes. They fulfilled the desires of Mrs. Darcy to see Matlock, Chatsworth and Dovedale, but were prevented from seeing the Peak due to bad weather.

Samantha and Jennifer Gardiner were very disheartened to say goodbye to Julia and Georgiana. Mr. and Mrs. Gardiner invited Julia and Georgiana to stay with them on Gracechurch-street the next time they visited London, for any amount of time to ease their daughters" sadness and satisfy their own genuine liking for the young ladies. Plans were made and secured for Georgiana and Julia to stay with them in October.

# CHAPTER 6

## SEPTEMBER 1813

Upon the departure of the Gardiners, Mrs. Darcy received a letter from Mrs. Collins.

"Husford Parsonage
"29th August

"Dearest Elizabeth,

"It causes me great distress to send you this letter, but your aunt and our attentive patron, Lady Catherine De Bourgh has taken terribly ill. Mr. Darcy is not expected by Mr. Collins" who insists he is paying Lady Catherine all of the attention she requires and is seeing to her every need and desire much in the way of a nephew or even a son, however, I thought it wise to inform you of the matter. It is quite alarming to have her so ill and Mr. Collins is in continual prayer and fasting for her wellbeing."

Elizabeth quickly showed the letter to her husband and they agreed it was time to renew their familial duties to Lady Catherine. After hasty preparations, an express post to Rosings announcing their visit, and arrangements for Julia to stay at Pemberley with Georgiana while they were away, Mr. and Mrs. Darcy went directly to Rosings.

They were greeted at Rosings by Miss De Bourgh who was quite transformed since they had last seen her. Her cheeks were no longer pale and severe but instead appeared tanned and healthy. Without the presence of her mother to constantly overpower her, she was rather unreserved. She had also lost the ever present Mrs. Jenkinson, who had been Anne's governess and was dismissed by Anne since her mother fell ill. Anne had recently discovered Mrs. Jenkinson adding laudanum to Anne's nightly bedtime tonic and was glad of the excuse to finally be free of her. At Elizabeth's previous visit, Mrs. Jenkinson had foreseen Anne's every possible need and assisted her in all daily activities which only proved to highlight Anne's illness.

"Cousins, it is so good of you to come whilst my mother is ill. She has greatly missed you, Mr. Darcy, since her disappointments in your circumstances, but I will say, Mrs. Darcy, that I am quite gladly rid of her expectations, with no offence to you, I hope."

Elizabeth had wondered how her husband's former betrothed would react to their first meeting since the wedding and she was relieved.

"Mother sleeps presently, but I hoped I might introduce you to a close friend while she rests. We will have dinner in one hour after you have both been made comfortable in your rooms."

They were shown to a very decorous set of rooms where they were meant to sleep separately. Elizabeth giggled at Lady Catherine's continued attempts to keep Mr. Darcy for her own family. Within an hour, they were seated, rather breathlessly, at the dinner table.

Mr. Rathwell was introduced to them along with his elder sisters at Rosings table. He was not handsome or tall and possessed a set of rather protruding eyes, however what he lacked in appearance, he made up for in exuberance. He was younger than Miss de Bourgh by a year and seemed to look up to her as one of his sisters. He talked excessively but so good naturedly that he could not be dislikeable. Miss De Bourgh watched him fondly and continually checked that Mr. and Mrs. Darcy were enjoying his tales as much as they should.

"My sisters will tell you, Mrs. Darcy, that I was the most spoilt child. With three older sisters and a doting mother, I was carried around the house until I was at least five years old. Roberta always says it is a miracle I can walk! Mother says they have certainly spoilt me for my future wife, but I say they have it all wrong, that with four women to raise me, I have become the perfect gentleman!"

Miss De Bourgh laughed prettily at this statement and both Darcys recognized her wish to be that woman. So far as they could make out, no engagement was presently expected.

"I understand you took Miss De Bourgh's husband from her," said Miss Lacey Rathwell.

"Hold your tongue, sister!" said Mr. Rathwell in mock alarm. "Is that any way to greet so respectable a man, but do tell us, Mrs. Darcy. How were you able to attain such a man?"

Both Mr. and Mrs. Darcy found the question highly inappropriate but to please their hostess, Elizabeth attempted a dignified answer.

"I had no intention of taking Mr. Darcy from anyone as I was never aware of any prior attachments and I believe the one to which you refer was never made official. The affection between my husband and I grew slowly over many months."

"How well you answer, Mrs. Darcy," said Miss De Bourgh. "It has always been my preference that couples be good friends before they marry."

Elizabeth recognized Miss de Bourgh and Mr. Rathwell seemed to get on as good friends, but wondered how such a match should ever be agreed to by Lady Catherine.

The Darcys soon grew weary of the vitality of their party, especially after a day of worried travel. Mr. Darcy was called to see his aunt after supper, but Mrs. Darcy was not invited to join him and was made to endure still more impertinent questions regarding her husband once he left.

"I understand you have a younger sister who made a rather hurried match," said Miss Roberta Rathwell.

"My younger sister Mrs. Wickham is most happily married," said Elizabeth, growing angry by the reference.

"Lady Catherine often bemoans her relation to such a woman," said Miss Rathwell.

Elizabeth made excuses then of fatigue and escaped to her rooms where she was shortly joined by her husband.

"How does Lady Catherine appear?" Elizabeth asked.

"Very grave," said Darcy. "I would not have believed such a woman could be so overcome. She hardly spoke two sentences of advice to me before she had need of more rest."

"It is rather unseemly that her daughter should be in such good spirits at such a time."

"Perhaps it is the relief of sudden freedom after a lifetime of careful watching and constant advising."

"I hope Miss De Bourgh will not behave foolishly." Elizabeth said, still burning from the questions at dinner.

"It is a good thing we have visited and I am grateful for your attempts to reconcile me to my aunt as this visit would not possible had you not," said Darcy, erasing his wife's worries with a gentle caress.

Darcy assured Elizabeth he would bring her to the very next meeting with his aunt. He had asked permission and was refused, but he felt it was in very bad form to leave Elizabeth out of Lady Catherine's company.

Mr. and Mrs. Collins were present at breakfast the following morning by the invitation of Lady Catherine passed through her daughter.

"How good of you to invite us during this time of worry and distress for your family," said Mr. Collins, bowing to Miss De Bourgh. "We were delighted also to learn of your coming to Rosings Mr. and Mrs. Darcy." Mr. Collins bowed twice more to each of his addressed.

"Did you travel well?" said Mrs. Collins.

"Indeed," said Elizabeth who embraced her old friend.

Mr. Collins began to speak in a whisper. "How fares our dear Lady Catherine de Bourgh? I have been in prayer for her since I woke this morning, as I have done every morning since we learned of her grave illness."

"Mother is the same, I expect," said Miss De Bourgh. "She will not see anyone until after breakfast and she has requested only Mr. Darcy see her this morning."

"Of course, it is fitting she will wish the company of her close relations while they are here. Did you see her last night, Mr. Darcy?" Mr. Darcy nodded. "How did she seem?"

"I confess I was much surprised by her altered air, but I cannot tell if she was better or worse than before I came."

"Oh, it is a grave concern for our parish, I assure you, Mr. and Mrs. Darcy. Why only this morning, I had not gone ten paces from the door when I was stopped by not one but two of our flock asking how Lady Catherine was. They do not know who would look after them should she leave us, heaven forbid, but I assured them, Miss, that Lady Catherine's daughter is as fine a woman as was ever known in the country and much like her mother in concern for her fellow man and could be counted on to be as fair and considerate a patroness as her kind and noble mother."

It was quite astonishing to see the attention Mr. Collins now lavished on Miss De Bourgh, which before had been directed at her mother. However, unlike Lady Catherine, Miss De Bourgh did not tolerate it so well.

"I should give no such promises myself, Mr. Collins. I am certain I would not run things exactly as my mother, for I have my own ideas on how best to support our estate and I am certain some might be made uncomfortable by my ideas."

"But of course, Miss De Bourgh. You are wise and formidable beyond your youthful years. I have always been a strong supporter of children holding different ideals from their parents. Why my own father had no education at all, you may recall, Mrs. Darcy. With no disrespect for my good papa, I might add I have turned out quite the opposite from him in all ways and none of them to any disadvantage."

While Mr. Collins made continuous attempts to ingratiate himself to his hostess and Mr. Darcy, Mrs. Collins and Mrs. Darcy had the opportunity to exchange pleasantries; the former in regards to their travels, her family and Miss Darcy, and the latter almost entirely regarding her child. Mrs. Collins was obviously in raptures over her newborn and insisted Mrs. Darcy and her husband visit at their earliest convenience as Lady Catherine did not believe in allowing a child out of the house before he was a full year.

"He is the most charming, chubby little angel you will ever see, though I must defer to the children your family is soon to expect. Have your sisters reached their times of confinement yet?"

"Only my younger sister as Mrs. Bingley expects to move from Netherfield before she must be confined."

"How distressing. Must they move so soon?" said Charlotte.

"I believe it is to their own relief to seek lodgings nearer Pemberley."

"Delightful! She will be so pleased to have you nearby, for I know you were both so very close. I miss my sisters terribly, I fear, though they have visited as often as possible. You may not have heard that my sister, Maria, will soon be wed to Mr. Collins" cousin."

Elizabeth remarked on the match and obtained many details of the upcoming nuptials.

After breakfast, Mr. Darcy was summoned to Lady Catherine, and ignoring the Lady's orders, insisted his wife accompany him. Mr. Collins made his apologies for intruding and gave so many requests for messages to be passed to her ladyship that the Darcys were forced to leave him without proper goodbyes. Mrs. Darcy promised they should visit before the day's ending.

Lady Catherine"s room was in complete darkness and had not been allowed to air since she had taken ill and was thus pervaded by an odour of sickness. Elizabeth resisted the urge to throw open window and instead entered quietly behind her husband.

"Who joins you, nephew?" Lady Catherine called in a weakened, but still stately manner.

"I have brought Mrs. Darcy to see you as well Ma'am, for I wish you to meet her since our marriage."

"I expressly asked for your coming alone," she began in fervor, but ended in weakness through a fit of coughing. Elizabeth whispered that she should leave.

"Stay, my dear," whispered her husband, reaching for her hand.

"Mrs. Darcy has traveled far to see you aunt, and it is she you must thank for our visit. She has encouraged reconciliation between our families and I have insisted upon her presence this morning."

Lady Catherine eyed Elizabeth, but only sniffed a forced acceptance of her presence.

"You have been sent many good wishes and concern for

your wellness this morning by Mr. and Mrs. Collins," Darcy continued.

"They are ceaselessly loyal," she consented. "Do they continue to follow my directions regarding Baby Collins?"

"Yes ma'am," replied Elizabeth. "This morning Mrs. Collins assured us the wee cherub would not be let out of the house before his first birthday."

"Humph," she replied, but seemed pleased with the news.

"Two of my sisters are expecting their first children shortly," added Elizabeth. "I would be most appreciative of your advice on their behalf."

"It is a pity your mother may not be more relied upon for such information," suffered the Lady, though she appeared pleased by the request. "I shall endeavor to dictate my advices to my woman as soon as I am up for it."

Mr. Darcy marveled at his wife's impeccable charms and was most grateful for his forethought in ensuring her company during his morning visitation. Lady Catherine grew too weary for conversation soon after and excused herself from her visitors. To the delight of both, she asked upon their leave,

"Fitzwilliam, I would request the presence of your wife at your next meeting here and each meeting thereafter."

"Yes ma'am," replied he and they quitted the room feeling the interview had gone better than could have been imagined.

# CHAPTER 7

The Darcys visited the Collins" parsonage for tea that evening. Mr. Collins was effusive in his delight at their granting such benevolence on a lowly clergyman, but after many apologies regarding their small home, he began to praise the improvements made during his station with generous thanks to the great workings of Lady Catherine. He requested Mr. Darcy's accompaniment on a tour of his garden with no room for refusal.

"I think, sir, you will be most pleased with the changes made since your last visit. Lady Catherine takes every opportunity to bestow upon us her wise council in regard to our everyday life. She has shared with me her wealth of knowledge in fashionable gardening trends and nearly insisted I develop a pinery."

Mr. Collins then gestured toward a sickly looking plantation of decorative pineapple trees where some lovely evergreens had once stood.

"You likely doubt the ability of these small plants to flourish in our climate, but Lady Catherine has it on authority from her gardener and the many publications she reviews that these will thrive within only a few years. I dare say my garden may one day be sought by visitors to the county, but I do not think I boast, for I have heard the statement directly from my patroness."

Here Mr. Collins paused to bow in reverence to her ladyship and then proceeded to ask questions regarding her health and wellness for the remainder of the time until tea was announced. Mr. Darcy was most relieved to return to his wife's company.

Mrs. Darcy had been given the pleasure of watching Baby William while he slept. Even in the plumpness of infancy and the bliss of sleep, Baby William had the great misfortune of a close resemblance to his father. Elizabeth hoped, for the baby's sake, this appearance would fade as he grew and he would instead take on the manner and appearance of his mother as quickly as possible. All of these thoughts were kept firmly within, however, as she listened to and gave her own effusive praises of the boy.

When the men returned from touring the garden and tea was served, Mrs. Collins, through great effort of her own as she preferred and was given to speaking almost entirely of her son since his birth, discussed the engagement of her sister to Mr. Collins" cousin.

"I am certain I have never seen two people so much in love as they appear to be," she said. "Although I am not entirely convinced so much attention need be paid between two people, I hope a short time of marriage shall dull their passion into a respectable regard for one another."

Elizabeth hid a smile in her tea as she considered Charlotte's own marriage and her utterly practical and passionless approach to all such unions. Elizabeth could not look at Darcy for fear she might laugh aloud if he were to read her own thoughts on passionate marriages.

The evening passed pleasantly enough, made more agreeable by the starting up of a casino which lessened the conversation regarding the sainthood of Lady Catherine and the angelhood of Baby William.

With such visitations were the Darcys chiefly employed for the following fortnight. Mr. Rathwell and his sisters were often found at Rosings and, to minimize the amount of time spent in such company, as well as to increase their own enjoyment while at Hunsford, the Darcys daily endeavored to take the air and frequently visited the well-loved path where they had met in days past. They told each other the story of their courtship and were enchanted with the secrets held by one another not yet revealed during their short married life. Elizabeth laughed at Darcy's first proposal of marriage and wondered how they ever saw to a second and Darcy wondered how he could first so offend and then so impress his dear Elizabeth. They smiled whenever they passed the room at the Collin's parsonage where the first proposal took place.

"I was never so devastated in my life," said Mr. Darcy.

"I was never so shocked," replied Elizabeth.

Thus, though the company they kept was at times trying and dull, the Darcys thoroughly enjoyed their second honeymoon.

Just as they approached the third week spent at Rosings and Lady Catherine had made her first appearance at breakfast, Mrs. Darcy received a letter requesting her return home due to the near arrival of Mr. and Mrs. Bingley to their new home within thirty miles Pemberley. With Lady Catherine out of danger, the Darcys felt it safe and appropriate to leave her to the ministrations of her increasingly independent daughter. They suspected Lady Catherine would soon discover her daughter's attachment to the Rathwell family and wished to be gone before such knowledge was obtained.

To her credit, Lady Catherine thanked them for their visit

and sent with Elizabeth a package for both her sisters and a number of pages on the proper care of infants. She insisted the Darcys visit again within a year, as she was yet unwilling to sully her reputation by mixing with the company of Mrs. Darcy's family. Elizabeth had grown quite fond of Baby William and was sorry to say goodbye to him and his mother, but could not quite bring herself to regret the removal of Mr. Collins from their daily routine. They left for Pemberley within a day of the letter.

Pemberley was in excellent form due to the careful attention of Mrs. Reynolds and Georgiana as well as the many other dutiful servants. Georgiana was pleased at their return and they spent a happy night comparing details of their time apart. Georgiana informed them she and Julia would soon leave for London to accept their invitation from the Gardiners. Julia's youngest brother, James, would accompany them on his way to Oxford in continuation of his studies. Georgiana also informed them the Bingley's were expected on the morrow for Michaelmas and that she had invited them to stay at Pemberley until they were well settled at Rundle Park. They spoke until late into the night and finally broke from their cozy trio to rest before the happy morning.

The Bingley's arrived by noon at Pemberley with Jane looking quite exhausted. They lunched together and then Jane was prevailed upon to rest in the guest rooms while Darcy and Bingley removed to Rundle Park to see to the set up. After a period of rest, Elizabeth joined Jane in her rooms to catch up with their news. Jane looked much improved and was pleased to hear her sister's trip to Husford had been so successful.

"I always knew any relation of Mr. Darcy's must be as kind and generous as he," said Jane when Elizabeth finished describing their stay.

"You give Lady Catherine too much goodwill, as you do

to everyone. I suspect it is her shrewd reasoning skills that forced her to accept me when she might regain the attention of her favourite nephew. She is quite taken with him and I heard her sigh once or twice as I supposed she considered the son she had lost in him."

"Did her daughter seem equally disappointed by the breaking of her expectations?"

"Quite the contrary! I think we will soon hear news of her own plans for the future."

Jane asked after the Collins's and their baby boy. Elizabeth passed on the packages sent for Jane both from Charlotte and Lady Catherine. Jane sighed over the sweet baby things and promised to read the advices from Lady Catherine with great care.

"You are too good, sister. I hope you will never change." Elizabeth smiled. Jane shared news of their family and, though she spoke not a single ill word, Elizabeth surmised their involvement in the Bingley's lives had been quite taxing. She sensed some relief mixed with guilt at their departure from Netherfield and hoped the increased distance would keep the Wickhams from continuing their demands on the Bingleys. Lydia was now confined to her own lodgings until the baby arrived. Elizabeth wondered how such events would alter the Wickhams' existence, despite Jane's confidence that a child would certainly ensure a proper responsibility to their duties.

The Bingleys and Darcys enjoyed one another's close company for only two days before the Bingleys became anxious to settle into their own home. Plans were made to visit them the following week. The same day, Georgiana left for London with the Lawsons and the Darcys were left alone in their own home for the first time in quite a while. They enjoyed it immensely.

# CHAPTER 8

## OCTOBER 1813

Mr. James Lawson was the youngest of the Lawson brothers at nineteen. He had followed in the educational footsteps of his brothers and was currently enrolled at Oxford. He was as different from Phillip and Barrington as they were from one another. Rather than being ironical and confident like the former and serious and pedantic like the latter, he was quiet and nervous. He lacked confidence and felt awkward in the company of almost everyone and tried with all his might to hide the artistic sentiment which lay deep within. Like his sister Julia, but unknown to them both, he greatly enjoyed writing poetry and was very curious to learn of her trip to the Lakes. He had never been there himself as he frequently summered with an aunt and uncle in the south. He had only been home a week before he must start school again. He felt a stranger in his home and, though he was not particularly eager to return to Oxford where he studied the law, he was not sad to leave Sunnings. He was fond of his sisters and looked forward to spending some time with Julia on his way to school. He was not greatly acquainted with Georgiana and was therefore somewhat afraid of her.

They took two days getting to London and James was relieved to find in Georgiana a thoughtful, quiet and kind traveling companion. He was always leery of women who flirted or joked with him. He was not sure how to respond and often only nodded at their chatter. He was rewarded by only a few questions regarding their trip to the Lakes with wonderful descriptions on the scenery they visited. He was especially interested in the Kiskstall Abbey, but neither Julia nor Georgiana were keen to give more than a vague description, explaining the day they visited had been very foggy. Georgiana questioned him about the south of England and seemed very interested in his description of the people and sights there. As James was so little accustomed to the kind regard of a woman due to his unassuming position as third son, accompanied by a certain lack of social courtesies, he soon fell deeply in love with Georgiana, though to his credit he was able to hide these feelings from both his sister and her friend. He was greatly disappointed to reach their lodgings at Gracechurch-street so quickly; however he was quickly comforted by promises from Julia to meet during their stay.

Mr. and Mrs. Gardiner were very pleased to welcome Miss Lawson and Miss Darcy to their home and upon meeting Mr. James Lawson, they eagerly invited him to dinner. Gracechurch-street was a lovely home with excellent decorations. Julia was most adamant in her praise and Mrs. Gardiner was soon appeased. She only hoped Julia and Georgiana would not lose their good opinion in the eyes of certain relations. The children were then allowed to greet their visitors and Julia was soon involved in games with them in the parlour. James and Georgiana were more reserved in their attention to the children, but nevertheless had the youngest between them on the floor to help him with a puzzle. In the presence of Georgiana, James was amazed to find children so appealing when they had held little interest to him before.

When Mr. Gardiner learned at supper that James intended to study the law, he was very pleased.

"It is a most worthy profession, Mr. Lawson, and I can see already by your disposition that you will be well suited to it. I would be honoured to give you any assistance in your studies or your procurement of a position when you have finished."

"I thank you sir," said James, taking Mr. Gardiner's interest in himself as a sure sign he would be a welcome addition to all Georgiana's family. After supper, Mr. Gardiner and Mr. Lawson retreated to discuss the law and politics further and, while James was pleased with the conversation, he regretted the loss of Georgiana's company. He left the home on Gracechurch-street with a promise to accompany his sister and Miss Darcy on an evening at the theatre in three days time. He could not remember ever before having looked forward to an outing so fondly.

JULIA AND GEORGIANA shared a room at the Gardiner's home. Mrs. Gardiner apologized profusely and promised her girls could share a room if the accommodations were in any way disagreeable. Julia and Georgiana were pleased to share a room as it would allow them many opportunities to share secrets and conversations over the course of their visit. They were both grateful to be treated as if they were sisters, Julia because she missed Penelope now that she was married and Georgiana because she had grown up the only girl in her household.

Mrs. Gardiner recommended a trip to the shops the following morning, knowing they would have much business in London after so long away. Both girls were familiar with

London and they went to the library first to look for gifts for their families. Georgiana was intrigued by a thin bracelet which she imagined Elizabeth wearing and stayed behind while Julia and Mrs. Gardiner went on to the hat shop. As she waited in line, she noticed a young man enter the store. There was something familiar to his walk and stance and as he drew closer, she recognized Mr. Phillip Lawson. To her surprise, she grew quite flushed and discovered her heart beat rapidly. She wished Julia were present to call him over, but did not think it proper for herself to do so. Just then, she was called forward to the counter and in much confusion did she face the clerk.

"How may I help you, miss?" said the clerk.

"I was looking . . . a bracelet . . . for my sister. Not my sister, but rather in-law. . ." She looked again at the door, while the clerk became impatient.

"A bracelet, you say. Which one had you in mind?"

Georgiana had lost sight of Phillip and worried she might not find him again. In desperation, she left the counter to find him, leaving the clerk quite annoyed, calling after her "Miss, Miss!", but she did not hear.

Georgiana realized she longed to hear Phillip's voice again. It had been so long since she had heard anything from him. Even Julia had not spoken of him. Where had he been and why had he not returned to meet with her? Had he really meant to propose, or had it been another of his jokes? In relief, she found him near a display of pocket watches and with great apprehension, she spoke.

"Good morning, Mr. Lawson." He turned and a quick smile overtook his features.

"Miss Darcy. What brings you to London?"

"I have come with your sister, Julia, and we are staying with some relatives of Mrs. Darcy"s."

"Is Julia with you?" He looked around quickly.

"She just went to the hat shop. We can go see her if you like."

"Of course, that would be grand. What luck you found me in the middle of such a city."

Just then a young woman with a fine figure and stylish red hair appeared at Phillip's side, holding a pair of gloves.

"What do you think of these, Phillip? Should I take them?" She spoke with an Irish accent, making her all the more mysterious and attractive.

"They are very fine, Bridget," he said, suddenly uncomfortable. "May I introduce you to my neighbour, Miss Darcy?"

"How do you do?" Bridget curtsied. "I am Miss Brill, come from Dublin."

"Very nice to meet you," Georgiana returned the curtsey; though she had felt faint from the moment Phillip called Miss Brill by her Christian name.

"It would seem that my eldest sister is town, visiting with Miss Darcy."

"Charming!" smiled Miss Brill. "Will we see her then?"

"Of course, I was just about to meet her. Won't you join me?" said Georgiana, but she found it difficult to keep her voice from breaking. It was a relief to lead them out of the crowded library to a fresh rain in the streets.

Neither Miss Darcy nor Mr. Lawson spoke on their short walk to the hat shop, but fortunately Miss Brill was a skilled conversationalist, though it became increasingly evident that she was not well-educated.

"It will be the first of your siblings I will meet, Phillip," she said as she held his arm along the muddy streets. "Will she like me, do you think?"

Before Phillip could answer, Miss Brill continued. "I have wondered what she would look like. Can you believe Miss Darcy that he travels without any likeness of his sisters?"

Georgiana wondered how he could do many things, but did not bother to answer Miss Brill.

"I am very eager to meet Mrs. Lawson, though Phillip tells me we will not visit another fortnight. He swears he has too much business. I, for one, am eager to leave this monstrous city. Dublin is not half the size and I was generally in the country rather than the city. I cannot wait to see Sunnings, for it sounds so dear."

Before much more of Miss Brill's excited talk, they arrived at the shop where Julia and Mrs. Gardiner waited at the door.

"Phillip!" cried Julia and raced to embrace him. "Where have you been, you devil and why have you not written in so long?"

"I have been detained at my business."

"You could not spare a line or two? Mother was half frantic when I left. But who is this?" She noticed her brother's companion. "Is she some friend of yours, Georgiana?"

"This is Miss Brill," said Phillip. "Our cousin and my fiancée." At which point Georgiana, looking hot and uncomfortable, fainted in the street.

Given the amount of mud in the street and the sudden increase of rain falling, it was not entirely surprising that Mr. Lawson picked up Miss Darcy. What was surprising was that he carried her all the way back to the Gardiners.

GEORGIANA WAS QUICKLY REVIVED in the comforts of her guest room; however, she waited as long as she could before returning to her party. Mrs. Gardiner attended her while Julia sat with her brother and Miss Brill.

When Georgiana could no longer excuse herself from her rescuer, Mrs. Gardiner supported her to the sitting room. Phillip stood at her entrance, looking both relieved and concerned. Julia took Mrs. Gardiner's place at Georgiana's side and assisted her to the sofa.

"My dear, however are you? Are you terribly ill?" Julia looked very uneasy.

"No, no. I think I will be fine. It was only the stuffiness of the library followed by the chill of rain, I suppose." She could not look in Phillip's direction.

"It must be this blasted city, I should think," spoke Miss Brill. "The air does not have the health of the country you are accustomed to. It is a wonder we all did not faint in the street."

"I am sorry I have not yet had the opportunity to congratulate you, Miss Brill. Mr. Lawson." Georgiana felt she must make up for her previous shock by assuring everyone she was not at all upset by Phillip's engagement.

"I thank you, Miss, to be sure. It must come as a surprise to you all. It is a wonder that men get anything done at all when they are not diligent in their letters. I would not have accepted if Phillip had not come with his family's consent already given. He told me he had asked their permission before he even left Sunnings, can you imagine! He arrived already carrying their letter of approval."

"Mother and Father knew before you left?" said Julia in amazement. "Why did they not say anything to us?"

"I suppose they were awaiting my letter of confirmation," muttered Mr. Lawson.

"You are very wicked not to send it then Phillip, for you have been gone from Sunnings these two months," said Julia.

"He took some time in convincing me, I will affirm," said Miss Brill. "For it has only been a se'ennight since the engagement. Still, that is enough time to get a letter writ."

"You forget we have been traveling most of the time," was Phillip's excuse. "I shall sit down to it directly upon returning to my lodgings."

"Where do you stay?" said Julia.

"At our family's home on Berkley Street. Miss Brill lodges with an aunt near you," replied Phillip.

"How lovely to be so close," said Miss Brill. "I should very much like to become better acquainted with you both, Miss Lawson and Miss Darcy."

The Gardiners were pleased to invite Miss Brill and Mr. Lawson to tea. Their only concern was the continuing paleness of Miss Darcy. They hoped she would be able to rest shortly.

Miss Brill seemed comfortable directing most of the conversation. Georgiana noted she was very pretty in her youthful exuberance, but noticed her dress was quite old and rather snug. She began to pity Miss Brill slightly for her ill speech and dress and wondered if she would be improved by the Lawson family. Georgiana tried to tell herself Phillip was being rather good in alleviating Miss Brill from a life of poverty and incivility. She only wished one of his other brothers had taken up the cause instead.

Tea ended eventually and plans were made for Miss Brill and Mr. Lawson to join them at the theatre the following evening where they would also meet James. Georgiana was then pressed to retire to her rooms to regain her strength and she was relieved to consider all of the morning's events by herself.

Georgiana reclined at her bed and contemplated all that had happened between her and Phillip Lawson. In truth, it did not amount to very much. She had been rather insufferable to him and when she considered the prank she played on him involving the pig, she realized Phillip might have sought revenge. His request to visit her on the morning of the dance was likely a trick to play with her expectations as she had with his. He must have known already he would seek the hand of Miss Brill, for he left that very morning with a letter of acceptance from his mother and father in proposing their marriage. Georgiana admitted it must be so and she had never been more to him than a friend of the family whom he enjoyed teasing. Georgiana shed tears of humiliation and disappointment for she realized then how much she had come to esteem him and in what anticipation she awaited his return.

After giving herself over to emotion for three quarters of an hour, Georgiana took hold of herself and resolved to accept her fate. It was only fitting, as she had previously settled to a life of solitude and she chastised herself for so easily building expectations of any man. She would befriend Miss Brill, forgive Mr. Lawson and regain her position as friend of the family. She would endeavor to do all she could to improve the situation and education of Miss Brill that she might be an acceptable partner to a deserving husband. It was only right and good for Mr. Lawson to seek a better life for his cousin and she would support it in any way she could. Thus decided, she washed her face, tidied her dress and descended the stairs to practice her pianoforte for the remainder of the afternoon.

# CHAPTER 9

Two evenings later, Mr. James Lawson arrived at Gracechurch-street a half-hour before he was expected. He was rewarded for his early arrival by finding Georgiana at the pianoforte. She had finished her toilette well before Julia and was passing the time in practice. Upon noticing James in the room, she quit her playing to greet him.

"Please go on, Miss Darcy. I would very much like to hear you play." Georgiana at first declined, but was prevailed upon to finish her piece and then play one other. At this point, Mr. Phillip Lawson entered without Miss Brill or the notice of Miss Darcy, who had become deeply involved in the piece. The brothers acknowledged one another and the elder Mr. Lawson saw something familiar in the way his brother regarded Miss Darcy. At the end of the melody, Miss Lawson entered the room with applause.

"Is she not the finest player you ever heard?" she declared. Miss Darcy looked up and was surprised at her audience. She blushed to wonder how long Mr. Phillip Lawson had been in the room, but was spared his notice by the entrance of Miss Brill.

"I have missed something, have I not?" she asked. "Please hold all future concerts until I arrive, Miss Darcy."

"I apologize, Miss Brill. I was only passing the time."

"And it is certainly time enough now," said Julia. "Shall we go to the theatre?"

The youthful party bid their goodbyes to the Gardiner's and took up their transportation – Miss Brill and Mr. Lawson in an open carriage and Mr. James Lawson, Julia and Georgiana in the Gardiner's chaise and four.

"Who is Miss Brill?" asked James as soon as they were off.

"Oh, did I not introduce you? But we were in such a hurry. He is our brother's fiancée and our cousin."

"Engaged? Cousin? Have I been missing for so long I do not know our own cousin or that my brother is to be wed?"

"She is a cousin from mother's side, apparently. She never speaks of her relations and I am sure we have never met them, but it seems Phillip asked for her hand before he left Sunnings in June. He has been these months visiting Miss Brill in Ireland and has recently proposed."

"Extraordinary! I did not realize our family held such secrets. Do mother and father know?" James smiled in delight.

"They knew of his intentions, to be sure, but at last meeting, Phillip only promised he would write as soon as possible. It is very unlike him, do you not think?" Julia was more suspicious.

"I fear I have been too often gone from home. I cannot say what our brother is likely to do lately. Do you like her?"

"She is very pretty, you could see yourself. Her manners are rather different from what we are used to, but of course she hails from a different country entirely."

"What say you, Miss Darcy?" he asked, hoping to entice her to intimacy.

"She seems very amiable and good, but I have only known

her such a short while. I can only take your brother's good opinion of her as my own."

"Very well said. Phillip is trustworthy and would not have proposed if she were not all she ought to be. Well then, we must seek to make her welcome as one of the family. I am certain our mother will be greatly pleased." said James with a wink at his sister.

James and Julia spoke of poetry for the remainder of the short ride and Georgiana endeavored to find a way of improving Miss Brill without offending either her or Mr. Lawson.

The party rejoined at the theatre and all that was left was to make their seating arrangements. Julia insisted upon sitting beside Miss Brill and Phillip must naturally sit beside her. As Julia left no space for Georgiana, she took the seat next to Phillip and was then joined on her right by James. It was a familiar seating arrangement to one she was accustomed to at Sunnings, only Barrington had been replaced.

Phillip was polite in asking how Georgiana had spent her summer and was pleased to hear she and Julia had toured the lakes. At this point, James cut into the conversation, and Phillip thought it very unlike his brother. James continued speaking with Miss Darcy until the play began and there was no further chance for her to ask Phillip of his time in Ireland.

The play was enjoyable and all of the party laughed many times during the show. Miss Brill seemed rather confused throughout and Julia and Phillip were kept busy in explaining different portions to her. James commented to Georgiana it must be quite different from what Miss Brill experienced in Ireland. Georgiana suggested they see more plays together so Miss Brill might become more familiar with them. James was very pleased with this suggestion and promised to make the recommendation to his brother and sister.

Georgiana found herself rather uncomfortable so close to Phillip. She wished she could sit by Julia, but thought it would be rude to change seats at the intermission. To her relief, Julia suggested it instead.

"Perhaps Georgiana would like my seat, for I am closer to the stage." All agreed to this and in private, Julia thanked Georgiana.

"I know she is to be my sister, but she is ruining the play with all of her questions and prattle. I half suspect she is only trying to gain my brother's attention. I hope you will not mind the arrangement."

"Not at all. I have seen this one before and I would be happy to assist her."

"Oh, you are too good, Georgiana. I know I am wicked to speak ill of a relation, but I have never been well disposed to hold my tongue." Julia hugged Georgiana in relief.

At that moment, Julia looked up and pleasure marked her features before turning to disappointment. She looked away quickly, but not before Georgiana followed her gaze.

"Mr. Black!" she called before considering the feelings of her friends. Mr. Black was well dressed for an evening at the theatre and was accompanied by an elegant young lady on his arm.

"Miss Darcy! How lovely to see you again. Miss Lawson." He bowed at each of the ladies and then turned to his partner. "May I introduce you to my sister, Miss Black?"

Julia's posture became very much relaxed at this introduction and she took over the introductions.

"Miss Black, how delightful. Do you live in London?"

"I am only here for school." When it was discovered she attended the same institution which both Julia and Georgiana attended, they quickly began comparing instructors and enquiring on changes made to the school. Mr. Black listened with an obvious smile to the talk and made no interruptions.

Intermission was come to an end, but before the group parted, Georgiana invited the Blacks to dine at Gracechurch-street at their earliest convenience. Miss Black promised to call and all returned to their seats.

The seating was adjusted and all but James were relieved by their neighbours. He, at least, could be mollified by the thought of future plays with his company.

# CHAPTER 10

THE BINGLEYS WERE BREAKFASTING AT PEMBERLEY THREE mornings after Georgiana's visit to the play. Jane planned to stay at Pemberley for some nights while her husband went to London on business. She dared not stay home alone in her condition and the sisters looked forward to some time together. The post which would change their plans arrived while they drank their coffee and chocolate. Both Mr. and Mrs. Darcy opened letters which affected their appearances.

"It is from father," said Elizabeth. "He will be coming this afternoon with Kitty."

"How unexpected," said Jane. "Do Mother and Mary join him?"

"Not if his letter is to be trusted, for it is only one line. I will read it, for it is just like him."

"Longbourn
"$8^{th}$ October

"My dear Elizabeth,

"Your mother's nerves grow tiresome. Expect Kitty and me for dinner on the tenth.

Father."

"How delightful that your father and sister should come while I am away." Mr. Bingley said. Jane looked at him in reproof. "I mean for your company while mine is to be missed."

"Of course," smiled Elizabeth.

"I beg your pardon," said Mr. Darcy. "I fear I must leave you all immediately."

"Whatever for?" said Elizabeth, fearful her news had upset him.

"I have had a letter of the most urgent nature, which calls me to London."

"Well, you must join me then," said Mr. Bingley.

"I am afraid I cannot spare a moment. I must leave instantly. Excuse me." With such ill manners did Mr. Darcy leave his wife and guests to make ready in haste. Elizabeth begged her company's pardon and promised to return to them promptly. She went after Darcy as he gave orders for his servant to gather some necessities.

"When can I expect your return?" she said.

"There are some things, Elizabeth, which I have been remiss in withholding from you. I have not the time to tell you now and I dare not send them by letter for fear their contents might be intercepted. Only trust me that I do what I feel is honourable. I shall send you notice of my safety, but you may not hear much else from me for some time."

"May I not join you, then?" Elizabeth was near tears over such a swift and mysterious departure. Darcy looked at her with regret.

"I thank you dear Lizzy for offering, but I dare not take

you where I must go. I shall explain all when I am returned. I love you."

One quick embrace was all he had left to give and he was gone before the coffee had gone cold in his cup. Elizabeth returned to the Bingleys greatly shaken, but endeavoring not to share her worries.

Mr. Bingley left shortly after Mr. Darcy and continually wondered aloud over his friend's hasty departure.

"He has always been so dreadfully independent. I cannot imagine why he could not wait half an hour for me to accompany him. Likely, we shall meet at an inn along the way. Be not sad my good wife and sister, I will take care of Mr. Darcy when I catch up to him in London. I will be gone only as long as is absolutely necessary."

Elizabeth excused herself to allow the newlyweds a goodbye exchange in private. She was somewhat relieved by Mr. Bingley's promise to watch for her husband, but Darcy's own final words left her unsure as to his being caught up to. She was glad she would not be left alone and returned to her sister as soon as she saw Mr. Bingley go.

As planned, Mr. Bennet and Kitty arrived before dinner on the tenth, the former looking quite proud of himself and the latter rather windblown.

"Would you believe, Lizzy, we made it here in only fourteen hours! Capitol, if I do say so myself. But where is your proud husband? Does he not welcome his visitors? I also make a practice of avoiding my own company. Introductions can be so taxing and greatly reduce one's privacy."

"Mr. Darcy was called to London on urgent business this morning. He sends his welcome and regrets his departure on your first visit to Pemberley."

"I dare say, there is a smart fellow. I must try that excuse myself in the future, only I think I dislike London more that I do my guests."

"Oh father! It is good to have you. How fare you, Kitty?"

"Father is impossible. I do not know how mother bares him! He would not stop near often enough for the needs of a lady. I fear I look deplorable."

"Mrs. Reynolds will show you to your rooms directly. We will dine as soon as you are refreshed."

As Mrs. Reynolds did her biddings, she wondered that Mrs. Darcy could be so different from her family. Only Jane was like her in manners and temperament.

Half of the Bennet family was reunited for dinner with much delight. Mr. Bennet was equally impressed to find Jane's husband also had business in London and could only regret that he was the only male in the company of so many women.

"I dare say, I will not stay as long as I planned. Kitty, you may stay at Pemberley longer, if your sister will have you."

Jane and Elizabeth attempted to persuade their father not to go so soon, but he could only be prevailed upon to stay three nights.

"It will not do, girls. I cannot make myself at home in another man's library if he is not present. You will be glad of my decision by tomorrow, I dare say. You girls will want your privacy to discuss female interests."

Kitty did seem rather improved to Elizabeth and they had an enjoyable dinner. She could not help but wonder if it would be as comfortable if her husband had been present, but she wished for his attendance none the less. They had not been apart for a night since they had married. She was glad for family to distract her from her melancholy thoughts.

The following morning brought two more letters of interest. Elizabeth read aloud her letter from Lydia.

"Dearest Lizzy,

"You must be awaiting this announcement on pins and needles, but your first nephew has finally arrived! We have called him George Henry for his father and grandfather Wickham. He is a delight, though he cries rather more than I had expected. You will wish to visit as soon as possible, I assume, but I would rather make the trip to Pemberley when I am ready. I fear our lodgings are not up to your preferred standards and I would once again implore you to recommend us to a better situation. I dare say, Georgie will be a favourite of his grandparents for he is the most handsome baby I have ever seen.

"I must end this letter, for I have yet to write Jane and mother. I will be coming as soon as I might.

"Yours, &c."

"And so I am a grandfather," said Mr. Bennet proudly. "And finally we are to have boys among us. If yours is also born male, Jane, we will begin to be equally matched in our family."

The second came from Mrs. Collins and after reading it silently; Elizabeth shared the particulars with some surprise.

"Mr. and Mrs. Collins will join us in four days time. They bring with them Miss De Bourgh, at the request of her mother, to stay at Pemberley."

"You must have made quite an impression during your stay for Lady Catherine to agree to such an arrangement," said Jane.

"I wonder if she would change her mind if she knew of your current visitors," said Mr. Bennet. "I think I might stay longer after all. It is too much to pass up a visit from such a distinguished guest and Mr. Collins might be borne for a day or two."

Kitty wondered if she would have to give up her rooms to Miss De Bourgh, but Elizabeth put her fears to rest.

"We have room enough for many visitors and I think Mrs. Reynolds shall be glad of a full house. I shall speak to her immediately. If only Mr. Darcy could be here to greet his cousin." Elizabeth left the room.

The rest of the party discussed the news at length.

# CHAPTER 11

GEORGIANA DECIDED TO BEGIN HER EDUCATION OF MISS Brill. The former sent an invitation to the latter to join the children's lessons for the morning, explaining her assistance would be most appreciated as Julia would be out for the day visiting friends. Miss Brill arrived by ten o'clock, when Georgiana was reading to the youngest Gardiner children while Samantha and Jennifer worked on their French.

"Good Morning, Miss Darcy," said Miss Brill, rather nervously. Georgiana had decided to do all she could to keep her intentions hidden from Miss Brill.

"How kind of you to come," she left the children for a moment to speak to Miss Brill privately. "I most need your help with the youngest. He is apt to distract all of the other children by chattering or asking to play. Can you see he listens to his lessons?"

"I will do my best. I have nine younger siblings of my own, so I have some experience."

"Nine! It is a wonder your mother could let you go to Mr. Lawson," and no wonder, thought Georgiana, that Miss Brill had not been well educated.

"She was happy for it, I should think, but I must not say more." Miss Brill looked ashamed of having revealed too much. Georgiana wondered what secret she could be keeping, but soon forgot it as she returned to their lessons.

Georgiana took up her reading. She had selected something simple yet full of moral lessons, keeping Miss Brill especially in mind. To her dismay, Miss Brill became the major distraction that morning. She began whispering to the youngest and then running a toy car about his small body. Georgiana could hardly reprimand her and so read slightly louder, hoping Miss Brill would remember herself.

"My brothers love this game," said Miss Brill. "How long must the children listen to their lessons?"

"Until twelve," said Jennifer. "Will you really marry Julia's brother, Miss Brill?"

"Oh yes," blushed Miss Brill.

"What will your wedding gown look like?" asked Samantha.

Miss Brill explained her wishes at length and Georgiana began to feel her goal of improving Miss Brill was ridiculous. She sighed rather loudly and Miss Brill stopped speaking.

"Oh! I must not keep you from your lessons. I will tell you more about it later."

Georgiana continued reading and then assisted the children with their printing. She had Miss Brill demonstrate to her charge after Georgiana had showed her pupil his letters. Miss Brill seemed rather delighted with her own as well as her pupil's progress.

"Would you look at that! My letters are nearly as good as yours, wouldn't you say?" The young Gardiner was enchanted with his teacher and repeatedly held her hand and looked into her eyes with great admiration.

Miss Brill was invited to lunch and all four of the Gardiner children crowded her to ask questions about her family in Ireland and her wedding to Mr. Lawson. Georgiana was pleased with their attentions and Miss Brill's enthusiasm; however, she was rather fatigued by the frequent references to the marriage.

Julia joined them for lunch with news that her family would be expected in London within three days time. They were very anxious to meet Miss Brill and to see Phillip after such a long time away. Georgiana found it difficult to rejoice at their expected arrival.

# CHAPTER 12

ELIZABETH HAD BEEN BUSY ENTERTAINING HER GUESTS AND preparing for the arrival of more for two days and decided to escape for an hour at twilight. She would have welcomed Jane's company, but Jane was sitting on the sofa to rest her swollen ankles. Elizabeth rejoiced in the freshness of a fall evening and the silence of the outdoors. However, as she passed favourite walking sites so often shared with Darcy, she began to wonder at his sudden departure. Could it be he only wanted to avoid the Bennet family? He had, after all, announced his intentions for London immediately upon hearing Elizabeth's letter from her father? But it was not like Darcy to lie. If he truly disapproved of their visiting, he would have sent word that they were not welcome – were his actions to Wickham not proof enough of this? What business could possibly call her husband to London at such short notice? Could he not have left a forwarding address or at least an expected return time? What would Miss De Bourgh think when she found her cousins gone? Could Elizabeth manage so many different personalities under one roof? She could only imagine how her father would relate to such a weak and disagreeable girl.

Elizabeth found herself deeper and deeper in gloom when she saw a horse and rider in the distance. Her features brightened in anticipation of her husband's quick return and she nearly ran to meet him, but on closer inspection, he was of lesser stature than Darcy and she slowed her pace to consider who it might be.

"Halloo there, Mrs. Darcy," came Mr. Wolfe's voice a moment later. "What brings you out alone on such a fine night?"

Elizabeth tried to hide her disappointment and endeavored to extend the civility due him.

"My husband has gone to London and I felt the need for air."

"Did he not take you along, Mrs. Darcy? That is a surprise; it must be dangerous business for him to leave you at Pemberley."

These comments did nothing to lift Elizabeth's spirits, but the darkness of the sky allowed her to hide her thoughts.

"I was just about to turn back to Pemberley. Some of my family is visiting if you could stay for tea," Elizabeth said.

"How very kind. I would be most delighted to meet your relations."

Elizabeth turned and Mr. Wolfe dismounted to walk his horse the remainder of the distance.

"I was hoping to find you and Darcy at home tonight. I wished to discuss some new farming practices I have learned on my travels. When do you expect him back?"

"It was a most unusual departure, Mr. Wolfe, for he left neither an address nor a return date," Elizabeth was embarrassed to admit.

"Ah, your Darcy was always one for secrecy, I fear. I

would not be surprised if he was off to buy you an important gift." Mr. Wolfe winked.

Elizabeth had not considered this idea. It seemed unlikely due to his countenance and manner upon quitting Pemberley, but it was a possibility to lift her heavy spirits.

"I am certain he will return soon, or at least write you a most becoming letter before another day has past," Mr. Wolfe voice was reassuring.

"Thank you, Mr. Wolfe. You are very kind."

They enjoyed the remainder of their walk to Pemberley with Mr. Wolfe regaling her with tales of Darcy's goodness since his youth. It was just the kind of balm Elizabeth's mind required.

Mr. Bennet was very pleased to have another man in the house and was even more delighted to find he was a man of sense and humility.

"Mr. Wolfe, do you play at billiards?" He asked after the proper time had been given to introductions and pleasantries.

"I do, sir."

"Smashing."

The two men excused themselves and left the women to their amusements.

"I wonder how mother and Mary get on," said Elizabeth after some time at their various employments.

"I dare say Mother will have all sorts of guests to keep her from being too long with Mary," said Kitty. "Mary is hardly the companion to keep anyone contented for long." She sighed. "I am so pleased father brought me here and is not Mr. Wolfe very handsome?"

"Do you think so?" smiled Elizabeth.

"He certainly is," said Jane.

"I have hardly seen a single man since you both left.

Father has been most disagreeable. Could you not host a ball while I visit, Lizzy? Father could not keep me from that."

"Oh, I could not go against Father's wishes," teased Elizabeth and Kitty pleaded. "Perhaps a small party would be acceptable when the Collins" arrive with Miss De Bourgh. We might wait until Darcy and Georgiana return, though."

"Oh must we?" said Kitty. "I have not danced in ages."

"I will consider it," said Elizabeth, though she had already made up her mind to grant her sister's wishes. "Why do you not read us something, Kitty? Whatever you have found of interest lately."

Kitty obliged her sister, in the hopes of swaying her favour. Jane and Elizabeth were most impressed with the improvements both of Kitty's reading and her nature.

The men returned shortly and Kitty blushed to continue reading in front of Mr. Wolfe. He gave her all the attention civility required, but Elizabeth detected a lack of interest on his side. She refused to meddle however and took joy instead in the comfort of friends and family. She decided to write Georgiana before going to bed, to confirm her return date and to inquire if she had heard from Darcy. She would plan a small dinner party upon her reply.

# CHAPTER 13

London had lost much of its enjoyment for Georgiana. Her daily lessons with Miss Brill and the children were a mixed blessing. She rejoiced in the improvements of all, but was constantly reminded of upcoming changes to Miss Brill's situation. The Lawson's were expected tonight and Julia had arranged for a small dinner including Georgiana and Miss Brill that evening. If only Julia knew how much Georgiana dreaded seeing the family united in Miss Brill's honour, she would never have orchestrated such an event. Georgiana received a letter from Elizabeth with much joy and discovered herself very homesick.

Pemberley
$14^{th}$ October

Dearest Georgiana,

I hope this letter finds you all well. I trust you are enjoying the company of the Gardiners and Julia. I imagine you all out and about, seeing plays, shopping and visiting. Your brother left for London almost a week ago and I wondered if he had called at Gracechurch-street? It was such urgent business that he was unable to leave a forwarding address and I have not heard from him yet.

My father and sister Kitty have arrived most unexpectedly. It is good company for Jane and me as Bingley has also gone to London on business. We also expect your cousin, Miss De Bourgh, and the Collins". It will be regrettable for Miss De Bourgh to find neither you nor Darcy at home, but of course I would not ask you to cut your trip short. If you could give me some indication of your expected return, I am sure it would give Miss De Bourgh some relief.

I miss you, Georgiana, but hope you will have all the enjoyment London can offer. Send my love to my aunt, uncle and cousins.

Yours, & c, Elizabeth.

GEORGIANA WAS SO RELIEVED to find an excuse to leave London she nearly cried. She spoke to Mrs. Gardiner immediately and arrangements were made for Georgiana to quit London the following week. Julia would go to stay with her family after Georgiana departed and Miss Brill would be left to continue her education on her own. Georgiana sent her reply to Elizabeth as soon as all was settled and only wished she could give some confirmation of her brother's whereabouts.

# CHAPTER 14

THE LAWSON HOME AT BERKLEY STREET HAD BEEN A favourite spot in times past for Georgiana, but when she arrived there with Julia, James and Miss Brill, she felt only a slight sense of dread. She was warmly welcomed by Mr. and Mrs. Lawson and with cool politeness by Barrington.

"How lovely to have all my children together at last!" said Mrs. Lawson. "And for such an occasion as this, dear Bridget! I have not seen you since you were a wee babe."

Georgiana recognized, then, a small lilt to Mrs. Lawson's accent. Could she have come from Ireland herself? It seemed completely obvious now that she and Miss Brill were together. It was surprising to Georgiana that Mrs. Lawson, who was always so open and kind, would not have mentioned such a thing.

Georgiana was seated between James and Julia and remembered her previous place between Barrington and Phillip with some regret.

"You look very well this evening," commented James quietly to Georgiana when all the other guests were engrossed in conversation.

"Thank you, James," said Georgiana, trying to ignore Miss Brill's shrill laughter over some comment Phillip had made.

"I wonder if you will be attending the opera Wednesday next?" said James.

"I fear I cannot, for I return to Pemberley on Monday," Georgiana forced her gaze away from Phillip.

"So soon!" James was alarmed.

"My cousin has come to visit from Rosings and I must attend her. She has not visited since I was a child, as she was always very sickly."

"Will my sister not regret your leaving so early? What of the Gardiners?"

"Julia will come to stay with your family here and the Gardiners will likely be glad to have their home to themselves once more."

"It is a great pity to cut one's visit short, in any case." James was distraught, though Georgiana did not notice.

"Indeed." Georgiana turned then to Julia, leaving James to his quiet meditations. Georgiana had noticed two empty seats to her right and asked Julia who was yet to be expected. Julia coloured slightly.

"Mr. and Miss Black should arrive directly. Miss Black called yesterday morning while you were with the children and I invited her to join us with her brother."

"You did not say anything to me," said Georgiana in surprise.

"I am sorry, Georgiana. I suppose with your sudden change of plans, I forgot to mention it."

Just then, the Black's were announced and warmly greeted by all the Lawson family. Georgiana noticed Mrs. Lawson appraised Mr. Black with very keen interest. Mr. Black sat beside Julia with his sister to his right. Georgiana wondered at his persistence in engaging Julia's attention.

"How do you do, Miss Lawson, Miss Darcy," he said, with his sister looking on.

"Fine, thank you. How lovely to see you both again," answered Georgiana.

"Did you know, Miss Darcy, I have just been reading one of Wordsworth's latest drafts. It is titled "Julia"." Julia choked on some wine at this statement and, beginning to cough, she left the table suddenly. Georgiana ran after her and attended her in a nearby room.

"Are you alright?" she asked when Julia had regained her breath.

"He is insufferable."

"Do you think he meant to tease you by mentioning your Christian name?"

"I cannot tell you, Georgiana, though I promise I will at a later time. We must return to our guests. I do not wish for mother to come looking for me." Mrs. Lawson was just then heard calling for Julia and they returned to the table expediently.

"Are you alright?" Mr. Black asked Julia who gave a slight nod.

"Do you often see drafts of writing before they are published? I thought I recognized your name on that book of poetry you so kindly lent me." Georgiana asked as the first course was served. Phillip looked over at her mention of a gift, though she did not notice.

"Indeed. My family is in the publishing business, you see. My father is attempting to train me to take over some day. I am surprised Miss Lawson did not mention this to you."

Georgiana began to wonder at the lack of anything said by Julia in regards to the Black family, but at this point Miss Black enquired of their time in London and their plans to attend future plays.

"I am afraid my friend Georgiana must return to the country before she can enjoy any more London has to offer," said Julia. "However, my brothers, Miss Brill and I have plans to see several more while we are in town."

The pair compared plans and found there were several nights on which they would be seeing the same productions. They made arrangements to meet and find seats together.

The rest of the dinner continued much as it began, with James attempting to gain Georgiana's attention, Julia ignoring Mr. Black as he sought her attention, and all of the women trying to speak to one another in between. After dinner, Miss Brill requested dancing and Georgiana volunteered herself to play. Phillip took Miss Brill to the floor, James looked disappointed, but asked Miss Black to dance and Mr. Black asked Julia. As Georgiana played for them, she wondered if this was to be her future, watching as others paired up and danced while she played. She noticed Julia seemed quite engrossed in what Mr. Black was saying to her. After some moments, she was shocked to find her friend responding to his conversation. She could not imagine what was being said and was very desirous of finding out when Miss Black took her side and asked to take over the piano. James made his way toward them, but before he could ask Georgiana to dance, Phillip requested her company.

"How good of you to come tonight," said Phillip once the dance began.

"I have always been grateful for the kindness of your family."

"You have been very good to my fiancée. She has greatly enjoyed your attention and I have had the occasion to discuss some of the books you have read with her in instructing the children."

"The children have come to like her very much."

He lowered his voice then. "Miss Brill, you see, is my cousin."

"Yes, she mentioned this." Georgiana was bewildered at his meaning.

"My mother and her mother are sisters and have always sought to keep watch over one another's families."

"They must be very fond of one another."

Phillip looked exasperated at Georgiana's response, but could speak no further on the subject.

"I was most regretful of being called to my aunt's house before I could meet with you the morning after the ball. I hope you will accept my apologies on breaking our appointment."

"Of course," said Georgiana who then curtseyed as the dance ended.

James quickly took Phillip's place and began in earnest as soon as the dancing began.

"Miss Darcy," he addressed her. "I hope I do not shock or offend you with what I am about to say."

Georgiana desperately wished she had kept her spot at the pianoforte.

"I had hoped to prolong our time of acquaintance, but as you have decided to quit London so early, I must take advantage of the little time you have left."

"Mr. Lawson, I do not wish. . ."

"Please, Miss Darcy, I must go on. Since the moment I met you, I have found in you a likeness to all of my firmest beliefs and values. I have come to admire you and even to love you. I am not a man given to long speeches and have not had the time to draw up a prettier proposal. I can only ask that you might agree to marry me at your earliest convenience."

Georgiana felt herself dizzy at the contrast of her feelings for one brother compared to another and especially to the contrast of each brother's words to her. In the absence of affection from the brother she suddenly realized she loved, she felt such infinite sadness that to keep the other brother from feeling the same, she could not refuse him.

"Mr. Lawson, I appreciate your kindness, and I accept your proposal."

James face grew radiant with happiness and instantly did Georgiana realize she could not follow through on her promise. Before she could explain her sudden change of feeling, however, the dance ended and James led her directly to his parents, who were nearly as happy as he was in the engagement. Georgiana was completely ashamed of herself and could hardly endure the rest of the party. She hardly heard the congratulations around her and felt herself the most foolish woman in England. Why could she not be already at Pemberley? Upon leaving the Lawson's an hour later with Julia at her side, she caught Phillip watching her sadly. What could that look possibly mean and why had he missed their meeting in June? She wished to confide her feelings in Julia, but Julia instead took up Georgiana's confidence the moment they were privately ensconced in the carriage.

"Georgiana, it is time I told you the rest of my secret, which I began to you after our swim in that glorious pond."

"Yes?" Georgiana could hardly make sense of Julia's words.

"You will remember I had a book of poetry in consideration of a publisher."

"Yes," repeated Georgiana.

"And that I was dependent upon the interests of a certain party to find a place for my book? Well, all this time it has been Mr. Black I relied upon."

"Mr. Black?" Georgiana began to forget her own worries.

"Yes, whom we both met while at school, but you quit

school early, on the advice of your brother, and I was left to myself for nearly a year. At which time, I became better acquainted with Mr. Black, much better acquainted, in fact, as I confided in him my love of writing."

"Mr. Black? Whom you never speak to?"

"Yes, well that happened later. Upon the night of our engagement, in fact."

"Engagement?" James was entirely forgotten.

"Yes, on the very night he proposed and I accepted, he insulted me by saying I might not write once we were married. I said "Of course I will write. There is no reason for me to quit." And he said, "but you might have children and then where will you find the time? I do not know any married women who write." And I said "Mr. Black, how dare you. I will not speak to you until I have found a publisher and then you will see a married woman can do as she pleases." So, you see Mr. Black became very desirous of finding me a publisher and with his connections to publishing through his family, he has found one after these two years in which I have not spoken to him."

"Does anyone know of your engagement?" said Georgiana.

"No one, for I would not allow it until I had proven myself a writer. Now we are free to tell everyone and I might have announced it to my family tonight, except for your own engagement!" Here, she hugged Georgiana tightly, just as the lady remembered her own promises and the weight they laid upon her heart.

"I am so glad I can now call you sister," Julia sighed and upon these sentiments, Georgiana began to cry and could not be stopped for an hour or more after she began. Julia hurried her friend past Mrs. Gardiner, whose worried look vanished when Julia whispered her friend was engaged to James.

"How wonderful," said Mrs. Gardiner. "Why, I believe I cried a good few days after my own engagement. It is such an emotional time."

When Georgiana finally stopped crying, Julia recommended a good night's rest and they prepared themselves and took to the covers, but neither slept. Julia smiled all the night in consideration of her future – imagining her published book in hand one moment and her wedding day the next. Georgiana heard many happy sighs as she tried to keep her own dreadful thoughts to herself. While some women might have spent the night in talking, Georgiana and Julia could not imagine breaking the spell of one another's thoughts.

Georgiana could not decide which of her two thoughts was more painful. The discovery she loved a man she could not have, or the task she must undertake at earliest convenience to break the heart of another. She considered writing James a letter, but did not wish to disturb Julia and felt it in much better taste to tell him in person.

Why had Phillip brought up their meeting in June? Had he meant to propose then? And what could he mean by mentioning Miss Brill was his cousin? These questions brought hopes to mind that Georgiana could endure least of all. If he loved her, but must marry another, how could either find happiness again? She found thoughts of Phillip overtook her dread of meeting with James and only confirmed what she must do the following morning.

James called before breakfast, looking possibly even happier than the night before. He was well congratulated by Mr. and Mrs. Gardiner and even the children. He was invited to breakfast and Georgiana felt she could barely withstand the meal. It was endured, however and Georgiana was relieved to be invited to a private walk with her intended as soon as it was over.

"How well you look this morning, Miss Darcy," said James, proving his love was blind as Georgiana had not looked worse since her broken elopement to Mr. Wickham.

"Mr. Lawson," she began.

"Please, do call me James," he pressed her hand as they walked.

"I –I fear that I cannot. . ."

"My dear, we will be married, certainly it is fitting for you to call me by my Christian name. With your permission, I might address you Georgiana."

"No. No, I must stop this now. James, Mr. Lawson, I am so dreadfully sorry."

"Please, let it not distress you, you may call me whatever you will, for all you say is as music to me."

Georgiana found herself irritated with the raptures of James" love and the ignorance it produced, but persisted still.

"Mr. Lawson, I must immediately tell you I cannot marry you."

James" face went so quickly from bliss to despair that Georgiana remembered why she had agreed to his proposal and quickly changed her tone.

"I have been so foolish, Mr. Lawson, and I do not know how I might ever gain your forgiveness. I was so surprised by your proposal I did not think straight and in fact, though I greatly admire you and think very highly of you, I have no affection for you."

Here James looked first crushed and then hopeful.

"Miss Darcy, I do not find anything to be lost then, for affection may grow once we have become better acquainted."

"I am sorry, Mr. Lawson, but I fear this is not to be, for in fact my heart belongs entirely to another."

James" took several minutes to consider this statement and finally spoke with angry resignation.

"Then it is finished. I hope you will be happy with him."

He walked away from her, before Georgiana could assure him her love was in vain. She was deflated and exhausted and knew she must immediately remove herself to Pemberley to avoid any accidental meeting with James Lawson.

# VOLUME THREE

NOVEMBER 1813

# CHAPTER 1

ELIZABETH RECEIVED GEORGIANA'S LETTER ALONG WITH ONE from Darcy. She was very relieved to see his penmanship and excused herself from her company to read it privately.

"My Dear,

"I am sorry to have caused you such anxiety at my rapid departure. I am well, but find that my business will keep me from you longer than I had hoped. As mentioned previously, I am not at liberty to share any particulars with you on my endeavors at present. Please trust that I will explain more when it is possible. I cannot give an expectation of my return as yet. You may write me at our London address, though I do not stay there. I will send my man to collect mail on Tuesdays and Thursdays.

"I miss your company constantly, my darling, and I will do everything in my power to return to you quickly.

"Yours, Darcy."

Elizabeth was relieved to hear him well, but found his continued secrecy disquieting. Why could he not stay at their London home and if he did not stay there, where was he? It was equally unsettling to find he had not contacted Georgiana, whom he knew to be in London. Still, she must be content with his continued safety and affection. She must focus her thoughts on the expectation of the Collins" and Miss De Bourgh who would be arriving today. She returned to the breakfast room to share news of Darcy's safety and Georgiana's expected return. Kitty was delighted to have a small party to look forward to and Mr. Bennet agreed to stay for such an event.

The Collins" arrived at three o'clock with their crying baby and a rather sour looking Miss De Bourgh.

"Let me see him!" said Jane, rescuing the howling child from his mother's tired arms. He immediately settled in Jane's comforting embrace.

"Silence at last!" said Miss De Bourgh. "I would not have believed in such a miracle the whole way here."

"I fear it is the colic," said Charlotte, quite beside herself with exhaustion.

"How correct was Lady Catherine in advising us never to remove our child from home in his first year," spoke Mr. Collins philosophically, with his hair in disarray.

"Yet was it not her idea to send you all here with your child?" said Elizabeth.

"Indeed, but only for the most urgent of circumstances," whispered Mr. Collins, eyeing Miss De Bourgh. Miss De Bourgh narrowed her eyes at Mr. Collin's attempt at secrecy and asked to be shown her rooms immediately. Elizabeth was surprised at Miss De Bourgh's change in personality yet again since their last meeting at Rosings, but excused it as anger against her mother and a long journey.

Mrs. Reynolds ushered them all to their quarters and Jane asked permission to attend to the baby while his parents were arranging themselves. Elizabeth joined her sister in the sitting room once her guests were safely out of hearing.

"The poor dear," said Jane. "He is dreadfully tired. He fell asleep so quickly."

"I can only imagine such a voyage with such a traveling party," whispered Elizabeth.

"I wonder what Mr. Collins means about urgent circumstances," said Jane.

"I can only surmise Miss De Bourgh has introduced her mother to Mr. Rathwell," said Elizabeth and then explained the situation as she found it during their visit.

The baby woke soon after, making obvious signs of hunger. His nurse was sent for and Jane let him go regretfully.

"You will make such a fine mother, Jane," said Elizabeth. "Your nurse will have nothing to do but stare out the window with you for her mistress."

"A baby is small for such a short time," said Jane with tears in her eyes. "I would not want to miss any moment of connection with my child in infancy."

"I cannot wait to meet him, or her," said Elizabeth, embracing her sister.

"It is a shame we cannot meet Lydia's son yet. Do you think she will arrive soon?"

"I find it a wonder she is not here already," laughed Elizabeth.

Dinner found their newly arrived guests is much better temper. The baby was safely removed with his nurse and Miss De Bourgh lost some of her peevish expression, but by no means all.

"Were my cousins not told of my arrival?" she complained after the first course.

"Miss Darcy will be returning early from her trip to London in your honour," said Elizabeth.

"What of Mr. Darcy? Was he kept from home on my

account?" Miss De Bourgh eyed Elizabeth as though she were in on Lady Catherine's scheme.

Elizabeth stiffened at this suggestion of her own jealousy. "He left on business before your intentions to visit were known. I have written him of your coming, but have had no word from him yet."

"I should not think my husband would find need to go alone to London so early in marriage," said Miss De Bourgh. Charlotte and Jane both took the opportunity to discuss the weather and Elizabeth was grateful for their presence, though her father wished she would unleash some of her temper on the peevish Miss De Bourgh. Mr. Collins then went on at length of Lady Catherine's miraculous recovery and his own small attentions to her ladyship. To Mr. Bennet's pleasure, Mr. Collin's was interrupted by Miss De Bourgh who asked if there was any form of entertainment to be had in such a home without master or mistress.

"We will have a small dinner party at Miss Darcy's return," said Elizabeth through a clenched jaw. "I will invite a few people from the neighbourhood to join us then, but for now, you may find the walks around Pemberley quite fine, or you may enjoy the use of our phaeton to tour the countryside."

Miss De Bourgh eyed her company and settled on Kitty, who had been quiet throughout dinner, and decided she would do for some form of companionship.

"I would invite your much younger sister to accompany me on a walk after dinner." Miss De Bourgh said regally.

Kitty looked both pleased and frightened by the request, but collected herself enough to assent to the proposition. All were relieved by the decision; though Elizabeth worried Kitty might find her companion more than she could manage.

# CHAPTER 2

One of the advantages of Miss Darcy's wealthy family was being able to come and go from anywhere at her own convenience. Upon sending a letter to Pemberley directly after breaking her engagement to James Lawson, she was able to give explanations to the Gardiners and Miss Lawson and take her leave by the following morning. In true friendship, Julia accepted Georgiana's news with no condemnation and promised her own engagement to Mr. Black would be announced soon as a distraction from James" disappointment. Still, Georgiana felt the weight of regret from all sides and could only begin to breathe again once her carriage was past the great city. Her letter to Elizabeth said only that Georgiana wished to return home quickly to welcome her cousin and the Collins", but she would confess all at her earliest convenience. She could not bear the fact that, at nineteen, she should have already failed twice in love. The only relief to her was that after a sleepless night and tense morning, she fell quickly to sleep along the road.

Mrs. Darcy was very pleased to have her sister-in-law so soon expected. Her father had begun to amuse himself with driving Mr. Collins to great feats. At the smallest suggestion, Mr. Collins was induced to move heavy furniture or adjust the greenery to Mr. Bennet's wishes. Elizabeth was highly embarrassed by her father's sport and recommended fishing to them; however when Mr. Collins returned damp and carrying no fish, she considered her suggestion a bad one. If only Mr. Darcy would return! She had one more brief letter assuring her of his safety, but giving no further instructions of his return.

To rescue Mr. Collins from further humiliation, Elizabeth invited Mr. Wolfe to Pemberley, but this brought about a new form of embarrassment, for though Miss De Bourgh had so recently thought herself in love with Mr. Rathwell, she found something in Mr. Wolfe to inspire her attraction. At dinner, she insisted upon sitting near him and monopolized all his conversation.

"Have you been to Bath, Mr. Wolfe?" she began at one point.

"Yes, only this winter. I meet friends there once a year."

"I thought I had recognized you! My mother, Lady Catherine De Bourgh, insists I visit once a year, for my frail health." She did not receive the attention she expected upon the high rank of her mother. Mr. Wolfe" only nodded and returned to his previous conversation with Elizabeth, but Miss De Bourgh was not deterred.

"I believe you know our friends, the Count and Countess of Sommerfield."

"Only faintly, I fear. They were better acquainted with my late wife."

"They are very amiable people, I assure you."

Kitty watched Miss De Bourgh's attempts with growing irritation. She had meant to draw Mr. Wolfe attention to herself, but could not compete with Miss De Bourgh's important acquaintances. Miss De Bourgh continued in her quest and was finally rewarded when Mr. Wolfe asked her to play for them. Miss De Bourgh was not an accomplished pianist, she explained, due to her ill health since childhood. Instead, she drew him to a corner to speak privately about their common experiences in Bath.

Kitty was quite disappointed and began to pout, but not to be outdone; she considered her own newfound love for the piano. She sat down to play a loud and raucous tune which soon drowned all attempts at discourse. Mr. Wolfe was relieved to move himself out of Miss De Bourgh's proximity and took Elizabeth's side until the music arrived at a more acceptable decibel. Elizabeth suggested the games tables be brought out and was careful to keep her father separated from Mr. Collins, and Mr. Wolfe separated from Miss De Bourgh. That left her at a table with the aforementioned and Kitty and Miss De Bourgh was forced to talk with Jane and Mr. Bennet. Miss De Bourgh quickly tired of this arrangement and stood instead behind Mr. Wolfe, commenting on all of his plays.

"A valiant effort, Mr. Wolfe."

"Played just as I should do in your place!"

"I would not recommend that card, sir."

Elizabeth felt her arrangement a failure and could only look forward to the end of the evening. Mr. Wolfe, however, was not entirely helpless to the wiles of women, and soon removed himself from Miss De Bourgh's attentions politely and forcefully. Miss De Bourgh announced she had a headache and left the group for the remainder of the evening.

All of Elizabeth's guests were visibly relieved by Miss De Bourgh's absence and the rest of the evening passed agreeably. After the first rubber of casino, Elizabeth invited Kitty to take her place at table and was pleased to see Kitty conduct herself prettily in Mr. Wolfe" presence. The party broke up before midnight and Elizabeth saw Mr. Wolfe to the door.

"Thank you very much for your kind invitation, Mrs. Darcy. It does an old widower well to get out on an evening."

"You are hardly old Mr. Wolfe and you are always welcome at Pemberley. It is good to have a friend of my husband's around in his absence."

"Have you heard nothing of his return?"

"I fear not," Elizabeth was wistful.

"I can only say it must be something very important to keep him from such a beautiful wife," Mr. Wolfe also had a wistful expression, but quickly hid it behind a tip of his hat. Elizabeth did not know how to respond. "Goodnight, then, Mrs. Darcy and may the morning bring you all that you wish." Mr. Wolfe left and Elizabeth watched him go for a moment longer than was necessary.

# CHAPTER 3

While the morning did not bring Elizabeth the news she wished for, Jane received word that Mr. Bingley would return on the morrow. She hid her feelings of elation as much as possible from Elizabeth, but Elizabeth put her at ease.

"I can only be thankful of Mr. Bingley's return. I see you will soon need to be in confinement and I am nearly as relieved at his return as I would be of Mr. Darcy's."

Georgiana was expected in the early afternoon and Elizabeth was very pleased to see Mrs. Highmore arrive for tea after breakfast. There was nothing like company to speed up the arrival of a long-awaited one.

"Mrs. Darcy, Mrs. Bingley, I am so pleased to find you both here. I have need of a little company this morning."

Mrs. Highmore's husband was also in London and their two children were causing her grief in his absence. Though she ran a very organized household and employed the best governess in the county, the children missed their father.

"I fear they grow tired of my constant remonstrance," said Mrs. Highmore. "I have always said a child needs his father as much as his mother, though my ideas are not popular in this age. How do you plan to raise your children, Mrs. Bingley?"

Jane's plans to see to her children's every need, especially in infancy, impressed Mrs. Highmore.

"I nursed my own babes," she whispered. "I could not imagine turning them over to a poor nursemaid. I think you will do very well, Mrs. Bingley and I can recommend several nursery maids if you desire. Even the most dedicated mother is required to leave her child once in awhile. You will need your rest in recovery at least."

Jane greatly appreciated Mrs. Highmore's attentions and suggestions. Miss De Bourgh entered the parlour then with a querulous expression.

"Mrs. Darcy, I request you advise me of your visitors in future," said Miss De Bourgh. Mrs. Highmore appraised her with amusement.

"Ah, Miss De Bourgh," Mrs. Highmore rose to take her hand. "I believe I met you as a girl. I am Mrs. Patricia Highmore."

Miss De Bourgh softened and curtseyed in acknowledgement.

"I fear I gave Mrs. Darcy no warning of my visit, but I would love to hear of your mother and Rosings."

Miss De Bourgh was won over by Mrs. Highmore's elegant manners and was delighted to talk at length of her home, though she did not give much more than the absolute minimal information of her mother. She even spoke of her friends the Rathwells, whom she had not mentioned since her arrival.

"Rathwell? I believe I know that name. Does their family have a home in London?"

Miss De Bourgh was overjoyed to discover the Rathwell's home was within a block of the Highmore's and gleaned as much information as possible from Mrs. Highmore. Elizabeth was again stunned by Miss De Bourgh's change of personality and silently praised Mrs. Highmore for her good influence. The visit was over all too soon, but not before Mrs. Highmore invited Miss De Bourgh and Kitty to dine at her home at their earliest convenience.

"Thank you, Mrs. Highmore," said Elizabeth as she saw her to the door. "Your visit has done us all a lot of good."

"I did not wish to speak of Mr. Darcy earlier, but as the wife of a man who is frequently away, I wanted to encourage you, my dear. London holds many temptations, but I assure you that men like our husbands are far above them. The best part of their being away is always their return. You have time to remember all that you love about them in absence and can appreciate them all the better on their return."

"I will remember this, Mrs. Highmore."

"You must call me Patricia, my dear, for we will be close friends, do you not think?"

"Yes, Patricia. I am so pleased to have you so near. Call me Elizabeth also, will you?"

"Thank you Elizabeth. It has been so good to speak to other women and I feel ready to raise my children up to greatness once more."

The two parted in high spirits and Elizabeth felt prepared to face her company and her continued absence from Darcy.

Georgiana arrived at two looking exhausted. After an interrogation by Miss De Bourgh of all the people and fashions of London, Elizabeth insisted Georgiana rest until dinner. After an hour, Elizabeth knocked quietly at Georgiana's door, and was warmly welcomed and soon told of Georgiana's trying ordeal in London. While she mentioned Phillip's engagement to Miss Brill, she did not divulge her feelings toward him. Those she could not admit and she explained only that she could not marry James because she had no affection for him.

"You need not have any shame in my presence for acting so admirably," said Elizabeth. "A woman cannot marry without affection, Georgiana. I am only sorry you had to realize this in so difficult a manner."

Georgiana felt a level of relief from their conversation, but her broken heart was still far from mended. Elizabeth quickly told of their plan for a dinner the following evening, but assured Georgiana this evening's supper would be small and quiet, if only the Collins's and Miss De Bourgh could be borne.

# CHAPTER 4

Mr. Bingley arrived early the next day after driving through the night so he might return to his wife as speedily as possible. Jane was overcome at his return and shed tears of joy. Elizabeth insisted they retire to their rooms and rest until the evening's party. She would send up trays of refreshment throughout the day. Jane and Charles enjoyed their reunion and Elizabeth's thoughtfulness immensely.

Miss Anne De Bourgh monopolized her cousin and in great relief confessed all circumstances involved in her removal to Pemberley as at last she had someone worthy of her confidence. She waited until they were well away from everyone via horseback.

"Georgiana, I am so glad you have finally returned home. I take it you must do all you can to avoid the new mistress of Pemberley."

"On the contrary, cousin, I love Elizabeth and believe she is the best thing to happen to Pemberley in quite some time."

Anne realized she must change her attitude toward Mrs. Darcy immediately.

"I am so pleased you have found her agreeable. A miserable sister-in-law would be such a trial. I, on the other hand, believe I have found a most worthy family in Hunsford."

"Really?" Georgiana was only listening as much as was necessary. She would much rather have been riding alone, but could hardly ignore her cousin on their first day together.

"You may have heard of the Rathwells? I am told they have lodgings near Mrs. Highmore in London."

"I believe the name is familiar."

"Did you hear nothing of them while you were in London?"

"No, I stayed with some of Elizabeth's family, who are not situated near the Highmores."

"How ghastly, but you are a most devoted sister. In any case, I believe they are very well known and fascinating company. I have been in close contact with two of the sisters and Mr. Rathwell since my mother took ill."

"That must have been comforting to you."

"Indeed." Here, Anne took a careful survey of her surroundings to ensure no chance of an eavesdropper. She lowered her voice.

"In fact, I may soon become very intimate with their family."

"I am pleased for you, Anne, but will your mother not miss you terribly?"

Here Anne threw up her hands and her horse startled. It took some effort to calm him, but eventually she could reply.

"You are well acquainted with my Mother, Georgiana. You must know her old fashioned standards of marriage – why she wanted me to marry your brother, for heaven's sake! She has guessed our plans and immediately insisted I come here with those awful Collins"."

"Mrs. Collins is very fine, I think," said Georgiana.

"Oh, you do not know her as I do. Any elegance she once

held has been completely destroyed by that baby and Mr. Collins takes over any civil conversation immediately. This is clear evidence that my mother's taste cannot be trusted."

Anne continued on in her disparaging remarks and Georgiana wondered at her once weak and sickly cousin. She considered love may have given Anne the strength she once lacked.

"I hope your mother will forget her prejudices toward the Rathwells," said Georgiana after Anne's tirade. "If you think so highly of him, I believe he must be worthy."

"Oh, I am so glad you see my way. If only you could meet him, Georgiana! I am sure you would love him and be proud to have him in our family. He is the most agreeable man in the world."

"Then you must marry him, cousin, for love is the only worthy reason for marriage."

"Thank you, Georgiana and I trust I may rely on your assistance in future to overcome my mother."

Anne continued describing Mr. Rathwell and relaying whole conversations they had shared. Georgiana was relieved she was not required to divulge any secrets of her own and could consider her situation in privacy.

To Kitty's delight, the night of the party finally arrived. Elizabeth had done her best to make sure there were equal numbers of men and women so no one would be left without a dance partner. Aside from the six women and three men who were staying at Pemberley, Elizabeth invited Mr. Wolfe, Mr. and Mrs. Spencer, Mr. and Mrs. Highmore and Colonel Fitzwilliam, who happened to be staying with Mr. Wolfe. That left one woman without a partner, but as Jane was not likely to dance much, she hoped the other women would not be neglected.

Elizabeth was pleased to have a new dress made for Kitty, who looked very well. Elizabeth felt Kitty had begun to take on Jane's appearance as she grew older and wondered how she had not seen it before. Jane had always been thought the fairest and so now Kitty must grow in admiration. Her manners were much more what they ought, since Lydia had left to marry Wickham, and Elizabeth hoped her younger sister would continue to acquire elegance. Georgiana also looked lovely, though Elizabeth noted Georgiana's face was drawn and pale. Elizabeth hoped being at Pemberley would restore Georgiana's spirits and return her to health and hope. Miss De Bourgh wore a very stylish dress, but it did little to improve her insignificant features combined with a thin and small figure. She would have to draw attention through conversation, which had taken a turn of improvement since Georgiana returned.

Elizabeth had wanted her sister to be guest of honour, but in deference to Miss De Bourgh, she had both girls assist her in greeting the guests. Kitty had little to say, but beamed with pleasure. Miss De Bourgh greeted all with an air of superiority not unlike her mother's. Only Mrs. Highmore and Mr. Wolfe received her warm welcome. Finally, all were assembled to dine and Elizabeth felt some satisfaction in her seating arrangements. Kitty and Miss De Bourgh were placed as far away from one another as possible. Kitty sat between Mr. Collins and Mr. Wolfe while Miss De Bourgh must content herself between her cousin Colonel Fitzwilliam and Mrs. Highmore. Elizabeth's only disappointment was her choice in sitting to Mr. Wolfe's other side. He chose to direct his comments chiefly her way and Kitty's attempts at conversation were politely answered, but hardly encouraged. Elizabeth did her utmost to remedy the situation, but found she had little to say about her sister that could interest a man such as Mr.

Wolfe and found herself drawn into his interesting dialogue.

"Tell me, Mrs. Darcy, what sort of place is your Longbourn?"

"I am certain Kitty could describe it better, for she was there more recently. Kitty?"

"It is a rather dull place, I fear. Not many young people for miles – just farmers and landowners." Elizabeth felt her sister's lack of effort in answering. There was only so much she could do!

"Mrs. Darcy, certainly there is something of your home which you miss?"

"Oh, of course! Pemberley is so artfully done, but I miss the wildness of the wood near Longbourn. The tangle of brambles beside the lane, the change of colours in autumn is more pronounced, I believe, than it is here, and the wildflowers are so plentiful in springtime. It is nothing I think anyone else might notice, until perhaps they were made to leave it a year."

"Home is always sweeter once one has left it. Tell me, what sorts of games did you enjoy with all of your sisters?"

How could anyone ignore such enjoyable topics? Elizabeth nearly forgot her absent husband in Mr. Wolfe's presence. She only wondered at his attentions when he asked the favour of a dance. Could she dance with a man who was not a relation when her husband was not present? He realized her apprehension and silenced it immediately.

"I am certain I would not have minded Darcy dancing with my wife should she be with us still. There can be no harm with your father present."

Elizabeth agreed to the arrangement and tried to ignore a whisper of guilt. Dancing began shortly after and Elizabeth began with her father. To her relief, Mr. Wolfe asked Kitty, and Colonel Fitzwilliam asked Miss De Bourgh. All husbands and wives were matched, leaving Georgiana to sit out. She suggested playing the first few dances and Elizabeth felt the arrangement could hardly be better with one less man. Elizabeth was pleased to see many smiling faces at her party and especially Kitty's. Only briefly did she regret Mr. Darcy's absence. Elizabeth took over the piano after the first two dances.

As the evening continued, Elizabeth realized Colonel Fitzwilliam's preference for her younger sister. While this had not been her intention, she considered his good manners and kindnesses to herself in previous times. Though he was not a man of fortune, he could certainly provide a small living for a wife. It was during these thoughts that Mr. Wolfe approached her to dance and she obliged him again.

"I have been observing your family this evening," he began. "Am I correct in supposing you were your father's favourite?"

"I would not say so," said Elizabeth.

"Ah, no, that would not be proper, but it is obvious. He delights in your comments and smiles whenever he sees you. He must miss your presence at Longbourn."

"We have always got on well, but I only saw this as fair considering my mother's disdain for me."

"I cannot believe that to be true," said Mr. Wolfe with a laugh.

"I caused her much disappointment when I rejected Mr. Collins" proposal of marriage," whispered Elizabeth.

"Great heavens! Your mother must be a fool to find disappointment in that. She must have checked herself when instead you found Mr. Darcy's favour."

"I believe she chose to forget her prior opinions."

The dance ended too soon and Elizabeth found herself laughing and enjoying herself much more than she had expected. Elizabeth sat out the next dance and was approached by Kitty in privacy.

"Thank you Lizzy for this lovely party."

"I am so happy you are enjoying yourself."

"You did not tell me what a gentleman Colonel Fitzwilliam is. He tells the most delightful stories." Kitty beamed.

"I must have forgotten."

"I had thought Mr. Wolfe the handsomest man at the party, but now that I see he is in love with you, I realize Colonel Fitzwilliam is much more to my taste." The Colonel approached at that moment to ask Kitty to dance and Elizabeth was left to consider her sister's statement alone.

# CHAPTER 5

THE PARTY WAS OVER TOO SOON FOR SOME AND AT LONG LAST for others. Elizabeth excused herself from any further dancing by complaining of fatigue. She had the opportunity then of watching Mr. Wolfe and realized his frequent attentions to herself. She tried to dissuade him, but had difficulty doing so without appearing rude. She sat with Jane in an effort to keep from being alone with him. If only Darcy could return. She sunk exhausted to her bed and wept silently with shame and loneliness.

Mr. and Mrs. Bingley left the following morning despite Elizabeth's insistence they stay longer.

"I do not want to wait longer sister, for I wish to make preparations for our child. I am sorry to leave you alone before Mr. Darcy returns, but certainly you have enough houseguests at present to keep you company."

Jane kissed Elizabeth and left in anticipation of coming changes. The post arrived shortly after with news to lift Elizabeth's sunken spirits.

"Dearest Elizabeth,

"I thank you for your patience, Lizzy. I am finally freed of my obligations and will return to you quickly. I fear you may regret my return however when you hear all I must tell you, but I must beg your continuing forbearance as there are changes at hand. I would request an hour's private conference with you directly upon my return. Assure the others I am in great desire of speaking with them, but there are things you and I must discuss immediately.

"I can say no more, but please know I love you always.

"Yours ever,
F. Darcy"

Elizabeth only saw he was returning and just in time. No news he brought could be as bad as being left without him. She was fortified to face the day with calmness and strength.

MR. WOLFE SENT word to propose a picnic at his home the following afternoon. Kitty was overjoyed and Mr. Bennet only commented he would enjoy some air. He found Colonel Fitzwilliam all that could be desired in a man without fortune. Mr. Wolfe was also a man of sense and after too many days in Mr. Collins" company, such men were very agreeable to him. Mr. Bennet, however, gave notice he would leave the day after Mr. Darcy returned.

"I have been too long from home, Lizzy, and I fear your mother may have gone completely mad in my absence. Kitty may stay as long as she is welcome or until her mother sends for her."

Kitty did not mention the letters she had already received from Mary asking after her return.

It was a lovely warm day for a picnic and though Elizabeth dreaded being in Mr. Wolfe" presence again, she planned to keep herself from any private moments with him and hoped the activity would hurry the return of her husband.

Elizabeth insisted Kitty and Miss De Bourgh travel in Mr. Wolfe" carriage with Colonel Fitzwilliam, while she rode with Georgiana and her father and left Mr. and Mrs. Collins to take the phaeton alone.

"If only my brother were here to join us," said Georgiana with a sigh. "You must miss him even more than I, Elizabeth."

"It is good for a man of his age and distinction to travel often to London, Lizzy," said her father. "You may have to get used to life without him by times, but he will never stay away too long, mark my words. You have found yourself a very worthy husband."

"Thank you father," said Elizabeth, who wished for nothing better than to keep talk of her husband going throughout the picnic. "Georgiana, how does Darcy prefer to be welcomed when he returns home from London?"

Georgiana took some pleasure in being thought an expert.

"I always prepared a new piece for his arrival. He liked to see what I had accomplished in his absence, but I should think he would only wish to see your face when he returns." Georgiana smiled in admiration of her sister.

"Perhaps we could practice the duet we were learning this summer," said Elizabeth and they continued in plans and preparations for Darcy's return the rest of the way to Mr. Wolfe's estate.

Chesterley was not as tall as Pemberley, but handsome and strong. The approach led through a fruit orchard on one side and a sparkling stream on the other. A well placed lawn sat directly before the house and it was friendly and welcoming. Mr. Wolfe led them on a tour through the house before the picnic. It was very recently decorated and carried treasures from his travels around Europe.

"I should be gone again soon, but have decided to delay my trip until after Christmas," he said, while pointing out Italian artwork and a German checkerboard. Despite her attempts to keep her distance from Mr. Wolfe, his efforts placed him directly beside her when they reached the piano.

"Please, Mrs. Darcy, will you play us that delightful tune from last night? I cannot seem to get it from my head."

Elizabeth obliged, but soon found herself alone with Mr. Wolfe as the rest continued exploring the house, yet she could hardly stop the song before it was over.

"Even more lovely than I remembered," said Mr. Wolfe when she finished.

"We should hurry to catch the rest," said Elizabeth, bustling out of her seat and thus, further from Mr. Wolfe.

"You know, my wife was an enchanting pianist." Mr. Wolfe pointed to a painting on the north wall of a young and elegant girl. Elizabeth felt she could hardly leave him after such a statement.

"You must miss her a great deal."

"I rarely come into this room. I cannot face that portrait for long."

"I am certain she would not wish you to remain melancholy." Elizabeth attempted to cheer him while drawing him away from the room and toward the others.

"Oh, I have tried to move on from her memory, but there has been no one to take her place in my affections, until. . ." He stopped there and looked, embarrassed, at his feet. Elizabeth refused to pursue his line of thinking.

"Perhaps we should move on with the rest." Mr. Wolfe took her elbow and walked with her. Elizabeth felt her breathing quicken, but could not pull herself from his touch, nor could she quicken the slow pace he set. She was in agony of her situation and could find no words to break the spell of their too intimate connection, when Kitty came rushing toward them.

"Lizzy, you must see the sun room! It is extraordinary. Oh!" She stopped short and looked confused at the sight of her sister so close to Mr. Wolfe. Elizabeth could not look at anything but the floor. Fortunately, she had reason to disengage from Mr. Wolfe" arm and she followed her sister to the aforementioned room.

"Lizzy, what are you doing with Mr. Wolfe? It is most unlike you." Kitty whispered. "Do you wish to show your husband a lesson on his return?" She smiled hopefully.

"No, of course not Kitty. He was only speaking to me of his late wife. I felt I could not leave him alone to consider her." Elizabeth was nervous and tired. She felt completely unsure of her own statements.

"It is tragic, but it has been several years now, has it not? He has plenty to offer another wife. Of his *own*."

"Kitty, I am certain you are mistaken. Mr. Wolfe is a great friend of my husband's." However, Elizabeth was far from certain.

"And you were a great friend of Charlotte's, but that did not stop her from stealing Mr. Collins the moment you refused him."

"I can only consider that a blessing," said Elizabeth before she could stop herself.

Kitty giggled and whispered to her sister. "Well, if you are so sure of yourself, perhaps you could tell me whether Colonel Fitzwilliam fancies me at all?"

"I believe I have noticed an appreciation on his side. Did you enjoy your drive here?" Elizabeth was relieved to have the subject changed.

"It was most pleasant and I think father approves – look they are talking together now!" Miss De Bourgh joined Kitty and Elizabeth so all previous subjects must be dropped and turned to the scenery and weather.

"It certainly is not as grand as Pemberley," said Miss De Bourgh with an attempt to diminish her surroundings, but her heart was not longer into belittling everyone and everything around her. "I received a letter from my good friend, Miss Rathwell, this morning – you remember her kindness and good manners, Elizabeth."

Elizabeth remembered no such thing about the lady, but gave a small nod in agreement.

"Her family is planning a ball within a fortnight and requests the pleasure of my attendance."

"How exciting," said Kitty.

"Of course, it would cut short my visit here, but I wondered if you might be able to do without me a little sooner."

Elizabeth tried not to appear too eager. "Of course, Anne, it would cause us some remorse to say good bye to you sooner than we expected, but we could not keep you from such an enjoyable event."

"I should also wish to ask Mr. Darcy, to be assured of his blessing and I might ask Georgiana to accompany me back to Rosings, I would not like to cut short the Collins" visit at Pemberley."

Elizabeth caught the end of Mr. Collins" ravings of Chesterley at that moment, with his steady reassurance that it was nearly as pleasing as Rosings and tried not to smile at Anne's obvious attempt to break free of her unwelcome chaperones.

"It is very kind of you to consider them, Anne, but I think you had better consult them yourself on the subject and send word of your change of plans to your mother."

Anne was disappointed by Elizabeth's words, but brushed off her duties with a wave of her hand.

"I will tell my mother when she needs to know. Perhaps you could speak to the Collins" for me." With that, she went in search of Georgiana to invite her to the ball.

"I hope you are not disappointed she left you out, Kitty."

"Heavens no, sister! I should not wish to go with her for the world, though with Georgiana's company, it might be bearable."

"We shall get you your own ball for Christmas, Kitty. And perhaps that will allow Georgiana to return quickly as well."

The tour finally turned outdoors where they walked a way towards a meadow where a bountiful picnic was spread for them.

"There is nothing like fresh air to improve one's appetite," said Mr. Collins after a solemn grace said over the meal with many mentions of Lady Catherine and her continued recovery. Elizabeth sat near them and told the Collins" of Miss De Bourgh's plan for an early return to Rosings. Mr. Collins looked very grave.

"I can safely say her mother would heartily disapprove of this invitation. You may have guessed, cousin, this is the family Lady Catherine was most desirous of keeping her daughter from."

"I do not see how we might keep her from leaving," said Elizabeth.

"You must speak to your husband of the matter directly upon his return." Mr. Collins advised.

"I will, but I do not see him especially interested in carrying out the wishes of his aunt."

"You do not see things, perhaps, in the same light as he, dear cousin. A female mind is easily led astray." Here Charlotte coughed and Elizabeth hid a smile in her tea. "I will write to Lady Catherine the moment we return to Pemberley, to make her aware of all that has passed."

Elizabeth left the subject and turned her attention toward

Mrs. Collins and talked of her knowledge of home and Baby William.

When the picnic was over, Mr. Wolfe stood to address his guests.

"I thought perhaps we might continue our outing with a surprise." He gestured to a small group who came forward carrying instruments. "I have hired musicians to play for us and I hoped we might enjoy a small outdoor dance."

A murmur of delight went through the party and the young ladies, especially, were overjoyed with the suggestion. Mr. Wolfe then turned to Elizabeth and held his hand to her with a look of such happiness she could hardly refuse. They led off the dancing and Mr. Wolfe began to speak to her in earnest.

"I understand Mr. Darcy returns tomorrow," he said.

"Yes, I am most anxious of his return," Elizabeth stressed.

"Of course, it is only right for a new wife to think this way; however, I wonder if you will feel the same in a couple of year's time. The constant demands of London can be a strain on any marriage."

Elizabeth was alarmed by Mr. Wolfe's increasing familiarity and boldness in her company. She must put him in place but felt weakened by the fatigues of constant houseguests and anxiety over her husband's whereabouts. Mr. Wolfe's continued;

"I said previously your husband might be secretly in London to obtain a precious gift for you and I pray it may be so, but I fear you may not be aware of the temptations of London."

"Mr. Wolfe, I.. ."

Mr. Wolfe continued in earnest. "I say this for your own protection, Mrs. Darcy. I know you come from a quiet and innocent country life and do not wish you to be surprised by the ways of our world."

"Mr. Wolfe. You have called yourself a close friend of my husband's and if you know him as well as you proclaim, you will know he is above any suspicion. I have the utmost faith in his actions when I am not present and must insist you quit this mode of conversation."

"Forgive me, Mrs. Darcy, I have no desire to upset you in any way. Only allow me one more word on the subject. If you ever need any assistance in obtaining a separation from your husband, please do not hesitate to approach me." The dance ended here and Elizabeth was never so grateful for a final note. She extricated herself from Mr. Wolfe and left the party immediately. She told only Georgiana that she must leave and would meet them all back at Pemberley. She complained of fatigue and Georgiana gave a small smile in hopes of what that fatigue might mean. Elizabeth ran to the phaeton and urged the driver to rush her home.

# CHAPTER 6

ELIZABETH WAS IN AN AWFUL STATE OF AGITATION ON THE road back to Pemberley. To have anyone suggest her husband was untrustworthy was an absolute insult – but from such a close friend as Mr. Wolfe it was injurious! If he had been merely an acquaintance of Miss De Bourgh's or a visitor from London, she could easily have put him in place and ignored any mention of fault in her dear husband, but Mr. Wolfe had known Darcy since childhood, while Elizabeth had known him less than two years and only very well in the last year. Perhaps if he had not been away for so long and under such strange circumstances, she might have been more in control of her senses. However, in her state of mind and situation, she could not easily ignore Mr. Wolfe's warning, even if Kitty suspected him of improper affection.

It was in this confusion of thoughts and beliefs that Elizabeth recognized her husband's carriage on her approach to Pemberley. Her spirits lifted and relief washed through her until, on closer inspection, she made out the form of a woman and baby entering the house with Darcy's hand upon the child's head. Her hopes fell while her agitation returned. She urged the driver on, but the horse was fatigued and Elizabeth continued the next quarter of an hour in agony.

At last she arrived and found Darcy immediately before her.

"Elizabeth, my love! I am so pleased to find you at home alone. You must have sensed my early arrival."

Elizabeth could hardly contain her emotions, but for a strong underlying belief in Darcy's honour. With great effort did she reply;

"Darcy, I am very surprised to find you here. Please, please tell me all that has passed since I saw you last."

Darcy was affected by Elizabeth's restraint at his return and realized his secrecy had injured his wife more than he knew.

"We best remove to a private room. When do you expect the return of our guests?"

"At least an hour," said Elizabeth.

"That will be time enough. Come." They left for their rooms and Darcy was finally at liberty to reveal all he had hidden from Elizabeth.

"I will begin by telling you, Lizzy, that I have another sister who is not known to many as part of our family."

Elizabeth's face filled with confusion and Darcy continued.

"Her name was Olivia and she was firstborn to my mother, but with tragic results. She was not well in body or mind and my mother, being somewhat alike her sister in prejudice and temperament did not wish to have the Darcy name sullied by an imperfect child. She told her friends the baby died at birth and had the child taken to a home in London."

"Did your father know?" Elizabeth was in awe at what she was hearing and found it changed her previous notions of Lady Anne Darcy entirely.

"Yes, as did some of the servants who helped my mother in keeping her secret."

Elizabeth marveled at what could be hidden by money and power. "How did you come to know of this secret?"

"My father told me when I was eighteen, but he was not able to tell Georgiana before he died."

"Is she still unaware of her sister?" Elizabeth felt all the tragedy this must mean for Georgiana.

"Yes, my father wished it be held from her until she also was of age." Darcy looked at his bride, seeking her acceptance.

"We must tell her immediately. It is not right I should know and not she."

This sentiment pleased Darcy. "I feel the same, however there is more."

"I saw you arrive with a woman and child. Who are they?"

"The child belongs to my sister Olivia." Here, anger marked his handsome features. "She was taken advantage of in the home she was placed and gave birth to him a month ago, which is why I went to London in such haste."

"Is the women, then, Olivia?" Elizabeth was hopeful.

"No, I fear she died in childbirth. The woman is a nurse, Mrs. Carter; I have hired to care for the child. Elizabeth, the child is now ours. In London, I made sure his father could never have claim to him. We are his only other kin and I could not leave him to be cared for by strangers."

"Of course not. Oh Darcy, if only you knew what I was thinking when you arrived!" Elizabeth flushed in shame at what she had considered only moments ago.

"What my dear?" Darcy looked so forlorn that Elizabeth at last embraced him as she should have upon his arrival.

"I will tell you later, Darcy, but now, I must see our child. Our son. What have you called him?"

"I waited to consult you, but I have been considering Henry. I have always been fond of that name."

"Henry it shall be and Fitzwilliam his second name after yourself. Quickly, Darcy, show me our son."

Darcy was overjoyed at Elizabeth's quick approval of this baby and her desire to have him as her son. He could not have hoped for better and upon seeing Elizabeth take the babe in her arms, her eyes filling with tears, he felt he had become a father and she a mother. Henry was perfectly formed and his brow held something of the Darcy appearance.

"My dear, you know this means he shall be considered the first son and inheritor of all the Darcy estate," said Darcy.

"Of course. It is his right. I would not wish it any other way," she kissed the sleeping child tenderly.

AN HOUR LATER, the guests arrived in good spirits. Elizabeth was relieved to see Mr. Wolfe had stayed behind while Colonel Fitzwilliam joined the party. Darcy and Elizabeth had discussed what should be told to them and decided an amount of truth was necessary without mention of the circumstances of Baby Henry's conception. However, Georgiana must first be told everything. Elizabeth attended her guests while Darcy and Georgiana met privately. After some hours, all in the house were told a portion of the past and present and all were given an opportunity to see the new child. Only Anne seemed to disapprove of this turn of events, but she had never been fond of babies and could not dampen the spirits of those around her.

After a lively dinner and visiting afterward, Elizabeth and

Darcy finally turned toward bed. They stopped in to peek at baby Henry and could not leave off watching him for some time. When they finally arrived at their own rooms, Elizabeth decided to leave discussion of Mr. Wolfe for tomorrow.

# CHAPTER 7

THE FOLLOWING MORNING WAS AS BRIGHT AND SUNNY AS THE moods of the inhabitants at Pemberley. Only Elizabeth felt a sense of dread at the sunlight streaming through her window when she remembered what she must tell her husband. When he woke, she sat with him to tell what had happened in his absence. When she had told all that passed between her and Mr. Wolfe, she said;

"I confess I began to doubt you, my dearest. I cannot say what convinced me most, but your unexplained absence weighed upon my mind."

Darcy's face was dark with anger.

"You must apologize for nothing, Elizabeth. You have been badly used and I myself am not completely blameless."

Elizabeth felt a whisper of coldness at this statement.

"What blame can you have in this, Darcy?"

"I should have told you of my sister Olivia sooner. I feared you would find me unfit to father if our children might be born deformed. I worried you might think my parents inhuman for sending off their own child to save their reputation."

"It might have helped," said Elizabeth gently. "Yet, you could hardly foresee her condition or the turn of events in her death. It had long been a secret in your family and it was habit for you to keep it hidden." She reached for Darcy's hand, but he would not take hers.

"There is more. I recognized Wolfe's affection for you at the ball. I had not seen him take interest in any woman since his wife's death until I saw him dance with you. I should have warned you."

"You could not have known he would act on such feelings."

"I could have, for his wife had once been dear to me." Here, Darcy became very uncomfortable and could not look at Elizabeth. Elizabeth was unsettled by the confession.

"I knew her before I met you. If fact, she married Wolfe before I met you. It was all very long ago." Darcy turned his back to Elizabeth and stared out of the window.

Elizabeth watched him nervously. "You never told me. Do you hold other secrets from me?" Darcy turned to her and took her hand in his. His voice returned to softness and he regretted ever leaving her.

"I may, Elizabeth, yet I do not now realize any. We have only just begun our marriage and have much yet to discover of one another. I hope you can trust me when I say I have far more affection and love for you than I have for any other creature in the world and I should do everything to keep and deserve your love for me."

They remained close for several minutes while Elizabeth considered all she now knew. Finally she asked;

"Did Mrs. Wolfe not return your affection?"

"I believe she did, but Wolfe was determined to have her. I think he had always been jealous of me at school and felt it a great victory to win her."

"He spoke of you with such praise, I thought him trustworthy."

"I am sorry he has deceived you. I will ensure he will not cause you any more distress. I shall visit him this morning to discuss his imprudence and insist he begin his tour of Europe as soon as possible."

Darcy left after breakfast to fulfill his goal and Elizabeth could finally relax and return to her new son.

GEORGIANA RECEIVED a letter from Julia after breakfast, which she took to her room and read in privacy. She wondered what she would write to Julia of all that had occurred since her brother's return. That she was now Aunt Georgiana caused her much pleasure, but that she had a true sister she could never meet was agony. She had wished for such a sister many times in her life. What was her appearance and how affected was her mind? She needed time to consider all this, but she put her thoughts aside to read the rather long epistle from her close friend.

"October 20
"London

"DEAREST GEORGIANA;

How are you, my friend? I have worried over you since you left in such low spirits. I wished to write sooner, but our home has been in such a state of business. Mr. David Black and I have announced our engagement and after some initial surprise at the length of our unspoken arrangement, my mother and father have found him a most deserving man of considerable wealth. He has purchased a home in London and has come into his share of the publishing business at his recent twenty-first birthday.

"We shall have to delay our wedding in deferment to my brother, Phillip, who has set his date of marriage to Miss Brill for December seventeenth. They will be married at Sunnings and so we shall return within a fortnight to prepare for the occasion. I am very anxious to see you again to determine your state of health and mind. To ease you, I hope, I will tell you James is carrying on. He has quite poured himself into studies at present, but he joins us for dinner or the theatre when he can. I hope you will not imagine him worse than he is. He will certainly heal in time.

"In other news, I have seen the first copy of my book of poetry! It is just a mock-up, but to see it printed and bound gave me such a thrill! The first copies are set to be sold in the New Year. I hope you will not mind a belated Christmas gift from me! I have not had as much time for writing poetry since your departure, but I am determined to keep it up to prove a married woman may write as well as a single one. I have even put off a walk with David to allow me an extra hour for my craft. He was rather vexed, but I insisted upon it!"

The letter went on to give details of her engagement and the parties, plays and operas they had attended. Georgiana found little comfort in Julia's insistence that James was carrying on without her, but that was little in comparison to the darkness she felt at Phillip's set date of marriage. It was now confirmed and she must give up all hopes of him. This was more difficult to bear than any guilt she had over the pain she caused his youngest brother. While she looked forward to Julia's return, she found the thought of Phillip's return made her wish they had planned for a London wedding. When Georgiana looked at the dates again, she realized she would be gone to Rosings with Anne when Julia returned, so she could put off seeing Phillip again a little longer. She wrote back to Julia, telling her of the ball as well as all the surprise and joy of finding a new nephew and the heartache at losing a sister she would never know.

# CHAPTER 8

After spending several hours with Baby Henry, Elizabeth turned to her writing desk to write first her mother and then her sisters about the addition of Baby Henry to their lives. She thought, but did not write, of how much she had been hoping for a child, without being able to speak of it to anyone. Now, she was even more impatient for the arrival of Jane's child. She realized why Charlotte could not stop speaking of her baby and wished for her sister to share in the joys and anxieties motherhood brought. Elizabeth quietly mourned the loss of Henry's mother and wondered when they would tell him of his circumstances. She hoped he would learn to be noble and good like Darcy rather than a rascal like his natural father. All these things lay heavy upon her as she attempted to sound light and cheerful in her letters.

Elizabeth's father would leave Pemberley after noon and carry the letter to her mother. He was quite delighted with the boy and was happy to sit with Elizabeth and speak in hushed tones while she held him. He looked forward to playing with his grandson when he grew older and hoped to live long enough to teach Henry to be a gentleman. The boy which had eluded him and Mrs. Bennet so long was now arrived to his daughter in the most unusual of circumstances, but he would not complain of such a grandson. He only hoped his wife would have the same sense.

"You must bring him to Longbourn soon, Lizzy," said Mr. Bennet. "Your mother will want to meet him."

"I will try my best, father, but why do you not bring mother here at Christmas?"

"You ask a very great thing, Lizzy, on my account and your husband's. Do you think he should like his mother-in-law nosing about and getting into all his business? And how should I bear her constant silliness the whole trip here without my study as escape? No Lizzy, I fear your mother will not see Baby Henry until he is brought directly to her. I, on the other hand, will likely see him at least once more before the new year."

Elizabeth was surprised by her father's attachment to Pemberley, but also pleased. A grand-father such as Mr. Bennet would be a blessing to his grandchildren.

Mr. Bennet left shortly after this conversation for Longbourn. "Your mother will want me now, Lizzy, if for no other reason than to parade her nervous condition during my leave. Thank you for your kindness, my dear. I have found you as happily settled as even I could desire." He kissed her goodbye and shook Mr. Darcy's hand, who had returned quickly after his meeting with Mr. Wolfe. Darcy brought Colonel Fitzwilliam with him when it was decided that Mr. Wolfe should leave immediately for his European tour.

An invitation for dinner from Mrs. Highmore inviting

Kitty, Georgiana and Anne left the Darcy's with only Colonel Fitzwilliam and Mr. and Mrs. Collins to entertain. Darcy was pleased by the opportunity of a small family dinner and a chance to speak to his cousin after a lengthy separation. Only Mr. Collins" constant expressions of gratitude and grandeur regarding Pemberley and its comparison to Rosings were left to cause irritation. Colonel Fitzwilliam told them of his good fortune in the past year and his plan to take a house in the near vicinity at Christmas. Darcy and Elizabeth insisted the Colonel stay with them until his home could be procured, much to the secret delight of Elizabeth, who hoped her sister might benefit from the arrangement.

Elizabeth had time to mention her plan for a Christmas ball and gained her husband's approval instantly. Now that there had been one ball at Pemberley, more could only be expected.

MRS. HIGHMORE'S home at Parkington was filled with the laughter of young ladies. She saw immediately the timidity of Kitty, haughtiness of Anne and secret sorrow of Georgiana, and sought to do away with it all. She regaled them with stories of her youth and had her two children perform a short play to entertain them. Patti was her eldest and Nathan her youngest and they were very comfortable performing for company. Patti was twelve and very tall with blond hair and pale blue eyes. She was a skilled seamstress, like her mother, and had created clown costumes for her brother and herself. Nathan was a reserved boy with dark hair and eyes who, nonetheless, was very fond of making and telling puns. They put on a delightful circus which made their audience laugh. Kitty lost her shyness, Georgiana's sorrow was briefly forgotten, and even Anne was charmed by the children.

"If only my mother could see children like yours. She always had me banished from company after I presented myself with a curtsey. She was firm that children be seen and not heard."

Mrs. Highmore greatly disapproved of such notions, but did not wish to offend her guest's family in any way.

"It was a popular notion not long ago, but I think such ideas have been changing in recent years. Mr. Highmore and I find our children have much to say which is enjoyable and even enlightening."

The children changed from their costumes and joined the company for dinner. They were both very polite and lost most of their bravado once the show was finished. They smiled, but said little during the delicious dinner and then they were excused. Mrs. Highmore showed her guests to a cozy drawing room and asked if they would prefer cards or a game. Only Anne would answer and it was decided the card table should be set up. Before Mrs. Highmore could deal, however, Anne began a lengthy discussion of her favourite topic – the upcoming ball at the Rathwell's.

"Mrs. Highmore, might I speak to you of my friends, the Rathwells?"

"Of course, my dear. They seem a very lively family."

"Indeed, such a change from my own reserved household. Perhaps Elizabeth informed you of their upcoming ball which Georgiana and I will soon be attending?"

"I believe she mentioned it."

"What style of dress might you suggest for a winter ball?"

Mrs. Highmore went to her collection of magazines and began showing Anne several designs and styles. While Mrs. Highmore and Anne studied the dresses, Georgiana and Kitty moved to the piano and worked at some duets which were left there. They had not been given much time to become acquainted and found they thoroughly enjoyed playing together. Kitty was not as accomplished as Georgiana, but Georgiana did not mind playing simpler pieces and giving an occasional suggestion for Kitty's improvement. Kitty was an eager learner and fond of lively dance pieces.

"I am sorry you will not be joining us at Rosings," Georgiana whispered between pieces.

"I should be dreadfully afraid of being in Lady Catherine's house," shivered Kitty.

"Perhaps you could arrange to stay with the Collins'?" Georgiana said.

"Oh, pray do not suggest such a thing!" Kitty cried. "How should I put up with Mr. Collins day after day with no one to silence him? Mrs. Collins is kind enough, but she only dotes on her baby and what would I be left to do?"

Georgiana laughed softly. "No, no. I should not wish you such a fate, I only think of myself, I suppose. How should I survive my time at Rosings? I can imagine my aunt's mood when she learns of our intent to attend the Rathwell's ball. I think Anne only brings me as a shield against her mother."

Kitty giggled and they returned to their playing to avoid being overheard.

While Mrs. Highmore and Anne looked over dress patterns, Anne sought Mrs. Highmore's opinion on other subjects such as jewels, hair designs, etiquette and finally the subject she was really concerned with.

"Mrs. Highmore," she whispered when Kitty and Georgiana began to play again. "May I confess something to you?"

"Of course, my dear."

"I believe Mr. Rathwell seeks my hand at this ball." Anne watched Mrs. Highmore's face closely to catch her approval of so great a secret.

"How lovely for you." Mrs. Highmore's face showed true pleasure.

"Indeed; however, my mother will be a rather large

impediment to such a union and I wondered how you felt about elopement?" Anne's voice dropped with barely concealed intrigue.

"Ah, dear Anne, I cannot endorse such ideas."

"But if it were the only way?" Anne became immediately defensive, which Mrs. Highmore saw and tried to soothe with gentleness of voice.

"It is never the only way, my dear. As overpowering as mothers can be, a lady must do everything in her power not to lose her mother."

"A mother like yourself would indeed be a pity to lose, but you do not know Lady Catherine." Anne flung a magazine away in disgust.

"Ah, but I do." Mrs. Highmore retrieved the magazine and smoothed it back into order. "I knew her as a younger woman when she would visit Pemberley, perhaps you remember?"

"I had forgotten, however you cannot know her as I do."

"Of course, yet I believe even she might be made to see the benefit of such a union. You may find she fears losing you even more than she fears gaining Mr. Rathwell." Anne turned to Mrs. Highmore with interest.

"What would you suggest, Mrs. Highmore?"

"You may call me Patricia, dear. I insist upon it when discussing matters of the heart." Her face was warm and kind.

"Thank you, Patricia, and you must call me Anne." Anne said eagerly.

"Thank you, Anne. Do you have an aversion to a long engagement?" Anne's face answered the question. "Very well, then you must make your marriage appear to be her idea. From what I understand of your mother, she is very fond of being in control of all her concerns." Mrs. Highmore explained her idea in full and Anne's face took on more happiness than had ever been seen in Derbyshire. Kitty and Georgiana continued their enjoyment at the piano and the evening was marked by Mrs. Highmore as a great success.

# CHAPTER 9

THE TIME PASSED UNTIL GEORGIANA AND ANNE'S DEPARTURE with trepidation by the former and great impatience by the latter. Elizabeth and Darcy grew in love for their son and for each other. Lady Catherine wrote insisting the Collins" accompany her daughter back to Hunsford, and Kitty was delighted to spend some of each day in the company of Colonel Fitzwilliam. Jane and Mrs. Bennet sent letters expressing their happiness over Baby Henry's arrival, though Jane's letter was considerably longer and more sincere. She regretted not being able to travel in her condition, but looked forward to meeting him as soon as possible. Baby Henry had caught cold and could not travel until he was well again. Elizabeth was distressed over her child's first illness, but Mrs. Carter, his nurse, assured Elizabeth the cold would pass shortly and did not cause him much discomfort.

The Collins", with their baby and the two young ladies, departed after an early breakfast on a clear morning in November and Elizabeth could only regret the loss of Georgiana. She was quite glad to be rid of Mr. Collins" constant prattle, and though she would miss her friend Charlotte, she admitted to herself they were no longer as close as they had once been. Elizabeth planned to devote herself to her ill son for the remainder of the morning while Kitty and Colonel Fitzwilliam walked in the country and Darcy saw to his many tenants.

The drive to Rosings was again made long by the wails of Baby Collins. Georgiana did her best to assist Charlotte with her son, but Anne's frequent complaints of the noise attested to the fact that no one could make him more comfortable. Mr. Collins frequently repeated Lady Catherine's advice on child rearing as they traveled, but was completely ignored by all his traveling companions.

At last they arrived at Hunsford where all the Collins" were deposited, and Georgiana and Anne were free to listen to the quietness of nature. As much as Georgiana desired to do so, Anne instead desired to pour out all her hopes and anxieties over the Rathwell's ball and all her plans of dress and jewellery. While Anne went on, Georgiana considered the Lawsons would be returning to Sunnings at about this time. She had written to Julia of her insistent invitation to Rosings. Georgiana wished now that Julia could have come along. Julia's company could make even this trip enjoyable, but Julia must assist her family with plans for Phillip's marriage and for Christmas. Julia's wedding was now set for the spring and she must be thinking frequently of this as well. Georgiana considered in fact it might be better not to have Julia along.

Lady Catherine greeted the young women at the door looking severe and diminished as she leaned against a cane.

"Anne, Georgiana, at last you have come."

"Mother!" said Anne with surprising delight. "It is so good to see you again." She embraced her mother who looked confused by the sudden show of affection. Anne began to cry and Lady Catherine patted her stiffly and said "There, there."

"Oh Mother, you do not know the trials I have faced at Pemberley. Those Collins" are insufferable and I had only Georgiana for companionship."

"Surely it was not as bad as you say," said Lady Catherine, but a small smile crept into her features as she considered the ineptitude of all others to please a daughter raised in a lavish home like Rosings.

"You must both be tired and hungry. Come to the drawing room and I shall call for tea." They were led through the great hall and anti-chamber to their usual sitting room. It seemed rather garish and stifling to Georgiana, who was used to the cheerful improvements her brother and Elizabeth made at Pemberley. To Anne, it seemed all comfort and stability once more. At last, she could breathe easily and relax in the comforts of home. If only Mr. Rathwell were here, all would be perfectly well. At this thought, she continued to implement Mrs. Highmore's plan, as she interpreted it to be.

"Ah, mother, I have missed your good taste and order of home. Do you know my cousin Elizabeth does not require her servants to present themselves to her for daily inspection?"

"I am not surprised, dear, as she was not raised in such luxury, but how do you find her hand at Pemberley, Georgiana?"

"I am very pleased to have Elizabeth at Pemberley. I cannot remember a time when we have all been so happy there." Georgiana tried to undo her cousin's complaints.

"Your poor mother would be disappointed to hear you speak this way. Can you not remember her expert graces at Pemberley?"

Georgiana's memory of her mother had been badly tarnished by the knowledge of her unknown sister. "I fear my memories of that time have grown dim as I grow older."

"For shame, girl! It is good you have come here then, for I

will remind you of all your mother was to you." Lady Catherine was firm.

"Thank you, ma'am," said Georgiana obediently.

Once the women were comfortably seated, Anne announced what they had learned of Lady Catherine's sister.

"Did you know, Mama, of Lady Anne's other daughter?" Georgiana grew pale and wished she were anywhere but this room. She was amazed at her cousin's ill breeding.

"What on earth do you speak of, Anne? She had only two children and if you must count him, that other rascal who aligned himself with your uncle Mr. Darcy." The tea arrived and Anne took over the pouring as Lady Catherine's arm was decidedly weakened.

"Of course, she wished to keep it all from you and I see she has succeeded, but it has all come out now, mother, about her first child." Anne passed the tea around and settled back to her chair while her mother attempted to correct her.

"Well of course, she was stillborn. My sister wrote to me of the great misfortune, but why should you bring this up now, Anne?"

"I fear she lied to you mother, for that very child has now born a son who has been adopted by Mr. and Mrs. Fitzwilliam Darcy." Anne watched her mother to catch her precise reaction.

Lady Catherine was visibly upset and Anne wondered briefly if this news may not help her cause.

"What are you speaking of, child? It sounds like a great fabrication to cover up some bad business on their side."

"Mr. Darcy heard the news himself from his father when he came of age. His older sister, Olivia, was born quite deformed of mind and body and was secretly sent to London, where they left her." Anne said.

"Impossible! My sister told me everything." Lady Catherine began to look very ill.

"Not this, mother. She did not wish you to know of the child, for fear of your disapproval." Anne began to wonder if she should have left this secret in Pemberley.

Lady Catherine was aghast. "My own daughter was born unwell. How could she think such a thing of me?"

"I came much later, of course Mother, and I was only unhealthy, not deformed."

"This cannot be – my own sister keeping such secrets from me! Where is this Olivia now?" Lady Catherine stood as if to run to her unknown niece's side.

"Unfortunately, she has died in childbirth, leaving her son to Mr. and Mrs. Darcy's care."

"They do not know how to care for children. Why was I not applied to for assistance?"

Here, Georgiana could no longer hold her tongue. "They are very doting parents, Aunt. I am absolutely confident Baby Henry will get the best care possible."

Lady Catherine returned to her seat in exhaustion. "A boy! Why have they named him Henry when there are plenty of family names to be used? He shall of course inherit all of the Pemberley estate; oh this is all too much." Here, Lady Catherine collapsed and needed to be assisted to her rooms. Anne accompanied her, leaving Georgiana to find the way to her own set of rooms. She was very grateful for the solitude.

Lady Catherine did not make another appearance that day. She allowed Anne a short conference that evening, but Anne had the presence of mind to mention neither Baby Henry, nor Mr. Rathwell. Georgiana took the opportunity to walk the grounds alone. She might have visited the Collins", but she was glad of the chance to consider the many thoughts which claimed her mind.

# CHAPTER 10

A WEEK PASSED AFTER THE DEPARTURE OF GEORGIANA AND Anne in which the Darcys took regular walks about the grounds with Kitty and Colonel Fitzwilliam. After one such walk, Darcy remarked to Elizabeth "I think my cousin grows increasingly fond of your sister. What do you think, dearest?"

"I believe you are correct, darling, but let us offer no interference and allow things to take their natural course."

Darcy smiled his approval. "Kitty is very much improved since I first knew her. I believe your good nature has had much to do with that."

"Your sister has also been a good influence."

While they smiled over their predictions, the footman arrived at their door with an urgent message.

"There is someone here, ma'am, and I believe it is your sister."

As Elizabeth considered which sister it might be, her question was answered by the arrival of Lydia into the room.

"Lydia! What a – pleasure. I did not expect you," said Elizabeth.

Lydia flew to the arms of her sister and began to sob.

"Oh Lizzy, it is terrible. Awful! Horrendous! I cannot stand it another minute."

Elizabeth patted Lydia's back and expected to hear of some treachery on the side of Wickham. "What is it, dearest?" Lydia broke from the embrace and complained;

"Is there no refreshment in this great house? I have come a considerable distance."

"Of course," said Darcy, who excused himself to arrange for tea and to escape the dramatics of his sister-in-law.

Lydia flung herself into the chaise and would not speak until she had drunk and eaten her fill.

"Now, tell me Lydia, what is the matter?" said Elizabeth.

"You can not imagine the worry, the work, and the stresses of my life!"

"Please tell me, then. You have not written us a word on the matter."

"How could I when he demands every moment of my life? I barely fall asleep when he demands all my attention, screaming and wailing all the while."

"Is something the matter with Wickham? He is not ill, I hope?"

"Wickham, ha! I have not seen him in a fortnight. You have no idea what afflication this is for a young bride and new mother. If only I could be with him, Lizzy. Everything would be so much better, but how can I leave my baby when I have no nurse."

"No nurse? What happened to Weston?"

"Weston was a pig! She ate us out of bread and milk and demanded I be at her beck and call. No, no. Weston left us just before Wickham and I alone have been left to care for that crying, screaming baby all to myself."

"Baby George has been the cause of misery?"

"Of course! Who else could it be? He cries all day and night and will not eat the broth cook prepares for him."

"Has he no milk?"

"We haven't any to spare and I cannot give him any. That was what the nurse was for and we could hardly afford another."

"Goodness. Where is Baby George now?"

"I had him taken to the nursery, for I could do nothing more for him."

"We must go to him immediately."

"I knew you would help, Lizzy," said Lydia and helped herself to more cake.

"You will want to accompany me, of course," said Elizabeth. Lydia yawned and shook off the suggestion.

"It has been such a long journey. I am sure you will know what to do."

Elizabeth could hardly contain the anger she felt toward her sister, but she controlled herself and left the room to see to her nephew.

She heard his wails long before she made it to the nursery. When she arrived, she saw Baby Henry safe in his crib and Mrs. Carter looking rather disheveled and trying to calm Baby George.

"Mrs. Carter. I am so sorry," said Elizabeth taking the crying baby from her arms.

"Who is this baby, ma'am and why has he been sent to me?"

"He is my sister Lydia's son, Mrs. Carter. I did not realize she was coming and she had him sent to the nursery before I knew she was here. I will take him to her now."

"That baby is not well, ma'am. He needs feeding."

"Mrs. Carter, my sister has lost her nurse. Do you suppose? Might I trouble you to feed him?"

"I do not wish to steal the milk from Henry, ma'am, but that there baby needs something right quick."

Elizabeth handed Baby George back and took Henry from his crib.

"I will go speak to my sister. We must arrange for another nurse, Mrs. Carter. Until then, however, I fear we must trouble you."

"It is alright, ma'am. I have nursed twin babies before. He will settle once he is well fed."

Elizabeth left Mrs. Carter with Baby George and took Henry down to the parlour so she could speak with Lydia. When she arrived, Darcy was standing there with a short note in hand and a dark countenance.

"Lizzy, is there no end to the impropriety of the Wickhams?" He took Henry and passed Elizabeth the note.

"DEAREST LIZZY,

"I have seen the concern you have for our dear son and so I can trust he will be in excellent hands. I must join my husband in London for he wrote requesting my disappearance. Of course, I cannot bring Baby George as he would not be safe and I do not know how we might obtain a proper nurse on our limited income. Therefore, I intrust him to your care until such time as we might be properly settled and able to call for him. He will need a nurse as soon as you can find him one. As you have no children of your own and a very insurmountable income, I trust this will be no real inconvenience.

"Take good care of our little angel. I have left a small bundle of his favourite things which you will find beneath this note.

"Until we meet again

"Mrs. Lydia Wickham"

Elizabeth flung the note to the floor and kicked the small bundle down with it.

"She came here meaning to leave her baby behind! I cannot believe we come from the same parents."

"I would have expected such a thing from Wickham, but it surprises me from Lydia," said Darcy darkly. "I fear his influence is overtaking any sense or goodness she once had."

"We must find another nurse, Darcy. Baby George is quite a charge to be left to and I do not wish to inconvenience Mrs. Carter."

"Of course, I know of a nurse nearby. I will give you the information and then I must go after Lydia, if she is alone, and try to get her to return. I will not have her leave her son here so easily, but it may require me some time to track her. I may need to return to London."

"Of course you must go, Darcy. We are obliged to ensure George's safety and health. I have my sister Kitty and Colonel Fitzwilliam for company and I know you will return as soon as you can. I will see to the nurse immediately."

Darcy kissed his wife and son and left on horseback after gathering a small bag of personal items. Elizabeth returned to the nursery fighting various emotions of anger, disbelief and pleasure over her new nephew. She returned to find George sleeping peacefully in Mrs. Carter's arms and returned Henry to his crib that she might hold her nephew. She could not indulge for long, however and after explaining her intentions to Mrs. Carter, left them to seek a second nurse.

# CHAPTER 11

THE DAY OF THE RATHWELL'S BALL ARRIVED AND ANNE'S wheedling and persuading finally obtained her mother's permission for their attendance. Mr. Rathwell had visited Rosings with one or more of his sisters every day since Anne's return, giving Anne the opportunity to acquire an invitation for her mother to attend the ball through Miss Rathwell, but Lady Catherine declined on behalf of her health. Anne and Georgiana saw Lady Catherine's constitution was not what it had been before her illness. This concerned Anne more than she would have guessed, and she was grateful she had reconciled with her mother, thanks to Mrs. Highmore's advice. Anne would certainly not wish to lose her mother's blessing at this point. Anne began to realize her mother's love beneath layers of control and propriety.

"Do you think mother might consent to my marrying Mr. Rathwell?" Anne asked Georgiana as they prepared their toilette.

"I believe you are doing much to persuade her on the subject. I am surprised at the change in my aunt and I think she is very concerned for your future at present."

"That is hardly an answer, cousin, but I see you mean well." Anne sighed as her hair was arranged in a coil about her head.

"I do not wish to leave mother, but I do so want to be married to Mr. Rathwell. He makes me so happy and I never wish to leave his presence."

"You may enjoy a long engagement if you wish to prolong your time at Rosings."

Anne snorted. "You have obviously never been in love, for a long engagement is the last thing I would wish. No, Georgiana, expediency in marriage is my first desire. If I could be married tonight, I could not be happier."

Georgiana only squeezed her cousin's hand in response, for she too could not imagine a better arrangement if she were engaged to the man she loved.

Georgiana continued to receive correspondence from Julia on the wedding preparations and Julia's desire for Georgiana's company. Georgiana found no comfort in Julia's letters or the task of responding to them.

A quarter of an hour later, the young women were ready and kissing Lady Catherine goodbye.

"Georgiana, you must ensure my Anne not tire herself with too much dancing. I insist she sit out at least every other dance." Lady Catherine said.

"Yes aunt, though I assure you, Anne's health has been much improved since visiting Pemberley."

"It is kind of you to say so, Georgiana, but you can not know her as I do and I believe she exerts herself before young company to acquire their approval. If only I were well enough to join you," she sighed heavily.

"Do not worry yourself, mother," said Anne, hugging her mother goodbye. "I will not dance every dance and I will be sure to keep away from any open windows. We will not be home too late, I promise."

Anne's behaviour toward her mother was so different from what Georgiana remembered; she concluded being in love had improved her cousin. The absence of Mrs. Jenkinson must also be attributed to Anne's change in personality and Georgiana considered governesses could become a detriment to their charges if retained too long.

The carriage arrived then and carried the young ladies away from Rosings with lofty expectation by one and resignation by the other.

Furdale was hardly the estate that was Rosings, but it had a charm and comfort which Rosings lacked. Georgiana could imagine a lifetime spent in the confinements of Rosings would make Furdale very attractive. Furdale was certainly lacking in fashion and order, but the Miss Rathwells and Mr. Rathwell overshadowed the chaos with their ebullient welcome.

"Miss De Bourgh! Miss Darcy! We have all been awaiting your arrival. Will you not stand with us as our guests of honour and help us greet the remainder of the visitors," said Miss Rathwell. Anne happily took her place beside Mr. Rathwell and Georgiana stood behind them, noting Anne's closeness to the open door. Georgiana was pleased, for her cousin's sake, that Lady Catherine was not present to witness such disregard for good health.

The dance began half an hour later and as expected, Mr. Rathwell danced the first and second dances with Anne. Mr. Rathwell's good friend, Mr. Ward, asked Georgiana to dance and together they formed a quadrille. Georgiana noted she had never seen Anne look lovelier. Her usually pale features had a lively glow and her small frame was light and pretty on the dance floor. Mr. Ward was a handsome partner who looked well in a burgundy coat. He was pleasant to speak to and very attentive to Georgiana. For a moment, she wished she had never met Phillip Lawson so she might return the compliment. Instead, she was merely polite and reserved.

As promised, Anne sat out the third dance with Georgiana. Mr. Rathwell and Mr. Ward joined them and they watched the other dancers together.

"My sisters will be sorry to see you sitting out, Ward," said Mr. Rathwell. "There are hardly enough young men for them all."

"I will dance the next one with Lacey, I promise, but a man cannot be expected to dance if he is in such good company. Tell me, Miss Darcy, have you been out for very long?"

"Only since June. I had been out previously, but my brother thought it prudent to recall me until I grew older." Georgiana hoped he would not ask why. There was nothing which could inspire her to speak of Mr. Wickham in the presence of strangers and especially her cousin.

"He sounds very wise. I have not sisters of my own and am rather baffled by the whole process, but I have found girls who are out too early can be rather silly."

"I am certain your mother would have a ready opinion on the subject," said Mr. Rathwell to Anne. "It is such a pity she is not well enough to join us."

Anne giggled and smiled, too happy for words.

"What do you think of Kent, Miss Darcy?" said Mr. Rathwell.

"It is lovely country. I have often visited in the spring and summer, but never so close to winter."

"I think I should like to settle here once I have made my fortune," said Mr. Ward. "It is so charming and full of good people. One grows so tired of people in London, do you not agree?"

Georgiana recognized his attempts to engage her conversation and though she did not wish to encourage him, she was glad for the chance to speak to someone outside of her small circle at Rosings. They spoke agreeably until the next dance when some relations of the Rathwells asked Georgiana and Anne to dance.

After the dance, Georgiana could not find Anne for the next quarter of an hour. Mr. Ward brought negus to Georgiana and they enjoyed another lively conversation about music and dance. She had not felt so carefree in months. They danced again and then Georgiana was approached by Anne.

"Georgiana, could you accompany me to the terrace."

"Of course."

They left the party and when Anne was certain no one could overhear, she confessed her disappearance.

"Mr. Rathwell began to ask my hand, Georgiana."

"Began?"

"Yes, I made him stop and insisted he first seek the permission of my mother. He is to join us tomorrow for breakfast, without his sisters." Anne hid a squeal of delight behind a gloved hand.

"Congratulations, then!" Georgiana hugged her cousin, but Anne stopped her.

"I would rather have your wishes of good luck, for convincing mother will not be without its complications. I recommended he bring along some symbol of his devotion."

"You mean jewelry?" Georgiana was surprised at her cousin's boldness.

Anne smiled and coyly lifted a shoulder. "Such things may have their influence on my mother. I believe it is in Mr. Rathwell's best interest to show his good fortune in life."

"You are a clever girl, cousin! I am quite surprised."

Anne smiled happily. "I might share some of my ideas with you, if you are interested in obtaining the interest of a certain young man." Anne giggled and Georgiana became serious again.

"No, thank you cousin, I have no need for such information."

"I see it is too early, but if ever you should need my discerning mind, remember my offer."

The girls returned to the dance shortly after and danced until ten o'clock, when Anne insisted they return home so as not to worry her mother. Mr. Rathwell and Mr. Ward saw them to their carriage and bowed their adieus to Anne and Georgiana.

ANNE HARDLY SLEPT that night and was up very early to prepare. She must look well on the day of her engagement and she wanted the breakfast room in perfect order for Mr. Rathwell's arrival.

"Oh William, do not fail me now," she whispered to her refection in the mirror. "You must present yourself well, my darling and keep your ridiculous laugh to yourself."

Georgiana soon joined Anne in the breakfast room where she was greeted with outstretched hands by her cousin.

"Oh, Georgiana, feel how cold I am! I cannot rest until it is done. Is it nine o'clock yet? Have you any sight of my mother?"

"I heard her voice when I passed her rooms on my way down. She sounds well enough and you may expect her in a quarter of an hour, I suspect."

Lady Catherine had attempted to await their return last night, but fell asleep in her chair. Anne walked her to bed, but did not mention Mr. Rathwell's visit of the next morning.

The next moment, they heard Mr. Rathwell at the door

and Anne hurried to greet him. He looked very nervous and held out a large box to her.

"Do you think these will do?" He asked, and his voice broke.

Anne peeked inside the large box and gasped at the wealth it beheld.

"They are beautiful, Mr. Rathwell, but I believe one well-chosen piece might be your best presentation. Where did you get these?"

"They are my mother's. She insisted I take them all to help my cause. She said you may have whichever you liked best."

Anne took Mr. Rathwell and the box out of sight of the servants into a separate room. After a quick perusal, she chose a bracelet of pearls and suggested it to Mr. Rathwell.

"It is perfect. Of course, you would know what is best. What shall I do with the rest?"

Anne suggested Georgiana might keep them safely while they were occupied. They left the room together to be greeted by Georgiana. Anne gave the box to her cousin with a brief explanation and then returned to the breakfast room to find her mother already seated.

"Good morning, my dear. Who have you brought? Ah, Mr. Rathwell and where are your sisters?"

"I-I have come alone, Lady Catherine," he bowed generously. "If I may, I would request the honour of a private conference."

"Not before breakfast, boy. You must all sit down to eat. It is not good for one's constitution to wait long for nourishment in the morning."

Breakfast was an awkward and distressing affair with Lady Catherine frequently encouraging the others to eat.

"I may be too unwell to enjoy what is spread before us, but you three must certainly indulge after your evening of frivolity. Mr. Rathwell, cook will make your eggs. You look very ill this morning and in need of sustenance."

Mr. Rathwell agreed to all of Lady Catherine's suggestions and was soon possessed of a full plate which he could hardly manage. His throat was constricted with nerves and even small bites made him choke and sputter. He was soon covered with a variety of breakfast foods and Georgiana took pity on him and Anne.

"Lady Catherine, do you keep my mother's likeness nearby? I know you have a different painting from the one at Pemberley and I desire to see it this morning."

"Of course, Georgiana. I have it in the next room. I shall send one of my servants for it."

Georgiana reached for one of Mr. Rathwell's many pastries and placed it on her own plate while Lady Catherine spoke to her servant. Mr. Rathwell smiled appreciatively.

Georgiana continued asking Lady Catherine questions of her mother, allowing Mr. Rathwell uninterrupted time to eat his food and she and Anne reached for anything they could when Lady Catherine's attention was diverted. At last, his plate was empty and breakfast could come to an end.

"You have a very hearty appetite," said Lady Catherine. "You must be careful you do not overeat, Mr. Rathwell. One can become too heavy, you know, and one never wishes to become heavier than he can be lifted, for what if you were to die in your sleep and need to be carried to the church for your funeral?"

With these happy thoughts, Lady Catherine allowed for a private conference in her library.

While Lady Catherine met with Mr. Rathwell, Anne chewed at her nails and paced the floor in front of the room.

"Anne, do sit down. The mail has just arrived and I am certain your pacing is not helping Mr. Rathwell with his speeches."

"I have only heard my mother's voice so far. She likely thinks he is here to seek her advice on proper care of roses or some such nonsense."

"He does well to listen to her first, Anne. Look, I have a letter from Pemberley." Georgiana opened her letter written in Elizabeth's hand and gasped after the first few lines.

"What is it, Georgiana? Is someone ill?"

"No, no. Only Lydia has come with her child and left him behind for my brother and sister to care for."

"Can she really be so awful! What else does it say?"

Georgiana read the letter aloud to Anne, skipping the lines which wondered how Georgiana was faring with her tyrannical aunt. It was the best possible tonic for what distressed Anne.

"Can you imagine such a heartless mother!" she exclaimed in wonder.

Georgiana most certainly could. "I must return to help Elizabeth," said Georgiana.

"She has her sister Kitty, though I dare say she is no better than Lydia. She might run away with some man at any moment."

"Kitty is hardly like her younger sister. If you had met Lydia, you could not compare them. Still, I do not like to leave her alone when my brother is away. Can you spare me, Anne?"

"Ask me later, once Mr. Rathwell has spoken to my mother, oh I had nearly forgotten."

Anne resumed her pacing and Georgiana reread her letter, trying to imagine what would happen at Pemberley. She loved babies, but could she love Wickham's? It was almost cruel that she would need to have his child in her home. But surely a newborn could not bear much resemblance to his wayward father? It must be a sure reminder of her devotion to remain unmarried.

Three quarters of an hour passed before Mr. Rathwell came beaming from the sitting room. Lady Catherine followed a moment later admiring a pearl bracelet on her wrist. Anne gasped – Had mother thought Mr. Rathwell's intentions were meant for her? Such worries were soon put to rest.

"Well Mr. Rathwell, I believe you have something to say to my daughter." She removed the bracelet and returned it. "This room is free, my dear." She ushered them into the study she had recently left and they followed her bidding. When the door was closed, Lady Catherine directed Georgiana to the east room and told her version of events.

"Mr. Rathwell is such a young man and I dare say young men lack sense and respectability, but my Anne has enough to guide them both. If he were asking for a lesser woman, I should not think their marriage capable of success, but where Anne marries; there can be no possibility of failure. I would not have thought myself able to let her go to a man less than herself, but she is to inherit all of Rosings and Mr. Rathwell was quite warm to my suggestion they settle here once they are married."

Georgiana wondered how Anne would react to this portion of the proposal, but only nodded in agreement.

"My mind has been swayed since your visit, Georgiana. I had so long expected Anne to marry your brother that I never imagined another husband for her. I believe it was learning of your poor mother and sister Olivia which opened my mind to new possibilities. I should hope my daughter never need hide anything so important from me, but here they come, the happy couple. William! Anne! May I be the first to offer you my congratulations?"

"Mother, I have never been so happy!" Anne embraced her mother while Mr. Rathwell stood back looking a mixture of fear and pride. "We will all live so nicely together."

"I knew you would agree, my dear, for how could I get on all alone in this big house without you?" William shook Lady Catherine's hand and then Georgiana's.

"Cousin, I am very pleased to have you present on this great day!" he said and it was obvious his usual good spirits had returned. He then turned to Anne and held her hand in his. "Just think of the many improvements we might make to Rosings together."

Lady Catherine's eyes widened, but for the happy occasion, she refrained from speaking. Georgiana hoped Mr. Rathwell's spirits would support him in the future.

The party enjoyed an hour of happy considerations until Anne suggested she and William must visit Furdale to share their news.

## CHAPTER 12

DARCY SENT WORD TO ELIZABETH THAT HE HAD NOT YET found the Wickhams. He now suspected Lydia lied when she told Elizabeth they were on their way to London. No Inn on the way had seen them and not one of their acquaintances in London had heard from them. He wondered if they had gone to the north instead or some other country entirely. He planned to stay in London two more nights in case they showed up eventually. Then he would return home and await some word of their whereabouts, for it could not be long before he heard of their ill-doings or was sent some note requesting funds.

Elizabeth sighed at her sister's continuing bad behaviour. Elizabeth had hoped a baby might settle Lydia, but she was still so young. Elizabeth found a second nurse for Baby George, who was now looking chubby and content after two days of frequent feedings. Kitty was equally outraged at Lydia's behaviour, and Elizabeth was mildly comforted to hear Kitty say how glad she was to have avoided that fateful visit to Brighton with Mrs. Forster when Lydia had run away with Mr. Wickham.

"I was as silly as she was then," said Kitty. "To think I might have made such an imprudent match. Imagine how devastated mother must be."

Elizabeth realized then she must write to her parents. She had hoped to avoid the task if Lydia shortly returned for her son, but two days passed with no hope of a quick resolution to the situation. She sat down to write them shortly after speaking to Kitty. Elizabeth wondered how her mother would excuse the behaviour of her favourite child this time.

The rest of the day was spent in cozy pursuits for it was a cold and windy November day. Kitty played piano and Colonel Fitzwilliam sang along occasionally. Elizabeth divided her time between the two boys and her plans for the ball. It was to be held a week before the wedding at Sunnings. It was as enjoyable a day as possible considering the upheaval which recently invaded Pemberley.

As Anne had previously expressed, a short period of engagement was to be the case. She would be married at Rosings a fortnight after the happy union was decided. Georgiana could not therefore be spared and so she remained at Rosings. Mr. Rathwell visited daily and frequently brought Mr. Ward who was an enjoyable, but occasionally troubling companion for Georgiana. She had no desire to encourage his advances, but he was an engaging young man who helped pass the time and take her mind from what was soon to occur at Sunnings. She still received frequent letters from Julia on the subject and between Anne and Rathwell, Julia and Mr. Black, Phillip and Ms. Brill, Georgiana felt rather bombarded by marriages.

Mr. Rathwell proved as insensitive to Lady Catherine's many strong opinions as could be hoped. His enthusiasm for the wedding and his subsequent move to Rosings had only increased since the proposal and acceptance. He brought gifts of cakes, jewels and books to endear him to his mother-in-law. This was exactly what she required and Georgiana came to believe Anne's choice could not have been better. For Anne's part, she continued to be cheerful and healthy and Georgiana could only wish her well. She still marveled at the change in her cousin and hoped no amount of badgering by Lady Catherine would dull it in future.

The day of the wedding arrived and Mr. Collins was called upon to perform the ceremony at Rosings chapel.

"It is my most humble duty to my great patroness, Lady Catherine De Bourgh, to join her daughter, Miss Anne De Bourgh to Mr. William Rathwell today. I cannot overemphasize the importance of this union to our parish and to all the people of Hunsford. From the moment I met Lady Catherine and her elegant daughter, I have hoped and prayed for this very day, for what could be better for Lady Catherine and indeed all of Hunsford than to have Miss De Bourgh properly wed?"

Georgiana restrained a heavy sigh and wondered if Mr. Collins" frequent visits to Rosings might be curtailed after the wedding. She took a quick look at Lady Catherine and discovered a hint of smiling pride beneath her regal composure. Mr. Collins was saying precisely what she could wish. A second look at Anne revealed she was so blissfully happy even Mr. Collins could not dim the brightness of her countenance.

The wedding was at last performed and the happy couple would leave Lady Catherine behind for only a fortnight while they took their honeymoon in London. Mr. Rathwell was insistent they not leave his mother-in-law for long during the winter. They would take Georgiana as far as London where she would meet the Darcy carriage and take it to Derbyshire and Pemberley. As they were leaving, much to

Georgiana's surprise and alarm, Mr. Ward joined their carriage and they all left for London.

"What a generous couple to bring their friends on honeymoon!" said Mr. Ward when they were a mile from Rosings.

"We could not think of two more enjoyable friends to have along. Could we not persuade you, Georgiana, to spend a week with us in London?" said Mr. Rathwell.

Nothing could induce Georgiana to spend another day away from her family. She had word from Elizabeth that her brother had found neither of the Wickhams and Georgiana was weary from being so long from home. More than that, she wished to remove herself from Mr. Ward before his attachment grew any stronger. They all spent the night at Lady Catherine's London home and then Georgiana left directly after an early breakfast.

"Miss Darcy," said Mr. Ward when he caught her alone in the hallway. "I must tell you how much I have enjoyed your company in these weeks since you have been with the De Bourghs."

"Thank you, Mr. Ward." Georgiana could not meet his eyes.

"Of course I am still young and in need of fortune, but I felt I might confess you are everything I could hope to find in a young lady and I hope we might meet again." Mr. Ward's expression was so hopeful and complimentary that Georgian could only say;

"I hope you achieve all you hope to, Mr. Ward."

Anne and William arrived then to kiss Georgiana goodbye and at last, Georgiana was free to return home. To her great delight, Fitzwilliam greeted her at the door and said he would accompany her to Pemberley.

"Brother! What a surprise. If only I had known, you might have spent a night with us here."

"You are very kind Georgiana, but I do not wish to be away from Pemberley any longer than absolutely necessary."

He spoke briefly to Anne and William expressing his and Elizabeth's best wishes and was introduced to Mr. Ward, who extended his hand in a warm greeting. After a minimal amount of pleasantries, they were off to Pemberley.

"I did not wish to speak of it in front of our cousins, Georgiana, but I spent last night again inquiring after the Wickhams."

"Of course," said Georgiana. "Have you found anything?"

"A small hint that they are in Scotland. It is not much, but it is more than I have heard since Lydia was at Pemberley."

"It is such a dreadful business, brother. How does the baby fare?"

"Fortunately, he is very well and thriving at Pemberley. We have found another excellent nurse and the two babies get along as well as infants can." The worry on Darcy's face lifted when he talked of the two baby boys. He found great delight in holding them and watching Elizabeth care for them. He could not be prouder if they were his natural sons.

"I cannot wait to meet George and to see Henry again."

Georgiana described her stay at Rosings and the wedding, especially Mr. Collins" long speeches. Darcy told of the growing attachment between Colonel Fitzwilliam and Kitty and mentioned the upcoming ball at Pemberley. They had an enjoyable drive until they needed to stop for rest at an Inn. They spent the night and began early the next day so they might be at Pemberley as soon as possible. Elizabeth was very glad to have them all home again and they spent a lovely evening together admiring the baby boys and discussing all that had passed since Georgiana left. Kitty played for Georgiana some new songs learned in her absence. Georgiana could not have wished for a better welcome and went to sleep in her own bed as satisfied as she had been in a month.

# CHAPTER 13

GEORGIANA WAS REUNITED WITH THE LAWSONS THE DAY AFTER she returned to Pemberley. Though she wished to avoid all but Julia, she could not put off her duty and visited with Elizabeth and Kitty the morning after her return. She was relieved to have Kitty and Elizabeth for company as she was told of all she had missed since she left London in October. Mrs. Lawson and Julia told them of the people they had seen and visited since the engagements and how each one reacted to the news. Mrs. Lawson was especially delighted by all of Miss Brill's responses to new people, new sights and new performances. They endeavored not to mention Mr. James Lawson, but Georgiana understood by little glances and looks he was quite heartbroken over his disappointment.

Georgiana answered many kind questions of her time at Rosings and Miss Brill was especially inquisitive of the wedding details. She looked very well and had been provided with new dresses since Georgiana last saw her. She was keen to tell Georgiana what she had been reading and showed her a letter she was writing to her mother.

"My family is most impressed by my penmanship, Miss

Darcy. I cannot tell you how much I appreciated your attentions to me in London."

Phillip was fortunately out riding with his father and they did not meet him during their visit. They stayed only half an hour as Elizabeth did not like to be long from her boys. Mrs. Lawson gave her several pieces of advice on the importance of warm clothing for babies in winter. Elizabeth thanked Mrs. Lawson and said how much she looked forward to seeing them all at the ball in a week's time. They said their goodbyes then and Elizabeth, Georgiana and Kitty returned to Pemberley.

IN THE DAYS before the ball, Julia and Georgiana reestablished their friendship, though Julia did not find in Georgiana all she wished in a confidante. Georgiana seemed vague about her thoughts and somewhat detached from all Julia's plans and ideas for the future. Only talk of Julia's poetry seemed to interest Georgiana. Julia feared marriage would separate them, so she put all her hopes into Georgiana finding a match so they could remain equally footed. For this reason, she asked after Mr. Ward frequently as he seemed the closest possibility. This did not prove wise, however, and Georgiana tried to express that Mr. Ward was not of great interest to her.

The evening of the ball was windy and cold, so much so that Elizabeth wondered if people would come and if they did, whether they would need to stay the night. Darcy assured her the wind would not cause much inconvenience and the ball would be a great success. She was glad, as she frequently was, of his calmness of nerves, especially when she contrasted them to those of her mother.

Mrs. Bennet had written them of her shock at Lydia's conduct, but only a few sentences later, she considered how fortunate Baby George would be to grow up at Pemberley and that after all, as the Darcys would not provide an ample home and situation for the Wickhams, it was their duty to at least provide for their poor child. And so, within a paragraph, Lydia was redeemed and all her blame put on Darcy and Elizabeth. Elizabeth could only shake her head over her mother's nonsense and was reassured by a note at the end from her father which said;

"Well done Lizzy in caring for your sister's child. I have seen your mothering skills and know you are up to the task."

Darcy's letters to Scotland increased suspicions that Mr. and Mrs. Wickham were somewhere in that country. He had yet to find their exact location and did not wish to leave Pemberley until he did so. He hoped to leave after Christmas to decide Baby George's future once and for all.

Kitty was placed at the entryway as guest of honour. She looked very well in a new gown and Elizabeth marveled at the good Pemberley had done for her younger sister. Elizabeth hoped to offer her sister Mary the same benefits, but did not feel she could ask Kitty to leave while her interest in Colonel Fitzwilliam remained strong. Georgiana joined the welcoming party as well and Mr. Darcy felt he presented the handsomest family in England. The Lawson's arrived as the third party of guests and brought with them a surprise. Mr. and Mrs. Lawson entered first and were warmly greeted, they were followed by Mr. Lawson and Miss Brill, Miss Lawson, Mr. Black and his sister Miss Black, and finally Mr. James Lawson with a friend, who made Georgiana gasp.

"Mr. Ward! Whatever brings you here?" she said before she could stop herself.

Mr. James Lawson made the reply. "Mr. Ward sought me out in London as a particular friend of yours, Miss Darcy. He also aspires to the law and when he mentioned his desire of seeing our county, I insisted he join me for the Christmas holidays."

Julia joined their conversation. "James and Mr. Ward arrived only this evening and we had not the chance of writing to tell you of his joining us tonight." Julia's eyes sparkled mischievously.

"You are most welcome," said Elizabeth. "We are pleased to have such a close friend of Mr. Rathwell's."

Georgiana was glad for her sister's welcome as she could find no words of her own. She had so dreaded seeing James Lawson again and to see him now with Mr. Ward, of all people, was a spectacular shock.

The guests were all assembled and well-fed. Georgiana's mind churned with the presence of so many of the men who consumed her thoughts. She reflected it could only be made worse if Mr. Wickham and Mr. Barrington Lawson were present. She made every effort to be attentive to Julia and Kitty who sat near her, but fortunately, they were distracted by the men in their lives so Georgiana had ample time to observe Phillip, James and Mr. Ward. She endeavored to do so without notice, but she often caught Phillip's eye and had to look down at her plate. As usual, Miss Brill was energetic in her speech and told many stories of her home in Ireland and her wedding plans. Phillip was as attentive as could be desired and Georgiana heard herself sigh loudly at the thought of their near future together. Would her feelings for him pass once they were wed? She could only hope so. She quickly looked away after the sigh and caught the glance of Mr. Ward, sitting across from her.

"Miss Darcy, I hope I have not acted improperly," he said across the noisy table.

"No, of course not. It was very good of you to look up Mr. Lawson in London. How have you enjoyed your time there?"

"It has been most agreeable. I have spent some time with

Mr. and Mrs. Rathwell, but I have tried not to impose on the newlyweds too greatly. They will return to Rosings in a se'ennight."

"Yes, I had word from Anne this morning. They seem very happy together."

"I have rarely met a warmer couple." Their conversation was interrupted by the removal of dishes and preparation for the second course. Georgiana took advantage of the confusion to glance at James and was surprised and relieved to notice his particular attention to Miss Black. She seemed to bask in his every word and frequently leaned toward him to hear him better or tell him some anecdote of her own. It helped to lessen some of Georgiana's guilt at her pervious conduct toward him. She fleetingly wondered if she should try to love Mr. Ward as a replacement for her broken heart, but upon seeing him smile across the table, she felt it would take quite an effort.

The meal continued with Mr. Ward attempting to engage Georgiana in conversation. She was very reserved in her replies and Elizabeth, Julia and Kitty wondered how long it would take for Mr. Ward to win her affection.

Mr. Ward successfully obtained Georgiana's assent to the first two dances. Phillip sat with his mother while Miss Brill danced with James. He considered James" comment on their way to Pemberley mentioning his prior acquaintance to Miss Darcy. His mother said to him;

"He seems an entertaining young gentleman. I wonder if our Georgiana might be able to love him."

"You do jump to conclusions, mother. Have you not had enough matches this year to satisfy you?"

"You must humour your mother, Phillip. I fear I am quite the romantic and am not satisfied until I have all my children well matched."

"Indeed," said Phillip and a moment's darkness passed

over his face before he set to providing his mother with good company. Phillip was then obliged to dance with his fiancée, but he decided he must later ensure a dance with Miss Darcy.

Georgiana; however, found her dances were quite taken. She wished for a pause to sit, but could not refuse requests by close friends and neighbours. For once, there were more young men present than young ladies and this caused quite an effect on the ladies. They were all quite fatigued by the end of the ball and so no opportunity came for Georgiana to dance with Phillip. It was also so busy as to prevent Mr. Ward from making more than general compliments to Miss Darcy. She hoped she could keep him from saying too much and avoid any private conversation with him.

To Elizabeth's great relief, the wind died down and no one needed either to leave early or to remain the night at Pemberley. Mr. Darcy whispered to her as the guests left she was a most elegant and beautiful hostess and he could not have wished for a more desirable mistress of Pemberley.

# CHAPTER 14

AFTER THE BALL, PLANS AND PREPARATIONS FOR THE MARRIAGE of Mr. Phillip Lawson and Miss Bridget Brill became all consuming for the Lawson family. Julia continued to visit Georgiana as frequently as possible and she was pleased to find they were becoming more comfortable together again. Julia stopped mentioning Mr. Ward and decided to let Georgiana keep some of her secrets. Mr. Ward had only stayed three nights at Sunnings and then returned to Hunsford for the remainder of the Christmas holidays. He had only the opportunity of speaking to Georgiana in company, so she was able to avoid any unwanted declarations. Julia also refrained from speaking too much of Mr. Black when she realized each mention of his name made Georgiana sigh.

So, when Georgiana noticed a young woman walking toward Pemberley three days before Phillip's wedding, she assumed it was Julia. It was a great surprise then to find Miss Brill in the front entrance.

"Miss Darcy, I hope I do not assume too much in visiting you alone. Julia wished me to tell you she is in bed with a headache this morning and will not be able to make her usual visit. I thought I might take her place." Miss Brill looked so hopeful, Georgiana could only oblige her.

"Of course, Miss Brill. How nice of you to come with Julia's message. May I offer you some refreshment?"

"You are most kind, Miss Darcy, but it is such a clear morning and I hoped for a walk about your spectacular park."

It was not a very nice morning at all, but Georgiana continued to accommodate her guest by donning her heaviest coat and boots and setting outside with Miss Brill.

After some polite enquiries after family and friends, Miss Brill arrived at the conversation she sought with Georgiana.

"Miss Darcy, you showed me such kindness and attention in London I hoped you might be the friend I have been seeking."

Georgiana hardly felt up to befriending the woman who would soon be Mrs. Phillip Lawson, but she was not one to disappoint.

"Please call me Georgiana," she answered.

"And you must call me Bridget. Oh, I am so relieved, for I could hardly speak of this to anyone in the Lawson family and most certainly not to Phillip. You do not know what a burden it has been to me these many months – since the very night of my engagement, in fact. Oh, I know I must forsake and forget all others, but I must confess it at least once before I wed."

Georgiana began to feel very awkward, but could do nothing to stop the lady.

"You see, I was very much in love when Phillip came to our home in Ireland. Mr. Sullivan was an acquaintance since childhood. Our homes were not far apart and the children of our families would often play together. Oh the happy hours of mayhem and make-believe! Weather and conditions could never keep us apart for long, but I must get to the point. You have likely guessed already that as we grew in size and mind, we formed an attachment. His family, you see, was even worse off than mine, though you may not have known, but you may have presumed that with so many children and a very small income, my family lived . . . *frugally*. I am therefore very obliged to Phillip for thinking of me and assisting my family when he asked for my hand. I could hardly refuse, but you see I was still very attached to Mr. Sullivan, and in fact I find myself thinking of him still from time to time. Oh, Georgiana, tell me I am not so very wicked."

Georgiana was stunned by the revelation and found she pitied both Bridget and Phillip their future together, for if they did not love one another, what kind of future could it be and why was money the root of so much unhappiness? She hurried to reassure Bridget of her goodness.

"I do not think you are wicked, no, but Bridget can you love Mr. Lawson if you still think of Mr. Sullivan?"

"Yes, oh yes. He is so kind and good and generous and he is my cousin, how could I not love him? I just wonder if I will still think of Mr. Sullivan once we are wed. Must I tell my husband of such thoughts or will our marriage be forever doomed?"

Georgiana wondered the same thing, but did not say as much. "I am hardly an expert on marriage, Bridget. There are certainly matches made with less love than you have for Mr. Lawson. I am certain thoughts of Mr. Sullivan will fade with time."

"Oh, thank you Georgiana. You are always so good to me. I knew I could trust you with this secret. I had hoped I was not so wicked, though I know I must repent of every thought of Mr. Sullivan once I am married, but if you only knew him, Georgiana, you would see what a good and deserving young man he is and so very handsome – Oh! But I must not speak of another man so. I see I will have much strengthening of mind to do in the days ahead. You have helped me immensely, but I must not presume further upon your time. I see I am at a point where I should move now toward Sunnings. I have many obligations there and I will leave you to your own responsibilities. Thank you Georgiana, thank you!"

Bridget grasped Georgiana's hands briefly and then flew off toward Sunnings, leaving Georgiana to breathe deeply for the first time since Bridget's confession began. Georgiana stood looking after Bridget for much longer than was necessary.

# CHAPTER 15

Over a month had passed since Mrs. Lydia Wickham gracelessly deposited her firstborn son with her elder sister at Pemberley. By this time, Elizabeth had spent nearly as much time with the child as his mother and had become very fond of Baby George. She was equally fond of Baby Henry and delighted over their growth and development. Darcy saw how well she cared for the boys and hoped and prayed she would not be badly wounded in regard to her sister's child. He had wished to avoid such attachment by finding his parents quickly and settling all matters decidedly, but it was not until December 15 that he finally located them and heard directly from Mr. Wickham.

"Mr. and Mrs. Darcy,

"We are very obliged to your family for caring for our young son during this time of upheaval in our lives. As you are well aware, I have never been provided the share of Pemberley I was once promised and due to unfortunate circumstances in my marriage, I have been stripped of my placement in the army. My wife and I have started out fresh in a new country, but I understand you already know this.

"At this time, we have acquired a home and cook to prepare simple meals. It is hardly what could be expected for a gentleman and gentleman's daughter, but we must make due. We are prepared to welcome our son back as soon as possible. Please send him by post if it is too much inconvenience for you to bring him yourself."

AT THIS POINT of the letter, Elizabeth was in tears and Darcy was outraged and paced the room while clutching the letter.

"By post indeed. To Scotland in the middle of winter! They are certainly mad."

"How can he be so heartless toward his own son? Oh, Darcy. We must do something." Elizabeth said.

"That is precisely what he wants, Elizabeth. Do not be deceived by him again. He has calculated exactly how he might hit us up for all he desires. He knew we would be won over by his son and would offer anything to keep him well and comfortable, but I will not have it."

"Darcy, you cannot mean to return little George as Mr. Wickham has suggested." Elizabeth grasped his arm.

"Never, my dear. You must not worry so. I will do all I can for little George, but I'll be hanged if I give one more shilling to his father." Darcy crumpled the letter and threw it to the floor before he stormed from the room, leaving Elizabeth to wonder what he might mean and to read the letter again and again in disbelief. She remembered herself then and went to the nursery to hold the children.

An hour later, Darcy joined Elizabeth in the nursery and asked her to join him in another room. He sat her upon a sofa and began pacing as he explained his plans to her.

"I must go to Scotland, Lizzy, but I will not bring Baby George with me."

"You will miss the wedding!" said Elizabeth before she considered what she said.

"I cannot wait, my dear. This is a very urgent matter and I am certain you can explain my absence nicely. I will meet with Mr. and Mrs. Wickham in person so they may see we are not to be trifled with. I will explain all we have done for our nephew and tell them he will stand to inherit the fortune of Pemberley as first son if they will agree to let him stay. I have reason to believe this is what Wickham seeks for his son."

"First son, but what about Henry?"

"You remember, my dear, Henry was born some weeks after George, so in fact George was the first born."

"You would do this for a son of the Wickhams?"

"Lydia is your sister and therefore mine as well. George is my nephew as much as yours and I would gladly welcome him as a son."

"Oh, Darcy," Elizabeth wept upon his shoulder for several minutes until she could speak again.

"Darcy, what if we have our own children, will you not be disappointed that they not inherit as they would?"

"George and Henry will be as much my sons as any we might produce, if you will agree to it, Elizabeth. We do not know if we might have natural children at all and if we do, we would not love George or Henry any less."

"No, certainly. But what will the Wickhams say? Surely they will not want to give up their son."

"We can only hope as much, but Lizzy, your sister is very young and I believe Wickham may have influenced her to give up George in the hopes of obtaining a better situation. Wickham wrote he wanted a new start, and I feel he might strive to better himself if he were cut off from all forms of dependence."

"My mother will not like it, but I cannot think of any

point on which I have ever agreed with her. I hope it will work out as you plan, my love. Please hurry back."

"I will write you as soon as I have any information."

The couple exchanged many other tender addresses and finally said goodbye.

# CHAPTER 16

DARCY WAS GONE WITHIN AN HOUR AND A HALF OF RECEIVING word from the Wickhams. Elizabeth told Georgiana of the letter, but the others were simply told Darcy had urgent business and, regrettably, would not be able to make the Lawson wedding. That left two days for Georgiana to practice the music she promised to play for the wedding and to walk the grounds with Kitty. Kitty was growing increasingly attached to her sister-in- law and she finally confessed her admiration for Colonel Fitzwilliam.

"He is such a learned and kind gentleman, Georgiana. To think I once thought your family full of pride and conceit, only to learn you all have such amiable and superior qualities. Do you think he could find anything worthy in me?"

"You think too lowly of yourself, Kitty. I have often observed my cousin watching you with animation and admiration. I am certain he holds you in high regard, but until he makes any declaration, I would advise you to continue to guard your heart."

"Oh, you speak very wisely, but it is so difficult! I have certainly learned the value of restraint from my sisters, from

Lydia's bad example and the good examples of Jane and Lizzy, but it requires so much effort on my part. Do you think he will soon make a proposal?"

"I cannot tell, Kitty. I wish I could for your sake, but I have often been deceived by the intentions of men."

"You, Georgiana, who are all elegance and presence of mind? I hardly believe it."

Georgiana wondered if she should tell Kitty of her experiences with George Wickham, James Lawson and even Phillip. It might bring some relief to share her regrets, but she was stopped in doing so by the approach of Colonel Fitzwilliam. He walked with them until Georgiana excused herself to practice her music. She left the couple smiling and walking in perfect harmony.

Elizabeth received word from Darcy the morning of the wedding. He was safely arrived in Scotland and would meet with the Wickhams for dinner. He assured Elizabeth all would be well and wrote he had known George Wickham a very long time and was wise to his ways. Baby George's welfare was uppermost in his concerns and everything would be done to provide the best possible life for the child. Elizabeth felt no other man in the world could be as caring and strong as her husband. If only Lydia had found a man with half of Darcy's integrity, all this upheaval would now be avoided. Elizabeth answered his letter and sent a short note to her father as well.

December seventeenth arrived and Georgiana prepared for Phillip Lawson's wedding with determined efficiency. She was about to have her hair arranged when she heard a small tapping at her window. She looked out and saw Bridget standing beneath her rooms holding a small assortment of pebbles. Georgiana leaned out the window in alarm.

"What is it Bridget?"

"Oh Miss Darcy, Georgiana, please come down as soon as you can. I must tell you something."

Bridget wore part of her wedding gown, but her hair was in disarray and she wore boots on her feet.

"I will be there presently."

Georgiana dismissed the servants so they might not listen at the window and then took the back exit from her rooms. She arrived at Bridget's side within five minutes.

"Tell me, Bridget. What brings you here in such a manner? It is freezing, we must go inside."

"I cannot be seen, Georgiana. I have received word only this morning from Mr. Sullivan."

"Mr. Sullivan – from Ireland? Is your family unwell?"

"My family is very well, thank you, though I am certain they may soon be displeased. It seems John, Mr. Sullivan, has acquired an inheritance and will soon make a comfortable living in the Irish countryside. Oh, Georgiana, he loves me and he has been regretting my loss all this time. He hated to write, but he could not avoid this one opportunity to share his feelings and he has in fact asked me to marry him!" Bridget's eyes shone in the waning winter sunlight.

"Bridget! What ill timing. What will you do? What can you do?" Georgiana wished she was not the bearer of such a confidence.

"I am all guilt and remorse, but I cannot marry my cousin when my heart belongs to John Sullivan." Bridget began to cry.

"You plan to break off your wedding? Bridget, everyone will be on their way already."

"I know! I tried, Georgiana, I tried to go on. Look, I am halfway into my wedding gown. This beautiful gown, but I had to stop and I wrote this letter to Phillip. He will understand, surely. But you must read it and make sure it is written proper."

Bridget thrust her letter into Georgiana's hand and Georgiana read it over quickly.

Dear Mr. Lawson,

"I cannot imagine the anger you must feel toward me after you receive this, but I hoped a letter of explanation, if it could not bring about your forgiveness, was at least your due. As you know, your mother was applied to for assistance against my connection with a Mr. Sullivan. Mr. Sullivan had been very dear to me for some time, against the wishes of my parents as he was very poor. You were a very obliging son, nephew and cousin in accepting your mother and aunt's wishes when you came directly to Ireland to assist in the matter. I accepted your offer of marriage only at the insistence of Mr. Sullivan, who knew he could not provide for a wife. Only two days ago, Mr. Sullivan came into a generous inheritance and he has asked me to marry him. I cannot refuse him, but in doing so I must greatly displease everyone else that I love. I will go to him this afternoon and I have only had time to write you this quick note.

I will likely be forever disowned by my family and yours. You have all been so good to me and I beg your forgiveness, though I do not expect it. I will send letters of apologies to your mother and mine as soon as it is possible. Please know that only the deepest love for Mr. Sullivan has drawn me from the goodness and kindness of my family and from you.

I must go in haste.

Bridget.

"Is it long enough?" Bridget said when Georgiana finished.

"Bridget, no length of letter could make your news any better. You must tell your aunt before you go. People will be arriving at any moment for your wedding."

"I cannot go back, Georgiana. Mr. Sullivan will meet me along the road to Sunnings in a quarter of an hour. He wrote he would wait there for me whether I came or not and I will go. I must now bid you goodbye, Georgiana, and beg you not to tell anyone until I am well on my way." Bridget embraced Georgiana who could not return the gesture.

"Oh, Georgiana, I see you are displeased. I am so sorry, but you would understand what I do if you loved a man such as Mr. Sullivan. I am so grateful for your friendship! I hope one day we may be reunited. I shall write to you."

At that, Bridget turned and ran off toward the road. Georgiana could only stare after her and then at the note in her hand. She must go to Sunnings.

# CHAPTER 17

GEORGIANA TOLD NO ONE OF BRIDGET'S VISIT AND WAS prevented from going early to Sunnings by the sudden arrival of a letter from Rundleston announcing the arrival of Mr. and Mrs. Bingley's first child. It was a boy and his name was to be David Charles. Elizabeth was ecstatic and could barely sit still long enough to be dressed. Georgiana wished to express her desire for an early departure, but she could not penetrate Elizabeth's joy.

"Three boys in one year! Mother and father will be delighted and now Henry and George will have a little playfellow nearby. Oh, what luck and how fortunate my sister and her child are both healthy. I wish I could go to her immediately, Georgiana, but she must rest nonetheless. Tomorrow will be soon enough, I am sure. Oh, I wonder if he has her eyes or his. Georgiana, I positively ache to hold him!"

Georgiana considered sending Bridget's letter ahead of them, but she could not bear to have Phillip receive such a letter from a servant and considered it might be intercepted. If only she could tell Elizabeth she might go to Rundleston as the wedding would not be happening today. Instead, she waited and tried to get Elizabeth to stay still while she was dressed. Finally, they left for Sunnings with Kitty and Colonel Fitzwilliam.

JULIA GREETED them and Georgiana asked immediately if she might see Mr. Lawson.

"I am afraid you are too late, Georgiana, anything you might wish to say must now be forgotten for my brother is already awaiting his bride at the front of the hall."

Georgiana followed Julia's gaze and felt her head spin at the sight of Phillip so handsomely dressed and expecting his bride every moment, when Georgiana held the message which would surely crush all his hopes. There was no private way of getting him the message and despite the questioning whispers of Elizabeth and Kitty, Georgiana hastened down the aisle and handed him the note. She noticed a flicker of happy surprise in his eyes before she escaped to sit with her family. When she sat again, she heard murmurings around her and stole quick glances at Phillip. His happy eyes soon turned dim. He read the letter rapidly and then whispered to the clergyman who grew suddenly pale. Phillip then dashed off in search of his mother. After several long moments of questioning whispers, the clergyman announced:

"Dearly beloved, I fear the bride has had a change of heart. The Lawson family will be pleased to see you in the main dining hall where dinner will be served shortly."

All eyes seemed to turn to Georgiana who could say nothing. It was not her letter and it was Phillip's news to share or not. She stood and led the crowd into the dining hall.

It was a very awkward dinner to say the least. Everyone attempted not to mention the reason for the gathering and sought to find some topic to fill the evening while Mr. and Mrs. Lawson looked ill with disappointment and no one could bear to bother them for more information. Elizabeth and Kitty gave up asking Georgiana to tell what was in the letter and spoke instead of their new nephew. Georgiana wished she could see Phillip to tell how he was, but he did not return for the meal. With true gentlemanlike manners, however, he met his guests at the door as they left and thanked each person for their presence and apologized for the change in plans. Georgiana could see no trace of tears in his eyes or any sign he had gone in pursuit of his wayward bride. She took his hand and felt he held it a little longer than necessary.

"Thank you Georgiana for bringing the letter yourself." She could say nothing before he turned to the next guest and so, she left the Lawson's home to spend a sleepless night at Pemberley.

# CHAPTER 18

A LETTER ARRIVED FROM DARCY THE MORNING AFTER THE wedding stating he would be arriving the following day with the Wickhams.

"I know I promised I would never allow Mr. Wickham into our house, Lizzy, but I fear it is absolutely necessary in this case. Please warn Georgiana and suggest she may wish to spend a few days with the Lawsons. We must endure this for the sake of our little nephew as nothing could be arranged here in Scotland. I trust you will make the necessary preparations."

Elizabeth shared this portion of the letter with Georgiana, never considering a few nights spent at the Lawsons would be worse punishment than a few nights spent with the Wickhams.

"It is very kind of my brother to suggest the visit," said Georgiana evenly. "However, he cannot be aware of what has recently passed at Sunnings and I feel it would be more prudent to remain at Pemberley. Mr. Wickham no longer causes me as much distress as he did once. The first meeting shall be the worst and then I suppose we may go on as mere acquaintances."

Once again, Elizabeth regretted causing Georgiana grief through her family connections. "I am very sorry Georgiana. Please feel free to avoid our company as often as possible." She paused a moment to consider what she had never shared with Georgiana before.

"I do not know, Georgiana, if your brother ever mentioned my own connection to Mr. Wickham?" She looked at Georgiana who shook her head in confusion.

"You mean beyond his marriage to Lydia?"

"Yes. When I first met Mr. Wickham, I felt he had a preference for me. I was flattered by his attention to me and found him handsome and agreeable. He deceived me by telling me half-truths of his relationship to Mr. Darcy and I was not at all aware of his ill behaviour to you. I thought him charming and fancied I might be in love. My Aunt Gardiner warned me a man with no fortune could never marry a girl like me and shortly after, I learned of his engagement to a Miss King which never came to anything, but I realized then he was not the man I thought him to be. Then your brother told me the truth of his connection to your family and finally he disappeared with my sister, so you see I can relate to your anxiety in his presence, only I have a husband to protect me from any further harm while you must still feel rather exposed."

Georgiana was very surprised by this revelation. If Elizabeth could marry after such deception, perhaps there was hope for her. However, she considered Elizabeth had never been persuaded into an elopement.

"My brother never told me," said Georgiana, thoughtfully. "But I am very glad you have trusted me with such information. I have been very embarrassed by my past with Mr. Wickham, but if even you could be deceived by him, perhaps

I am not possessed of as much ill judgement as I had thought."

"No, no, Georgiana. You must not judge all men by Mr. Wickham." Elizabeth held Georgiana's hands and looked steadily into her eyes. "You will find a man worthy of you, my dear. I am certain of it."

ELIZABETH TOLD Kitty next of the plans and Kitty was torn between joy at a reunion with her sister Lydia, who had once been very close, and repugnance at Lydia's behaviour since her marriage.

"I hope they will not stay very long, Lizzy, but it will be nice to see Lydia again," said Kitty.

Elizabeth also hoped the Wickhams would make a short stay, but she felt it would take a lot of effort to accomplish such a feat.

A day and night passed and by noon the following day, Darcy and the Wickhams arrived at Pemberley.

"Oh, how good it is to be home again," said Mr. Wickham when they entered. "It is lovely to see you Elizabeth. Georgiana, I believe you have grown since I saw you last! Kitty, you have become very pretty and Colonel Fitzwilliam, it has been a long time." Wickham bowed toward the Colonel and then gave him a warm handshake.

George Wickham was as smooth and charming as ever and Elizabeth and Georgiana wondered at his ease. Lydia's manners had only worsened.

"I do not think you look so very pretty, Kitty, though your dress is very fine. I suppose Lizzy bought it for you. I do not imagine she has considered my want of a new dress." Lydia pouted like the child she still was.

"Please take some refreshment in our parlour," said Elizabeth, attempting to disguise the outrage she felt toward Lydia.

"It is very good to be with family for Christmas, do you not think Georgiana?" Mr. Wickham spoke as they walked. Georgiana wished she had not been so close to him and merely nodded in agreement.

"I cannot believe how long it has been since I have seen you, Georgiana. I hope you have found yourself able to forgive me for my past imprudence," he smiled.

"Of course. It is not Christian to bear grudges, especially against one's family.

"Very true – I wonder, then, how your brother continues to keep me from Pemberley. He should take a lesson from your example, Georgiana."

Darcy caught the end of this conversation and took Georgiana's arm, leading her as far away from Wickham as possible.

"If only mother and father could be here," said Lydia. "I know mother should be proud to see me and my little son. Oh, Lizzy, do fetch him at once, for I have been very anxious to see him." Lydia clapped like a little girl expecting a present.

Elizabeth feared what might happen when George was settled back into his mother's arms, but she could not refuse and went herself to the nursery.

"Oh Little George," Elizabeth whispered when she held him. "I promise we will always take care of you." She struggled to maintain a calm exterior and returned slowly to her guests.

"Oh Lizzy, it has taken you an age to return. Bring him to me at once!" Lydia shouted when Elizabeth entered the sitting room.

Elizabeth glanced at Darcy, who nodded slightly and she brought the baby to her sister.

"Goodness! Look how fat he has become!" Lydia's loud

voice startled George and he began to cry. Lydia rocked him a moment and then thrust him toward Elizabeth.

"My, what a temper he is in. What have you done with him, Lizzy? He was such a contented child when I left him with you."

Elizabeth bridled at the comment and could not keep herself from saying,

"Your son was nearly starved and screaming from want of food, Lydia. He only cries because he does not know you."

Lydia laughed. "Nonsense, Lizzy! A baby knows his own mother." George had settled in Elizabeth's arms and Lydia reached for him once more to prove her point.

"Come Georgie. Surely you have missed me." Lydia spoke quietly and George remained settled when she took him from Elizabeth. Lydia rocked him a moment before turning to her husband.

"See, George, how well he knows his mother. Is he not the handsomest baby you ever saw?"

"Certainly," said Wickham "though I have always thought one baby looks similar enough to another. Still, he looks particularly well to me. How is your little Henry?"

"He is well. The two babies seem to enjoy being together," said Elizabeth.

Little George fell back to sleep in his mother's arms and they resumed talk about family, weather and Scotland. Lydia noticed Colonel Fitzwilliam's special attention to her sister Kitty and set about flirting with him, much to Kitty's dismay. Colonel Fitzwilliam responded politely, but was certainly not in any danger of Lydia's advances. Tea ended and Darcy suggested the Wickham's meet with him and Elizabeth to discuss some business in the library. Georgiana was soon called to the door to see Julia Lawson, and Kitty and Colonel Fitzwilliam remained in the sitting room to play music and cards together.

Darcy took control of the conversation as soon as Baby George was returned to the nursery and the four brothers and sisters assembled in his library.

"I do not wish to delay what we have gathered for," he began.

"We want our baby back," said Lydia with her head held high. "You have no right to embezzle him from us."

"Certainly," said Darcy, before Elizabeth could speak. "He is your son and we could never deny your right to him."

Lydia's sense of evil was deflated and she considered her next statement. "Well then, what more is there to discuss? Let us partake in some Christmas festivity. Lord, but Scotland was dull."

Wickham interrupted his wife. "A moment, Lydia, we are in no state to care for a son at present. I believe Darcy was willing to enter an agreement with us as little George's uncle."

"Certainly our baby has grown accustomed to grandeur while he has spent these six weeks in your care," said Lydia. "You would not wish to send him away with nothing."

"I should not consider that we owe him any more than we have already provided. We shall send gifts as we would any other nephew, but I would not consider anything else to be required." Darcy spoke quietly.

"Well, and what would mother have to say about this?" Lydia began to cry. "Certainly you, who have so much," she gestured about the room "should provide for your indestitute relations."

"My husband has already provided a great deal for you and your husband, Lydia. Perhaps Mr. Wickham has not mentioned all the debts which have been paid on his behalf."

Wickham interrupted Elizabeth. "Let us not veer into the distant past. I am grateful for all you have done, Darcy, but certainly it is no less than would be done for any brother."

"I believe it is a great deal more than would be done for any true brother of mine," said Darcy. "I am a firm believer in taking care of one's own affairs, but let us return to the matter at hand. Are you able to provide a safe and healthy life for your son?"

"What more could a baby need than his parents?" said Lydia defensively.

"Then you should be off with him at once," said Darcy pounding his desk and Elizabeth gasped. He silenced her with a serious look. "I do not wish to detain you from your travels. Mr. Wickham, I have only asked you to Pemberley to discuss this matter, though your wife and son are welcome whenever they wish."

"Let us be going, then, Lydia, unless you wish to stay behind while I go on to London?" Wickham looked hopeful.

"Lord, no! Why should you go to London without me? That would certainly not do. You did not tell me, Wickham you planned to go to London. Oh, I should like to be there for Christmas. What a delightful scheme!"

"Shall I send for Baby George's things, then?" said Elizabeth dully.

"Heavens, no! We could not take a baby to London. Where should I find a nurse on such short notice? No, no, he had best stay here until we are settled somewhere more permanently. Well, you should not mind, Lizzy when you have servants and nurses to spare!"

Elizabeth looked at Darcy in confusion, but he showed the faintest trace of a smile and she wondered if he had foreseen the Wickhams reaction.

"We are very fond of little George and are concerned for his well-being," said Darcy. "We should like to offer him a permanent place in our home, at least until you might be more happily settled."

"That sounds very obliging," said Wickham "but what of

his future? Surely you cannot expect a boy who is brought up in such opulence to live a pauper when he is older?"

"I should hope we never live to be paupers!" exclaimed Lydia. "Lord, I should not like that at all."

"I only say pauper in comparison to Pemberley," Wickham barely concealed his impatience with Lydia.

"If George should wish and you should give permission, we are prepared to offer him an income upon his eighteenth birthday if he is to spend the majority of his time at Pemberley. We should be happy to consider him as a son of sorts."

"How am I to trust a promise from a man such as you?" Wickham sneered.

"This need not be a mere verbal agreement," said Darcy. "I have taken the trouble of consulting a lawyer who has drawn up a contract detailing the arrangement. You have only to read and sign the papers if it pleases you."

Elizabeth then realized her husband's forethought and good intentions. She could finally take a deep breath and stop her various imaginings of doom and poverty for little George. Lydia and Wickham were shortly persuaded to accept the agreement with a provision that they should visit him frequently and have him to visit their home as soon as they were possessed of one. These intentions would prove weak and their visits and attentions to little George would grow fewer as the years passed and stop altogether when Wickham was persuaded to seek his fortune in the Americas upon George's fifth birthday. An occasional letter, usually seeking some support or other, would be all George would receive from his parent's as he grew. To the Darcy's relief, the Wickham's produced no more children and, though little George knew his parentage early on; he was never made to feel less than a true son of Pemberley.

# CHAPTER 19

Julia came to Pemberley to invite Georgiana for dinner. It was exactly the invitation Georgiana wished to avoid, but she could not deny her friend after such an unfortunate occasion only two days earlier.

"Shall we take some air?" asked Julia when Georgiana agreed to the dinner.

The pair headed out into the wooded area of Pemberley Park.

"I wanted to tell you, Georgiana, that though I always wish you to visit Sunnings, it was not my idea to invite you this morning. I did not want to make you part of the despair at Sunnings so early after our misfortune."

"Then who has sent you?"

"Can you not guess, my friend? You must, it will give me some enjoyment to hear you stammer." Julia smiled as she always did during a prank.

"Come, Julia, can you not just tell me?" Georgiana pleaded.

"No, you must humour me this morning for I have been

forced to be pensive for far too long." Julia tossed her golden hair decisively.

"Alright, does your mother wish me to come and offer comfort?"

"No, indeed, she finds enough comfort at present, I believe."

"Does your father wish me to come as company for yourself?"

"No, no, though it would be very thoughtful of him."

"Does Mr. Black tire of your ways and wish for you to have someone else to sport with?" Georgiana teazed her friend back.

"Georgiana! You have changed since we were girls. I am most pleased at you, but no, Mr. Black has not yet tired of me, though I dare say it will not be much longer."

"Miss Black, then, desires a fresh face at Sunnings?"

"No, I fear, Georgiana, my brother James has become quite attached, despite his ardent admiration for you, and from what I can see; Miss Black has no use for anyone but him. If I am correct, we will soon have another engagement at Sunnings."

"I had thought as much. Do not tell me Mr. Ward has returned to Sunnings? Really, Julia, I want nothing to do with him."

"Oh, that is a pity for he is so agreeable, but alas no, I believe you have left all but the very person who has asked the pleasure of your appearance tonight. You must say his name now, Georgiana."

"Phillip? Why should he wish my appearance?"

"If you will not speculate, then certainly I must not. However, I do see him ahead and I must leave you now for mother will want me. Good day, Georgiana. I look forward to your visit tonight."

Julia smiled brightly and flounced off toward Sunnings before Georgiana could protest. She felt suddenly small in Phillip's presence. What could he mean by coming to her? She must have patience, though her heart was beating wildly within her.

"Miss Darcy, you must think me very ill for visiting you this morning," he smiled despite his words.

"No, of course not. I am only a little surprised."

"I could not let another minute pass before I saw you again, for I cannot delay as I have reason to believe Mr. Ward will propose to you soon."

"Mr. Ward?" Georgiana struggled to stay fixed in her goal of serenity.

"Georgiana, you have put my brothers in their places, but foolishly, I must seek what they had desired. I wished to do so several months before, as you may have imagined, the morning after the ball, but I was prevented by an urgent letter from my aunt in Ireland. I suppose you have put the entire story together, knowing Miss Brill as closely as you did, but I wish still to make it entirely clear. I was called upon to relieve Miss Brill from her attachment to a Mr. Sullivan. My mother had always promised to do what she could for her sister, Mrs. Brill, and when it seemed her daughter, Bridget, would make an unfortunate match, my mother decided I should make every effort to marry her. Unfortunately, I was not yet attached and I could not refuse my mother or the needs of my cousin. I had hoped Miss Brill would refuse me, but it did not take as long as I thought to secure her hand. I believe you know all the rest, we were engaged and nearly wed when Mr. Sullivan wrote to tell of his fortune and she agreed to his proposal and gave up mine." Phillip watched Georgiana to be sure she understood it all.

"It was very good of you and quite ill of her to use you so."

"Thank you, Georgiana, but now I am free of all obligation and I may tell you what I thought when you walked down the aisle two days ago carrying her letter. Perhaps you will recall I smiled as I watched you, for Georgiana, I thought I must be dreaming and decided I would enjoy what my heart truly desired, if only in a dream. And when I read the letter, you will remember I spoke to the clergyman and left our guests immediately, but did you suppose it was because I was disappointed?"

"Of course, what else could you be?"

"Elated, Georgiana. There, now I have said it aloud at last. For you had brought me the best news I could have imagined. I could not face guests who believed me to be in love with my cousin. Certainly she was an agreeable and pretty enough girl, but I had no love for her beyond a brotherly sort. You had freed me from her at last and I have come, Georgiana, to insist you marry me, for it is you I have loved for so long I do not know when it began. It is you I want beside me always to care for and argue with, to laugh with and comfort. Please, Georgiana, will you have me, despite all my faults and ill-timing? Can you possibly love me at all, please tell me quickly."

Georgiana sat down upon a rock and could not speak for two full minutes. Tears fell down her cheeks and Phillip offered his handkerchief and began to apologize for upsetting her. At last, she spoke and relieved him of all his fears.

"You cannot know how happy you have made me, Phillip, for though I did not realize it until you were engaged, I love you also and have lived in agony these several months. I will have you, yes of course, my love. Oh, I am so happy I may faint."

The couple spent a quarter of an hour in happy proclamations until Georgiana wondered how his family would feel about their engagement so soon after the demise of their expectations.

"I will not make you part of that scene, Georgiana, for I will return home to make all explanations, but I believe you will find them most agreeable when you visit us for dinner tonight, for I believe it has always been my mother's favourite wish to have you a legitimate daughter and now it will be done. No, you must not fear my family, Georgiana, but do you think it wise to announce our intentions to yours?"

"Of course. I imagine they may now be in need of some good tidings, yet I have remembered something you said. From whence did you hear Mr. Ward intended to propose to me?"

"Why from Julia. She said you spoke of it to her yourself."

"I did no such thing," said Georgiana, smiling.

"Why then do you smile?"

"I believe my dear friend and soon sister, has assisted in speeding up this engagement, Phillip. She always had the greatest interest in Mr. Ward and she was always one for arranging a scheme."

"I have been had! It has been some time since I have fallen for one of her tales, but I must have overlooked her ways when I considered only you, but I must pay her back the compliment, with your permission."

"Only if I might be a part of your plans."

"Then you must write her a letter." Their plot was set forth and done before they parted. Phillip would be sure to visit Julia before he said anything to the rest of his family and Georgiana would hear of it all at dinner.

Dearest Julia,

I had not time to mention that I have been engaged to Mr. Ward by letter only this morning. It is with great regret that I have refused your brother. Please comfort him as best you can. Although it shall be very awkward for me, I insist upon keeping my engagement at Sunnings tonight.

With love,

Georgiana.

# CHAPTER 20

The jest with Julia regarding their engagement went remarkably well and she was very pleased at their fun. She would not repent of interfering with their affairs and insisted she would keep up her ways even once she was an old married woman. Unbeknownst to them all, Mr. Ward had at that moment found his fortune in London in the close friend of Mrs. Rathwell, a young woman of considerable beauty and 10,000 a year named Miss King. He would vaguely regret the comments he made to Miss Darcy on his intentions, but soon forgave himself when he heard of her engagement. It could not have fit him better and he doubled his efforts to attract the very good Miss King.

After some time spent in reasoning and discussion, the rest of the families were completely satisfied with the engagement, though Barrington was seen to cast an occasional glare his brother's way.

There was snow at Pemberley for Christmas and all were merry to see such beauty on the joyous day. Phillip Lawson came early to spend as much of the day as possible with the woman who held all his hopes and dreams. Elizabeth was very pleased to have so much love and joy around her and was greatly pleased when she later found a covered canvas in her rooms. Darcy watched as she carefully removed the covering and exclaimed at the painting beneath.

"Why it is the very cottage we saw in Skelwith-fold on our tour of the Lakes. Darcy, how thoughtful of you to remember my admiration of such a place and to have it painted for me."

"This is not all I give you, Lizzy. For with it comes the knowledge that I have purchased this cottage for our little family to visit whenever we wish."

Elizabeth embraced him and wondered at his extravagance.

"Thank you Darcy, you have surprised me well and it shall be a perfect accompaniment to my gift for you."

"How so, my dear?"

"I have nothing to show yet, but I will tell you our family will soon be a little bigger. I am to have a child, Darcy, who will be born to us sometime in June."

The couple could not imagine any greater happiness and they spent several moments exclaiming of their great fortune in life, though Elizabeth did not speak aloud the rest of her thoughts on the fulfillment of her expectations. She felt she could fully enjoy the realizations of her expectations as they were countered by the continued vexations of the wayward Wickhams, a foolish mother, and an unmarried sister who held little hope of finding married bliss. In the midst of embracing Darcy, she promised herself she would invite Mary to Pemberley in the New Year. Happiness at Pemberley would increase at dinner when Colonel Fitzwilliam and Kitty announced their engagement.

When Mary received her invitation to Pemberley along with news of all that had recently passed there, she remarked to her mother;

"It may be observed that married women come to appreciate their unmarried sisters when they begin to fill their homes with children."

Mr. Bennet sat with his wife and middle daughter in a comfortable room warmed by a tidy fire. He gave a short review of all that had occurred during the year and remarked his letter to Jane and Elizabeth certainly had the desired effect, for their husbands were now well provided with male heirs.

"Oh, Mr. Bennet! Did you hear, Mary, he wrote a letter advising Jane and Elizabeth and said nothing to us about it. Is that not just like you, Mr. Bennet to keep us all in suspense? I say, I had no knowledge of any such letter. Elizabeth and Jane did not share a word of it with me. Well, well, I am all felicity and good feelings for you have gone and got a husband for Jane and grandchildren for me. You are most kind, Mr. Bennet."

Mr. Bennet allowed a kiss and settled into his chair to enjoy the pleasures of hearth and home, but before he was very comfortable, Mrs. Bennet remembered her news.

"Mr. Bennet, I nearly forgot, you will never believe the news I have had from Lady Lucas."

"Confound Lady Lucas. Can she not keep her knowledge to herself?"

"Oh, Mr. Bennet, you pretend to have such a temper! Surely you will wish to know that a new tenant is to take Netherfield in a fortnight and would you believe he is another single man of large fortune! What luck, what opportunity, oh Mr. Bennet we have surely been blessed."

"Heaven help me, Mrs. Bennet. Will I never be done the work of having five daughters?" With that, he quit the room in a very foul temper and Mrs. Bennet remarked to Mary;

"You see, you shall not be pitied of your sisters! Though when you marry, Mary, you must promise to stay closer to home, for what am I to do when all my daughters have gone and left me?"

Mrs. Bennet was low for a quarter of an hour considering the great sacrifice of losing all her daughters until she considered her assistance should be wanted in procuring partners for her brothers' children. She returned to pleasanter thoughts as she began reviewing the Gardiner and Phillips children and imagining her efforts in obtaining their profitable matches.

# WORKS CITED FOR EXPECTATIONS


Austen, Jane. Lady Susan/ The Watsons/ Sandition. Penguin Classics. Ed. & Intro.

Margaret Drabble: Penguin Books, 1974.

Austen, Jane. Northanger Abbey. Penguin Books, 2003.

Austen, Jane. Pride and Prejudice. Oxford University Press, 1970.

Austen, Jane. Sense and Sensibility. Introduction and Notes by Anne Rowe.

Wordsworth Classics: Wordsworth Editions, 1996.

Blashfield, Jean F. England: Enchantment of the World. 2nd Series. Children's Press,

1997.

Hibbert, Christopher. The English: A Social History: 1066-1945. Grafton Books, 1987.

MacKinnon and Chapman. "Chronology of Pride and Prejudice."

Purvis, Jane. A History of Women's Education in England. Open University Press,

1991.

Ross, Josephine. Jane Austen: A Companion. Rutgers University Press, 2002.

Stone, Lawrence. The Family, Sex and Marriage in England:1500 – 1800. Abridged

Editions. Harper Torchbooks, 1979.

Wordsworth, William. A Guide Through the District of the Lakes in the North of

England. Greenwood Press, Pub., 1968.

www.KirkstallAbbeyHistory.webarchive

# GET YOUR FREE EBOOK

Join the City Lights Press mailing list for information on new releases, updates, discount offers and a copy of the historical romance novel, Jasmine Passion: http://citylights-press.com/get-your-free-copy-of-jasmine-passion/

Thank you for taking the time to read Expectations. If you enjoyed it, please consider telling your friends or posting a short review. Word of mouth is an author's best friend and much appreciated. Thank you.

*Samantha Adkins*

# A LOOK AT SUSPICIOUSLY RESERVED

Emma Woodhouse is one of Jane Austen's most beloved heroines. She is smart, well-dressed and rich. But what about Jane Fairfax, her poor, orphaned nemesis? Would the story be so light and sparkling from Jane's point of view?

Suspiciously Reserved in Jane's story, set in present-day Canada. Jane has felt uncomfortable living off the goodwill of her wealthy benefactors, the Campbells. Now that their daughter has found the man of her dreams, Jane wonders what her future holds. She feels she must return to live with her grandmother and Aunt Hetty. Before she goes, however, she has one blissful week by the ocean where she meets handsome, charming Frank Churchill. But can she trust him?

*COMING SOON FROM CITY LIGHTS PRESS AND SAMANTHA ADKINS*

## ABOUT THE AUTHOR

Samantha Adkins is a Canadian story-teller. She studied journalism and professional writing at Mount Royal College in Alberta, and is inspired by the works of Jane Austen, Lemony Snicket (aka Daniel Handler), Judy Blume, Louise Penny, Roald Dahl, Bodie Thoene, and Lois Lowry.

*READ MORE ABOUT SAMANTHA ADKINS HERE:* http://christiankindlenews.com/our-authors/samantha-adkins/

Manufactured by Amazon.ca
Acheson, AB

16323949R00192